OTHER BOOKS BY ARTHUR HERZOG:

fiction

THE SWARM

nonfiction

THE B.S. FACTOR

McCARTHY FOR PRESIDENT

THE CHURCH TRAP

THE WAR-PEACE ESTABLISHMENT

SMOKING AND THE PUBLIC INTEREST (CO-AUTHOR)

ARTHUR HERZOG

Earthsound

SIMON AND SCHUSTER · NEW YORK

DESIGNED BY EVE METZ
MANUFACTURED IN THE UNITED STATES OF AMERICA

1 2 3 4 5 6 7 8 9 10

LIBRARY OF CONGRESS CATALOGING IN PUBLICATION DATA
HERZOG, ARTHUR.
EARTHSOUND.
I. TITLE.
PZ4.H58EAR [PS3558.E796]   813'.5'4   75-6702
ISBN 0-671-21993-6

ACKNOWLEDGMENTS

I have profited immensely from the generous and knowledgeable counsel of the following individuals and organizations I now wish to thank.

Drs. Chris Scholz, Lynn Sykes, James Kelleher, Paul Pomeroy, Mark Sbar—all from the Lamont-Doherty Geological Observatory.

Messrs. Ed Simmons and M. L. Brashears, geologists, Leggette Brashears & Grahame, Inc.

Lord Pentland, Richard H. Brower, of Hunting Geological Surveys, Inc.

Dr. John Carmen, geologist, United Nations.

Dr. Gregory Herzog, Dr. Lawrence Cohn, Alan Buchsbaum, architect, Mr. and Mrs. David Goodrich, Rev. Samuel Southard.

The Consolidated Edison Company of New York.

The Anchorage (Alaska) *Times*.

My special thanks to Scholz and my brother Herzog, who read the manuscript for accuracy.

As before, my deep gratitude to my superb editor, Phyllis Grann. And, always, my love and thanks to my wife, Betty Rollin.

FOR FATHER, DOLORES, DAYTON,
GREG, ELAINE, LEE AND JOE

Contents

11

Part Seven
QUAKE
Page 227

An earthquake is of its very essence terrifying, more terrifying than nature's other dreadful outbreaks, since more than any other it sets the stability of the underlying basis of human life itself in question. But for anyone who has not undergone the extreme terror of a very great earthquake, and whose mind has remained youthful enough to feel delight at being at grips with some great upheaval, there is a certain exhilaration in being made aware of the earth's enormous power in this way and in saying to oneself that perhaps one is about to live through an extraordinary experience. We watched, torn between reason, which urged us to rush out before everything collapsed, and a childish fatalism, which held us back, almost happy at being so close to disaster —we were restrained as much by a juvenile sense of invulnerability as by a kind of gambling spirit, a half-formed feeling that this was a wager.

Haroun Tazieff
When the Earth Trembles

Most of the human race takes the stability of the earth for granted. Even those trained to recognize the dynamic nature of the lithosphere seldom consider how cycles of human life and death are related to the geological times involved in cumulative dislocations of the earth's crust. Human adjustment to earthquake hazard thus requires adaptation to phenomena that confuse man's senses and confound his beliefs.

Robert W. Kates
"Human Adjustment to Earthquake Hazard,"
in *Human Ecology; The Great Alaska Earthquake of 1964*,
National Academy of Sciences, 1971

God uses earthquakes to shake people up, out of their complacency and overconfidence. Some earthquakes are natural, but sometimes when God wants to get a point across, He speaks through earthquakes.

Rev. Billy Graham

PART ONE

TREMOR

Saturday, June 15 Vail was up on a high stepladder, pruning a dead branch from a tree with a saw. He said, "Good to get outside for a change. This is the first Saturday morning it hasn't rained in . . . how long would you say?"

"More'n a month."

"Easy. Maybe two."

The blade bit into the tough wood of the elm. He put his shoulder into it and then stopped. "Can you hold the ladder tighter, Dun?" He began sawing again, and again the ladder shook. "Dun!"

He looked down. Dun had vanished. From the barn Vail could hear hammer blows. The legs of the ladder seemed firmly planted in the moist ground. "What the . . . ?"

It was as though the earth had shrugged gently, like an animal twitching its hide. The ladder swayed and Vail dropped the saw and held on with both hands, mouth open. Then he scrambled down as fast as he could.

Not far from the ground, the toe of his boot must have slipped on a muddy rung. Flailing out with his foot, he lurched drunkenly and fell. His lips parted of themselves and shaped his cry.

He broke the fall with his hands. Stunned, he lay with his eyes shut, big frame outstretched, head pressed against the naked soil. Through his earth-fused ear he thought he heard a tiny sound, like a grunt—a small grunt, far away, and yet he sensed incredible power.

"Mr. Vail?" the voice implored.

He did not want to be interrupted. He needed to remember, record the experience indelibly. He squeezed his eyelids and flattened his ear to the ground.

"Son?" The voice lost its indecision. "Better get the missus."

Shuffling feet. Piano music that stopped, then a child's cry, a dog's bark, more footsteps. Damn! He wanted to hear the earthsound again.

"Harry! Are you all right?"

Magic Fingers, he thought. You put a quarter into a slot in a motel room and the bed vibrates. That's what the shaking was like. What was the grunt?

"Are you all right?" Kay demanded once more.

A tongue, wet, warm, furtive, touched his lips. Dog breath. Opening his eyes, he could see his own bushy brows. He muttered, "Yes."

"Daddy's okay!" Mark shouted.

The old man stepped forward, hand outstretched, but Kay stopped him. "No. He might be hurt. I'll call Dr. Bjerling."

Harry wiggled his fingers and toes and questioned the rest of his body. "I'm all right," he said, standing up to prove it.

"What happened?" his wife asked anxiously.

"I slipped coming down the ladder." He glanced at Dun.

The handyman mumbled, "Should have held the ladder for you. Shouldn't have gone off." Watchful gray eyes blinked.

Harry reached out and shook the ladder, which seemed stable enough. "Not your fault," he said to Dun. He started for the stone house and stopped. "About the time I fell, did either of you feel anything funny? Hear anything strange?"

18

Dun and Kay exchanged glances. Kay said, "No."

"You, Mark?"

"No, Daddy."

"Why?" Kay said.

"No reason."

But he had been positioned up on a stepladder while Dun had been hammering and Kay playing the piano. And Mark was only six.

In the kitchen, Kay cleaned dirt from his head and ear with a moist towel, while Mark watched. Harry showed square teeth as he said, "Ouch!"

"You have a bump," Kay fussed as she touched his skull gently. "I hope you haven't really hurt yourself. Have you a headache?"

"No," he lied. "Funny what happened up there."

"What's funny about falling down?"

"Before that. The ladder shook exactly as though there were . . ." He paused in surprise at his own words. ". . . an earthquake."

"In Rhode Island?" Kay said with a small smile.

"I didn't say there *was* an earthquake. It just felt like one. It must have been the saw."

"Saw, Daddy?"

"The saw stuck on a knot and the ladder shook when I pushed. Come to think of it, sawing is something like an earthquake." Harry gazed solemnly at his son.

"Explain."

"I'll try. The saw scrapes on the wood. When the blade sticks, it cuts. In an earthquake you have two big pieces of stone trying to push past each other. The stone slabs stick. When the pressure gets too great they finally slip and the ground shakes. Buildings can fall down."

"With people in them, Daddy?"

19

"Sometimes." His big hand ruffled the child's red hair. "I'd better get moving." He started to rise, felt wobbly, and had to sit again.

"You ought to check with Dr. Bjerling," Kay said, eyeing him. "People can fracture their skulls and not know it for days."

Harry smiled and this time he gained his feet.

"Lie down for a minute, at least," Kay begged.

"I'm okay," he insisted.

The boy and the shelty went outside, while Kay returned to the grand piano in the living room. She played nicely, but a bit too heavily for the state of Vail's head. Also, the piano sounded out of tune. He went to his study and closed the door.

The room was simple and small, containing an old couch, a desk with a swivel chair, a filing cabinet. A bookshelf ran along one wall. Below it, Vail found books scattered on the floor. Could Mark have reached the shelf from which they had fallen? He was into everything these days. Or the cat. Judy sometimes jumped from the back of the armchair to the bookshelves, where she perched, watching him work. Or the books might just have been unbalanced. Still . . .

Vail replaced the books, took a few short steps to the desk, and sat down, nerves twitching. It was unreasonable to be upset and yet his eyes scanned the smaller collection of shelves above his desk, the ones containing books on geology and seismology. He reached for a volume but pulled back his hand. No, he warned himself, don't. That episode is over. Forget about it— you fell from the ladder. End of story.

But the room suddenly seemed constricting as a cell, and he fled. Outside, he stood indecisively, unable to put the earthsound from his mind. It was a damp morning, cool for the season. Bunches of clouds scudded in under a gray tarpaulin of sky. Shoulders hunched, he started toward the sea.

The stone house stood on six acres of land. The trail led

through an overgrown field where farmers, and Indians before them, had planted corn—occasionally Vail found arrowheads. He hopped on the stepping-stones over a stream known as Torturous Creek, swollen by recent rains, and skirted a long, brackish pond lined by sedges rustling faintly in the light breeze. Swans paddled aimlessly. After the pond came a marsh, then a copse of trees and a small field, and finally a ten-foot bluff that overlooked their rocky beach.

He waited until he reached a spot curtained by a grove of trees, aware how odd he would look if seen from the house. Abruptly he dropped to the ground and placed one ear to it: the earth was mute. He got up and continued until he reached the bluff, where he stood at the base of a shallow coastal indentation. To his left down the coast, close to the sea, loomed the Demming mansion, three stories high; on the right lay Shonkawa Point, the tip of Old Brompton peninsula, where the village of Old Brompton was, on the far side of the cliffs. When the wind drove in hard straight from the east the sea became rough here, but otherwise, partly protected, the water was calm. Today a big surf ran.

On the edge of the bluff was a chairlike rock, with arms and a back, in which he sometimes sat immobile, watching the waves, studying their shapes, hypnotized by the unending motion. He stared intently at the surf splattering the exposed rocks, turned his head so that his ear pressed against the stone slab, and listened once again.

All right, all right, think about it if you have to, just don't think about it too much. The shaking he felt on the ladder was easy to explain; it was the earthsound that bothered him. He must have imagined it as he lay in a daze, and yet he was not normally given to flights of fancy. Supposing he had actually heard such a noise, what could it have been? The earth for Vail was familiar terrain, and he ticked off conceivable causes— blasting, excavation, underground water, deposits of natural gas

21

struggling to reach the surface . . . None of these answers was plausible. In the clearing and again on the stone chair, Vail had tested still another notion, however unlikely—that a mineral conduit of some kind could carry the vibrations of surf. This idea, too, had to be discarded. Close as he was to the sea, he could barely feel it pulsate through the rock.

Had he then experienced a tiny tremor? Vail had been a seismologist at the California Institute of Technology before he had quit academic life and moved east a decade earlier to become a working geologist; he knew that noise sometimes accompanies quakes and that even stable Rhode Island was not entirely free of seismic activity. He took a deep breath and tried to remember the Modified Mercalli Scale of earthquake intensities as they affect human observers. Slowly the categories came back:

I. Not felt except by a few under especially favorable circumstances.
II. Felt only by a few persons at rest, especially on upper floors of buildings. Delicately suspended objects may swing.

And so on up to the maximum intensity:

XII. Damage total. Waves seen on ground surfaces. Lines of sight and level are distorted. Objects thrown upward into air.

Little earthquakes—premonitory tremors, earthquake swarms —could be precursors of big ones, deadly ones. . . .

Stop! The reels of his mind balked, refused to turn. Nor would his deepest self give authorization to continue the profitless self-torture. When the memory he tried to keep buried stirred, he forced it back, since it undermined his normal self-image. Because he had another, secret image of himself, as shaken and helpless.

When Vail returned from the ocean, he found his son in the backyard poking a patch of yellow mud that lay along a narrow strip. Dun had dug for a pipe to the studio. The mud was new.

"Mark! You're getting yourself filthy."

Kay appeared from the studio. "Where did that mud come from? It hasn't rained today yet."

"It will." Harry compressed his lips. "I guess the new pipe is leaking for some reason. Is there water in the studio?"

She vanished and returned. "No."

"That's the answer then. Where's Dun?"

"He left right after you did. He said he had something to do and seemed in a hurry."

"I'd better get him back. People will slip or track mud all over the house, and I don't know anything about pipes." He surveyed the yellow patch. "It's funny—Dun doesn't usually make mistakes."

They expected company that evening, and Kay said, "If you're going to the village I'll give you a small list." She added anxiously, "Head all right?"

He sensed that the ache was there, dormantly. "Do until I get a new one."

Under a canopy of trees, Vail maneuvered his twenty-year-old Rolls Royce. The car, which he kept in perfect condition, was rather an affectation—it gave him a country squire look he didn't deserve—but he had so few airs, he thought, that one wouldn't matter. The long driveway was filled with holes, exposing rocks sharp as drill bits. He would have the drive graded and graveled when the rain stopped.

The Rolls Royce turned onto Point Road, the only thoroughfare down the narrow four-mile-long peninsula called Old Brompton Township. Between the stone house and the village lay a half-mile section of empty land. Fred Demming owned it and would never sell. The stretch was like a buffer zone between the rich summer people up the peninsula and the villagers, whom none of the others wanted to know socially. The Vails were neither rich nor summer people, since they lived on the peninsula the year round, but socially they allied themselves with the rich because the villagers were, well, impossible.

Nobody appeared to have counted how many people lived in Old Brompton Village—or Shonkawa Village, as its inhabitants called it, using the Indian name. A hundred or so, Vail guessed, the descendants of the early settlers. Farming in the area had long since declined because of the sandy, low-yield soil, and the more enterprising local people had broken with the past and moved away. Those who remained took a bare livelihood from the sea, and from occasional work for the summer people, who arrived in June and left after Labor Day. Except for a small general store and a grubby, unfriendly bar, the village had no stores nor even the inevitable shore restaurant. The few tourists that came turned around and departed.

Bleak against the slate sky, the village appeared after a bend, almost as though whoever laid out the road had wished to keep the place out of sight. The buildings consisted of shacks and old trailers set on cinder blocks, and everything needed paint. Vail could imagine how the town green, which testified to the village's self-image, had once looked, with grass and trees and a proud cannon from the War of 1812. Now filled with abandoned vehicles, torn fishing nets, stripped machinery, staved-in boats, old lumber and weeds, the square was nothing more than a dump that happened to be in the middle of town.

On the square appeared a faded white church, the village's only vaguely presentable building. Too large for the present population, it had no minister and so Dun, as deacon, performed the services. The church, the old man said, housed a valuable old Aeolian-Skinner pipe organ, and Vail took his word for it, having never been inside. Like the others who lived above the buffer zone, the Vails were not churchgoers, and the place was always locked except on Sunday mornings. Nobody from up the peninsula ever attended services.

The town looked deserted except for Sam Wilbore a tall, long-haired, athletic-looking youth who stood on the ramshackle pier, a pile of flat white stones beside him. He reached down, took a stone, and launched it across the bay, where it skipped a half dozen times on the water. When Vail parked the car and got out, Wilbore turned suddenly to reveal a face in which hardness mixed with craft and stupidity. It seemed surprised.

Uncomfortable with most of the villagers, and especially with the Wilbore clan, Vail made himself say, "Where is everybody?"

Wilbore hesitated, as if uncertain whether to respond at all. "Church."

"Saturday?"

"Memorial service," Wilbore mumbled. He turned his back and launched another stone.

Vail's eyes, following the trajectory, saw a distant column of smoke, barely discernible against the overcast horizon. "What's that?" he asked.

Wilbore said over his shoulder, "Tank farm blew up near Newport."

"Anyone hurt?" The kid shrugged. An idea jabbed at Vail's brain. "What time did it blow?"

" 'Bout an hour ago."

"An hour!" That was when he had fallen from the ladder. He calculated: the storage tanks were about five miles across the water, too far for shock waves to have traveled through the ledgerock below. He said, "Thanks."

The Wilbore General Store was locked: Mrs. Wilbore, Sam's mother, must be in church, toward which, Vail noticed, the boy now sauntered, leaving the village to Vail. Try as he might, he could not rid his mind of the earthsound and the suspicion that went with it; if there had been a tremor, mightn't it have left clues? He began to prowl the street looking for cracks in the pavement—broken windowpanes, fallen objects—but found nothing unusual. As he approached the church he heard the bleat of the pipe organ; the music suddenly stopped, and the villagers poured out.

In their plain-colored clothes, they regarded him with blank eyes, as if he were a curiosity. Such strange folk, he reflected, from another culture almost, in some other time. How little he had learned about them in the three years he had lived in Old Brompton; but after all, they kept to themselves.

"Looking for something, Mr. Vail?" Dun inquired, appearing from the throng. Vail explained about the mud and the leaking pipe. Creases deepened in Dun's weathered face. "Wonder what went wrong. Go right over." Vail regarded the liverish sky. "With all this rain, Dun, maybe you should build us an ark."

Vail returned to the store. Mrs. Wilbore was a tall, strongly built woman with short dark hair and a lined, stony face, the face of someone who never changed her mind. As long as the Vails had lived here he had tolerated her vague chill, her taut refusal to smile, his own discomfort when their gazes met. Invariably, he wondered what went on behind the red-rimmed eyes. There were several possibilities. Conveniently overlooking the fact that her store did not carry meat, she might be piqued because the Vails did their major shopping elsewhere. His vocal objections to the driving habits of her teenage sons, Sam and Cy, might have annoyed her. The boys tooled down Point Road day and night, honking, tailgating, driving fast, and someday, he told Mrs. Wilbore, somebody would get hurt or killed, but she wouldn't listen. Also, perhaps, she lumped him with the rich summer people whom the villagers appeared to resent and envy. But Vail believed what really bothered Mrs. Wilbore was his purchase of the stone house from her spinster sister-in-law, for Mrs. Wilbore had been cold from the start. Vail had questioned Dun about her, but the old man failed to enlighten him.

In the back of the store, Vail almost tripped on a can, then

26

saw that several cans had fallen from a stack against the wall. Some cereal boxes were down from a high shelf. Putting his purchases on the counter, he said to Mrs. Wilbore, "Some things have fallen down in the back of the store. Just thought I'd tell you."

She stared at him bleakly and began punching the register. "Oh?"

"Mrs. Wilbore, this might sound silly to you, but do you remember hearing the cans fall?"

"Pardon?"

"I'm trying to find out when they fell."

"No idea, Mr. Vail."

"Or why they fell?"

"Somebody must have knocked them down." Her glance included him among the suspects. "That'll be six twenty-seven."

Absently, Vail produced six dollars and fished in his pockets for change, coming up with a quarter, which he placed on the counter.

"Six twenty-seven," she repeated without touching the money.

He blinked, felt a surge of annoyance, found a ten dollar bill in his wallet and handed it over silently. Mrs. Wilbore made change without speaking. He swung the box under his arm and left the store hurriedly.

Two cents! Two cents! And the way she overcharges! He'd see to it they shopped there even less often. Feeling demeaned, he slipped too easily into what happened next.

Cy and Sam Wilbore leaned against the fender of the carefully polished Rolls. Cy was about eighteen and Sam about two years younger; both were almost as tall as Vail but lean, without his heft. They had dark hair and pointed faces like their mother's, with the same narrow, congenitally red-rimmed eyes. Vail said, "Get off the car."

Neither boy moved. " 'Fraid we'll scratch your fancy buggy,

Mr. Vail?" Cy Wilbore said. He asked his brother, "Sam, you got a burr on your ass?"

"Why, have a look," Sam clowned. He bent and turned the seat of his Levis toward Vail.

Cy Wilbore leaned over and looked. "No burr." He settled back on the fender.

"You kids are too much," Vail said, his deep voice tight with anger.

Cy Wilbore laughed. "Lose something? Saw you poking around."

"Well, it's a free country."

"Yeah? Never know it from all you rich folks' signs that say 'Private Property—Keep Out.' "

"I didn't put them up," said Vail, who didn't have one, though the summer people all did as a way of keeping outsiders off the beaches. He was losing his temper, and he surveyed the peeling shacks and the town square deliberately. "Though, considering the looks of this place, I can see why people do."

Cy's face twisted. He extended his middle finger and made an X on the hood of the Rolls. "Fuck you," he said distinctly.

The ache jerked in Vail's head like a muscle spasm. *"Get off the car!"* he roared. Neither boy budged. He lunged, grabbed their necks, and with all his two hundred pounds behind him, lifted them from the Rolls and threw them on the ground. Sam Wilbore lay gasping for breath while Cy got to his feet and backed away, the whiteness of his face exaggerating the red rims of his eyes.

Vail jumped into the car and drove off. He hit his driveway too fast and the Rolls shuddered in the holes. The dog barked as he sat in the car trying to calm himself. Even after a decade in New England Vail still thought of himself as a Californian—easygoing, essentially unflappable—as opposed to Easterners, who in his stereotype were tense and erratic. As he considered the scene in the village, he wondered if he had become an hysterical Easterner, too. Surely there must have been a better way to handle the Wilbore kids.

The barking persisted, and Vail, himself again, left the car. "Shut up, Punch. Don't you ever know it's me?" he growled playfully as he picked up the dog by its long bushy tail, an act to which Punch never seemed to object though others had. He put the groceries in the kitchen and went to the backyard where Dun was digging an oblong trench. "I'll give you a hand, Dun," he said.

Kay's face appeared in the doorway of the studio. "Oh no you don't. No physical exercise until we're absolutely sure there's nothing wrong with that head of yours."

"No problem, son. Ground's soft. Almost finished already."

"Well, all right."

Vail joined his wife in the studio. Over the winter, the renovation of the stone house finished at last, Dun had converted part of the barn—a small building probably used once for holding corn—into a studio for Kay. In what had been the storage room, Dun installed insulation, wiring, new flooring, plasterboard walls, a lavatory, spotlights in the ceiling and, because a skylight would have been too expensive, a picture window that overlooked the massive gray rock in the backyard. Neat and cozy, the studio would replace the cramped bedroom she had used before. If the past few summers were any guide, between now and Labor Day Kay would gradually sell off her winter's worth of acrylics and watercolors to the summer people, earning enough to pay for her paints, canvases and frames plus the yearly upkeep of her mare, Brioche. Vail hoped that the studio would help keep Kay busy during the long winters, which were hard on her, especially the last one, with Mark in first grade and himself away frequently on business trips. She sometimes complained of being lonely, nervous, depressed, and waited eagerly for spring when the skunk cabbage, marsh marigolds, dogtooth violets and shadbush blossoms told her that the summer people were on the way like a rescue mission. Unlike Harry, Kay was very gregarious.

During the morning Kay had been hanging her pictures and for the first time the studio looked like one. Harry said, "Terrific."

"Isn't it? Thank you—it's a wonderful present." She kissed him. "Like the arrangement?"

He inspected the pictures in their clear plastic frames: perhaps because of his geological training, he often displayed a better spatial sense than she did. He said, "They're all at a slight angle."

"Angle?" She stepped back.

"Look at the frames in relation to the floor."

"You're right. How spooky. I'd have sworn I had them straight. Well, what about the layout?" she repeated.

He pointed to a picture. "That's too high. It ought to go there—to the left of the one of the boulder."

"Will you change it?"

A hammer and picture hooks lay on the table. He put in a new hook and took down the picture. He stared at it. As time passed Kay's work had constantly become more literal—this painting was almost photographic. It showed part of a wall of the stone house. "Have I seen this before?"

"It's new. I just painted it. Like it?"

"Yes, I do. It's just that . . ." Something seemed wrong—some minor detail he could not quite extract from the pattern of stones and mortar. Dun entered the studio and Vail's head turned.

"Found the problem, Mr. Vail. Care to come outside?"

Vail followed the short, spare figure. It had started to drizzle. Dun pointed at the trench he had dug and said, "Leak in the coupling. Guess I messed up." He kicked the ground playfully

30

and his smile revealed small brown teeth. "Fix it now before the rain gets too bad."

"What about the hole?"

"Put a piece of plywood over her so nobody falls in and finish up tomorrow."

Vail looked away from the open trench. "Okay," he said.

Vail was shaving in the bathroom when Kay said, "You'd better hurry."

"They never come on time." He combed his hair, slipped on clothes and said, "Your turn to step on it."

"I'm ready," she said from her dressing table. She inserted the other earring through her pierced ear, did a final flourish with her comb, and stood up to be appraised and to appraise, cocking her head as she studied her husband.

Vail was a muscular man a little over six feet tall, with a round, friendly face, pea-green eyes and a complexion ruddied from the outdoors. He wore an old tweed jacket over a sport shirt, cavalry twill trousers, brown suede shoes. "You have your own look, God knows, and what a look! When the weather gets warmer you'll wear the new summer blazer I bought you," she said firmly. She turned to scrutinize herself in the full-length mirror. "Anyway, it's how *I* look that matters."

Kay was thirty-four, three years younger than Vail. Like him, she had reddish hair and ruddy skin. But she was eight inches shorter and not much more than half his weight. Somehow the leap of her breasts from a thin ribcage seemed structurally sound. Her lean nervous hands fingered her pearls. "I'm wearing a new bra," she went on. "a bra that isn't a bra. Do my nipples show?" She turned to face him.

"A little."

She seemed disconcerted. "I don't want them to show. They're for your eyes only. I'll change."

31

"You don't really show—there's just the suggestion. It's what you want," he said.

They were still as they examined each other's faces. "You're a good strong man, Harry Vail," she said. "I'm lucky to have you. We have a fine life."

"Yes," he said. "We have everything anybody could want, just about. We're awfully lucky."

"It's true." She became subdued. "I just wish the rain would stop. It's like summer hasn't started yet, and the winter was so long." She looked brighter. "The real summer will start soon."

"We'll go on a trip next winter, I promise."

"That's what you said last winter and the winter before. It always costs too much. I wish we had as much money as our friends."

"The Demmings and the Pollidors? Well, I guess they'd be even unhappier without it."

"Stop that. I hate it when you sound superior. Smug even. I think you actually enjoy being middle class."

"We're the backbone of the country," he said with a round smile. "And I'm *not* smug. We're perfect, that's all."

"Oh, I don't know. You're overweight and I have a mole on my behind."

"I'm going to say good night to Mark." His gaze slid past her to the window. "Look, it's stopped raining. See how lucky we are?"

She pressed her body to his. "Do I look nice? Answer me."

The Pollidors, who had a relative as a house guest, and the Demmings were the Vails' closest neighbors on the peninsula. As Harry predicted, all were late. Kay fluttered around the living room, patting the couch cushions, changing positions of ashtrays, pouring birdseed in the brass cage, rearranging flowers that stood on the grand piano. Harry put wood in the fire and lit it. Smoke billowed. Using tongs that hung on a metal plate screwed in the wall, he pushed the logs deeper into the fireplace; smoke continued to pour into the room. "Christ," he said, "the flue is shut. I don't remember closing it."

"I didn't," she said, "so you must have."

"I could say exactly the same thing," he retorted.

"Better open the window," she said, and he did, with effort. The smoke cleared.

When the shelty's high-pitched barks telegraphed guests, Big Ben, the grandfather clock, said 9:30. "Shhhh, Punch," Kay scolded as she opened the door. "Darlings!"

Polly Pollidor entered first, talking as usual. A short, pretty woman in her late thirties or early forties, with shoulder-length brown hair and a straight profile, Polly contrived to look simple and expensive at the same time. Her forehead was split down the middle by a sharp vertical frown line which she tried to hide with makeup. Polly and her husband Bill had married young and recently celebrated their twentieth anniversary. They had no children. Polly was an heiress from a manufacturing family. She was saying to Kay, holding her arm, "My dear, don't you look glamorous! How do you keep your hair so nice in all this damp? Me, I look like a wet mop, and not a hairdresser in Old Brompton. I swear I'll import one from New York. Not that it will do any good, with all this rain. Have you seen the like? I hear it's the beginning of a new age, with the ice cap melting, the seas expanding, the continents drifting around like rafts. Pretty soon Old Brompton will be under water and we'll have to move—or grow gills. Why, the peninsula's half submerged already. Torturous Creek is close to overflowing. . . ."

Bill Pollidor stood behind her. A balding man in his middle forties with a narrow, shell-like head and blue veins webbing his cheeks and the sides of his nose, he was a New York tax lawyer. He spent most of the summer in Old Brompton, conducting his business by phone and getting drunk every night. Not gently, he tapped his wife's shoulder and said, "You're forgetting our guest."

Polly said quickly, "This is Jeffrey Carmichael. We've been in love for years, even though he's my first cousin."

In a tartan blazer and white sandals, Carmichael stepped forward, hand outstretched. A handsome man about Vail's age, he walked on the balls of his feet like a sprinter ready to run in any direction. His brown eyes looked inquisitive. He was a television reporter for one of the networks and his wife had recently left him, Polly had told the Vails. He needed warmth and reassurance, she said.

"We've seen you on the tube, of course!" Kay told him.

"Always glad to hear that," Carmichael said with a bright smile under his mustache. As they entered the living room from the foyer he exclaimed, "What a lovely place!"

Kay looked pleased. "When we fixed it up we tried to keep it pretty much as it was."

"You were right." He glanced quickly at the Pollidors, who had done the opposite the year before, gutting their old farmhouse and converting it into a modern dwelling with glass walls and high ceilings. "Not that starting over isn't all right, too!" He examined the beams nestling in white plaster, the marble fireplace, the old peanut vendor's cart on sturdy wheels, which Kay had converted into a bar. "What a good idea!" He pointed at the brass birdcage. "That's a pretty bird. What kind is it?"

"Nobody ever asks me that," Kay said warmly. "It's called a green singing finch. It's supposed to have a nice voice, except this one doesn't seem to know how to sing. It never has, anyway."

"Maybe it needs another finch to sing to," Jeff said, wrinkling his eyes. He nodded toward a row of squat jugs with painted faces and three-cornered hats that gleamed on a lighted glass shelf above the bar cart. "What are those?"

"I picked them up at an auction. They're real antiques," Kay explained. "They're called Toby jugs after one Toby Philpot who is a character in a poem, I think. The faces are all different, but they're modeled after an eighteenth-century Englishman whose name I've forgotten. He's supposed to have drunk two thousand gallons of beer without eating."

"Bill Pollidor could do that," Polly chuckled. "Oh, you won't believe what Bill's done. He bought a bar with a computer! It was supposed to come today from New York—but it didn't, which will ruin Bill's weekend. Wait till you hear what it cost!"

Pollidor broke in. "It can be programmed to make a hundred kinds of drinks, if you provide the liquor. I wonder if it ever gets drunk."

Harry laughed and took the drink orders while Carmichael asked Kay, "Are there many stone houses around here?"

"No. We have the only one on the peninsula."

"You must be very special. How old is the house?"

"That's a bit of a mystery," Kay said volubly. "Around here they documented the pedigree of the houses very well until just after the Civil War, when the local archivists suddenly got lazy. Some say records got destroyed in a fire, but we can't seem to find out exactly when the house was built, or who built it. The woman we bought it from three years ago—funny little thing, she was—wanted the money in cash, all of it. Fortunately I had a small inheritance from my father and Harry his savings. The woman vanished as soon as the deal was máde. We know the family, the Wilbores, but they're not very, well, communicative. Anyway, the builder must have been a Wilbore because most of the property on the peninsula has stayed in the same families except those that were forced to sell when farming went bad. The house is definitely post–Civil War, and it was certainly a farmhouse, like most of the old houses here, since it stands at the end of a long drive and farmers always built in the center of their fields, right, Harry? Harry believes the house must be built on the foundations of another house, because it's a good location."

"Why did this particular farmer use stone?" Carmichael inquired.

"Who knows?" Kay said. "Maybe he wanted to show off a little, but my bet is that the stone gave him a feeling of stability, of security." Under Jeff's stare she blushed beneath her freckles. "You *do* ask a lot of questions."

Carmichael replied gaily, "Of course! It's my business." As if to prove it, he asked, "Where did the stone come from? Or is that a mystery, too?"

"Yes, that's a mystery, too," Kay confessed with a sigh. "The stone looks local because it's the same color as the seacliffs, but it couldn't have come from there because the cliffs are crumbly, or something. But Harry can't find a quarry anywhere on the peninsula. Stone is Harry's thing. He's a geologist, you know."

"I was told. Are you also interested in geology?"

"Me?" Kay cried. "What do I know about science? My thing is people. People are a lot more interesting than rocks, though Harry doesn't think so. He's fascinated by the earth, aren't you, honey? He believes it's alive."

"Alive?" Carmichael's mustache turned toward his host.

Just then Punch exploded like a string of firecrackers and the door opened. Wende Demming's low voice said, "Surprise, surprise. It's us."

Each Demming rated a superlative.

Fred had money, much of it inherited. With extensive real estate in Boston and elsewhere, including the peninsula, Demming was surely the richest man in affluent Old Brompton, but he seemed to have paid a price. His hands shook as though from a mild palsy; his gruff face looked older than his fifty years and he wore thick glasses. Remote in manner, he was no longer interested in wealth, only the uses of it, like power, and women, in the person of his wife.

Wende was a former beauty queen and still reigned as one in Old Brompton. Twenty years younger than her husband, tall, small-boned, she had a narrow waist and long, supple legs. Her face, white-skinned, blue-eyed, oval, looked fragile, deceptively. Wende was an immensely competitive woman who delighted in being a general at games. Sometimes she would glance at her own breasts, arms, fingernails or legs with a little onanistic smile: she was capable, she had joked, of becoming aroused simply by inspecting herself in the mirror. She was not entirely happy, however, she once confessed to Kay, who had a way of bringing people out. There was some deep need in her that Fred failed to satisfy, and sometimes, impetuously, she would depart in her cream-colored Mercedes convertible for several days at a time. In Vail's judgment, Wende didn't want to grow up.

He brought the newcomers into the circle, introduced them to Carmichael and made drinks, including a fresh one for Pollidor.

Kay was silent, Harry saw, and understood. She had kept them from the new studio for tonight's unveiling and now she was eager to show it. "Come see the new studio," he said.

Chattering, they trooped across the lawn toward the square of light from the picture window. Harry had to push hard on the door to open it. "I thought you were going to straighten the pictures, Kay," he said as they filed in.

"I thought I did," she said. "I guess I didn't."

To all but Jeff Carmichael the scenes on the walls were familiar, yet in a sense they were new to the summer people too, since they depicted winter in Old Brompton, when they were not there. The brackish pond with a lone swan huddled in the sedges; the jutting block of granite behind the house that looked like a giant gravestone; a single deer by the little house in the woods; the big elm in the backyard, soaring black and desolate with the little clay bell hanging from a branch.

"Kay, you've changed your style!" Polly exclaimed.

Kay smiled gratefully as she straightened another picture. "I'm trying to be more realistic, that's all."

"Do you exhibit in New York?" Jeff asked.

"I wish I did! No, I'm just an amateur. Painting's therapy for me. It keeps me from going crazy when Harry's away on business and our son's in school."

"Pretty good for an amateur," Jeff said. He pointed to the picture of the little house. "What's that?"

Wende answered, "It's a playhouse Fred built for his children when they were small. It's like a real house, in miniature, with a little kitchen and living room with tiny furniture. It's in the woods, right where the Pollidors', the Vails' and our property all meet." She added lightly, "His kids by his first wife."

"You didn't need to tell me," Jeff said. His gaze rested on Wende's clear face a little longer than necessary. "What's that big rock? I haven't seen anything like it around here."

"It's a hunk of granite in the backyard," Harry explained. "You're right—there's nothing like it around here. Nearest granite that shade of gray is probably thirty miles to the south. It was carried here when the last glacier receded and dumped when it melted. That was about 10,000 B.C. Can you imagine the power involved? It weighs tons."

"I guess Mother Nature hasn't got the stuff she used to have," Jeff observed. "She's all worn out, here in the East anyway."

"Oh, I don't know. The trouble is, tucked away in our cities we're losing the feel of the earth. If Mother Nature gets in a bad mood, we don't know what to do. And things can happen."

"What things?" Jeff demanded.

Harry shrugged. "Hurricanes, floods, droughts . . . earth-quakes."

"Earthquakes? When has there been an earthquake anywhere but out West?"

"You can get tremors everywhere."

Jeff said impatiently, "Sure, sure. But I mean a *real* earthquake."

"A tremor, even a tiny one, *is* an earthquake. As for severity, one in early Salem was strong enough to knock down chimneys. There was a good-sized earthquake in Boston last century and a serious quake in Charleston, South Carolina, about 1875. A tremendous earthquake hit the Midwest in 1811 and 1812. Some said the Mississippi actually flowed backward for a brief time. The Indians under Tecumseh took it as a divine sign and rose against the whites."

"Well, that's a long while back," Jeff argued.

"By what standards? Ours, maybe, but by the earth's it was just a second ago. You never know what Mother Nature is up to."

"Oh yes, you think the earth is alive, your wife said."

"The earth isn't exactly alive, but in many ways it's like a living organism. The crust would be its skin, rocks its bones, veins of metal its nerves, water its blood. And it does have a heart—its core. There's movement under the earth, just as living things move, and it changes, too, as living things change."

They moved to the next watercolor, the one Harry had rehung, depicting the stone wall of the house. He stared at the stone mosaic intently. "Kay," he said, "I thought this was your realistic year."

"It is. Why?"

He had been aware before of a peculiar detail in the painting. Now, inspecting the canvas closely, he saw that Kay had painted a tiny crack, like a series of diagonal *W*'s, in the stones near the roof of the house. "There's no crack like that. Not in our house."

She glanced at him. "Of course there is."

"Since when?"

"Since always."

"I'm sure it wasn't there when we bought the house. Where is it?"

39

"On the wall outside Mark's room." Kay smiled with her mouth, not her eyes, and said, "Maybe you don't get to that side of the house much. Maybe you've forgotten."

He shook his head. "When did you finish the picture?"

"This morning." She turned to the others and said kiddingly, "Harry fell today and whacked his head. It's affected his memory, which is usually sharp."

"Nothing's wrong with my memory," he insisted.

She sucked in her thin cheeks. "Well, darling," she said sweetly, "you can see the crack for yourself tomorrow. And ask Dun if it hasn't always been there."

She turned to leave the studio, but Harry insisted, "Kay, didn't we take pictures of the house and grounds with your Polaroid when we bought the place?"

"I don't remember."

"Try. I'm sure we did."

"Maybe we did at that. We were going to make a 'before and after' album but never got around to it. Why do you ask?"

He said, trying to keep his voice even, "Where are the photos?"

"How should I know?"

The others had stopped speaking. "I just asked if you remembered, that's all," he said.

Kay said to the others, "Shall we go?"

"Your work is really improving, Kay," Polly Pollidor was saying. "You ought to think about a New York show. Why, the awful stuff they're selling in the galleries these days, and the prices! It's scandalous. . . ."

Vail remained in the studio to turn off the lights after the group had found its way to the house, but even after voices faded he stood by the picture window, thinking about the crack. Why couldn't he quite bring himself to believe her? And if by some dreadful chance he was right, the implication of a new crack could be serious. It could mean that the house was shifting

40

in subsoil turned to treacle by the unprecedented rains. He told himself to stop imagining things.

About to leave the studio, he heard the mare champ in her stall on the other side of the barn and, almost simultaneously, Punch's staccato bark. He turned again to the picture window. Usually he put the Rolls in the barn, but this time, preoccupied when he returned from the village, he had left it outside. It stood behind the Demmings' and Pollidors' cars, on the edge of the pool of light. His eyes probed the darkness. Did he detect movement behind the Rolls, the white of a hand, a retreating figure?

He went outside. Clouds curtained the sky and the dark behind the Rolls was almost total.

Vail turned off the studio lights, closed the door and returned to the house. Heads raised a little too quickly when he entered the living room. Kay said, "Why did Punch bark?"

"Wild animal—deer, fox, owl. Happens all the time," he said for the benefit of Carmichael, the newcomer.

"Sure it wasn't a prowler?" Kay asked.

"Didn't see anybody." He looked at her. "Why?"

"Polly says there have been robberies on the peninsula recently. And Bill thinks he's seen people walking in the woods."

"I wouldn't take that too seriously. He sees a lot of things after he's had a couple," Polly said lightly.

"Listen," said Pollidor, "you were the one who insisted I install the burglar alarm."

"No sense taking chances."

"A burglar alarm?" Kay said. "But who would hear it?"

"That doesn't matter. The important thing is that thieves *think* that people can hear it, or that it's hooked up to a police station. That's what the man who installed it today told me. What a joke, because it runs on batteries and isn't hooked up to anything. Another joke is the local police!"

"What's wrong with them?" Jeff asked.

41

"Them? We have exactly one cop, and he's practically senile."

"Police, burglar alarms," Kay said, her face showing concern. "But who would be in our woods?"

"The village idiots, who else?" Pollidor shouted. "I hope they keep their distance, because if they don't, bang! bang!" He extended his left arm and placed his right fist to his cheek, as though sighting.

Jeff broke in. "Who are these villagers?"

Demming leaned forward and spat out one word: "Fools!"

"I don't get it."

Demming replied, "You have to know the situation. The so-called summer people like myself own much of the land on the peninsula but by no means all. The locals come from farming families and, though they no longer farm, they still own land—quite a bit of it. On the theory that the price of land will rise, some time ago they made a collective decision to hang on, not to sell until the price went higher. And it was a good idea, so far as it went. The price of land *is* rising."

"Then why don't they sell?"

"The fact that the price rises confirms their expectations that it will rise still more. And so it will, slowly, again confirming their view. If the price of land dropped, they would sell at once, but it won't drop, and so we have the status quo. They will always hope for a still higher price, and we do our best to preserve the expectation."

"Oh?"

Demming waved his cane. "Some of us—I don't mean the Vails here; they're a little naive about such things—have influence on the town council."

"Run it, you mean," Bill Pollidor said.

Demming ignored him and went on, "We see to it that the zoning laws are so strict you can't put a vegetable stand on the road, and that real estate taxes stay dirt cheap so as not to strain

42

the locals' pocketbooks. The summer people pretty much finance the town, through various charitable donations."

Harry and Kay bartered glances. Carmichael exclaimed, "So!"

"And from time to time," Demming continued, "blind offers to purchase the villagers' lands are made through us. The price is always high enough to be interesting and low enough to be turned down."

Jeff said, "But surely there comes a time when someone wants to sell. How do they keep each other in line? Social pressure?"

"Oh, it's a matter of a handful of families, really. Any one of them who thinks of selling faces ostracism. They did it in the case of the Wilbore woman who sold to the Vails here. She vanished immediately after and hasn't been heard from since. Forced to move away, I suppose. That was the last land sold in these parts—three years ago. They haven't forgiven Vail yet, just for buying the property."

Harry whirled as something crashed at the bar. Bill Pollidor had lurched against it, upsetting a bottle. " 'S okay," he said, righting it.

Polly said quickly, "They're practically like an Indian tribe, clinging to their old ways!"

"She's right," Kay remarked. "They *are* like the Indians. The village is almost a reservation, and in it they're dying off. I just hope they don't come back to haunt us, too."

"Haunt us?" Harry asked.

Kay said wanly, "A few weeks ago Mrs. Wilbore got talkative for a change, and she told me that people hereabouts used to believe that Indian ghosts haunt the peninsula, seeking revenge on the early settlers who squeezed them off their lands. Eventually the whole tribe died of starvation." She shivered slightly.

Polly chirped, "It would be just like the villagers to believe in ghosts."

"A surprising number of people do in one form or another," Jeff remarked. "They don't admit it because they're afraid they'll sound foolish."

He happened to glance at Kay, who said quickly, "Not me! I don't believe in ghosts."

Said Jeff, tilting his mustache, "Did I say you did?"

Kay faltered. "Well, no. But . . ."

"Anyway, it's *how* you die that counts—not what comes after. Don't we all pick our own form of death in a way? I mean, don't we willingly choose our death zones? Say, I know a game . . ." Jeff stopped speaking, as if he had thought better of what he was about to say.

"Let's come back to life," Kay said. "Who's hungry? I have sandwiches in the dining room."

They cleaned up in silence after the others had gone. Kay said finally, "Have a good time?"

"So-so."

"What did you think of Jeff?"

"Kind of a know-it-all."

"Wende liked him. I hope nothing's starting, for Fred's sake. Say, the tap water's running brown. I wonder why."

"Water from the pond must be getting in the well—it's happened before."

"I hated all that talk about ghosts." She straightened up from the dishwasher and looked at him. "You weren't yourself tonight, the way you carried on about the silly old crack. It was embarrassing, Harry."

"Was it? Would you be embarrassed if the house fell down?"

"Mortarfied," she joked. "Harry, I just don't understand why the crack bothers you so."

"It's just that I don't remember seeing it. I'd still like to look at those photos."

"All right!" she snapped and set down a pot with a bang.

"I'll look for them in the morning. In the meantime try to remember the crack is in your head! I'm going to bed."

"I'll put the cars in the barn."

"Hurry."

He took a flashlight from the hall closet and went outdoors, rounding the house until he stood below Mark's window, where he shone the light, seeing nothing except tangled patterns of shadow and stone. He put both cars in the barn and started back to the house, when the light picked up the whitish oblong shape on the lawn.

He stopped still, wrestling with his emotions. Something inside him demanded that he look beneath, into the open hole, into the earth. No, no, he argued helplessly, but it did not lie within his power to prevent himself, so strong was the compulsion. He knelt, put the flashlight on the grass, and lifted the plywood with both hands. His skin cringed at the outline of the cadaverously thin body at the bottom of the trench. *God damn you, it's only a pipe!*

He replaced the plywood and entered the house, alarmed by his own reactions. Inside, he became aware of Kay's half-fearful cry from the bedroom, as though she had called before.

"Harry?"

She lay in bed. As he began to undress she said, "You were gone forever. Where were you?"

He hadn't been aware of time passing, and he wondered how long he had knelt by the open hole. "Checking the house," he muttered.

"Poor baby," she said as he got into bed. "I'm sorry I snapped at you. Can we make up?" Her breasts were taut against his chest as they made love in the silence of the bedroom. When it was over, she said, "That was wonderful."

"Yes." He sat up.

"Didn't I satisfy you?" she said plaintively.

"Of course you did."

45

"What's the matter then?"

"Kay, I felt the bed shake."

She laughed without restraint. "Of course it shook. The whole world shook. That was us making it shake."

His mouth had opened into an *O*. "No. In some other way."

"It was *us*, damn you," she cried. "Harry, are you getting back your trouble?"

He lay coiled like a watchspring on his side of the bed, listening to her breathe. Normally after sex, and especially after sex on top of a few drinks, he slept like a petrified object. Once as he started to doze something seemed to fall on him, and he woke with an involuntary start. Vail knew he was in for a siege.

The room was still except for the soft sounds entering the open door, sounds to which he was so accustomed as to be usually unaware—the grumble of a pump, the whine of the refrigerator, the patter of a little animal somewhere inside the walls, the creak of a beam, the faint clanging of the clay bell in the tree. Every house has its own sounds, like its own personality, he thought. His was old, slightly complaining. Vail shifted uncomfortably, senses alert, waiting.

Ever since he had hurt his back playing football he had sat on hard chairs and slept with a board beneath his mattress, and he was uncertain whether the rumble reached him from outside, far away, or from the bed, transmitted by the board plate. He ran to the window and threw up the shade, scrutinizing the night. For just an instant he thought he saw on the road two dots of red that danced and vanished. *Must be a truck, has to be a truck.* But why a truck at that hour?

He returned to bed. Sweat rose on his forehead. Careful not to wake Kay and let her see him in this state, he stayed as motionless as he could.

Dawn breaking behind the windowshade found him immobile

and exhausted. The wind had ceased; the room was utterly still, as if Kay had stopped breathing. Nothing had happened, just as nothing could have happened, would ever happen, to justify his dread. He sighed and started to sleep, and then he felt it: quick, nervous, light, evasive, almost gentle, a shudder in the bed. Kay rolled over without waking.

Vail woke on Sunday feeling terrible. Kay entered the bedroom and he asked her what time it was. "Nine-thirty." She put her palm flat on his forehead. "The sheet's wet as if you've been sweating, but you don't have a fever."

"I'm all right," he grumbled. "Dun here?"

"Yes. He's finishing up before he goes to church."

He dressed and had breakfast, though he lacked appetite. Mark was watching TV in the living room as permitted when the weather was bad. Vail went outside, eyes on the unavoidable clouds.

"Watch out!" Dun shouted.

Vail walked gingerly around the open trench. Dun set down the wheelbarrow and said, "Don't want no more accidents, do we? Feeling all right, Mr. Vail?"

"I've been better," he said. "Tell me, Dun, did a truck come to the village late last night?"

"Yes, as a matter of fact. Something to deliver to the Pollidors from New York."

"At that hour?"

"Supposed to get here yesterday afternoon, but the truck broke down on the highway," said Dun. His universe, however small, seemed to hold few secrets. "Slept in their truck in the village and waited until morning to ask directions. Come here, did they?"

"No. I heard the truck on the road." It showed how capable he was of misreading evidence. "Come with me, Dun."

"Oh, Mr. Vail." Dun, walking by his side, seemed eager to speak. "Your car has a flat tire."

"Thanks. I'll fix it this afternoon."

"No, I'll do it for you, Mr. Vail . . . son. Tire has a gash in it."

"Oh?" Harry said, moving rapidly on his long legs. "Maybe one of those sharp rocks in the driveway. Hit it too hard," he surmised. "Drive needs grading."

"Come look at the tire, Mr. Vail."

"Later."

They turned the corner of the house and stood below Mark's windows. Looking up, Harry saw a thin, steplike crack up near the roof, exactly where Kay had painted it. "How long has that crack been there?"

Dun had been working around the place since the Vails had bought it. He scratched his cheek with yellowed nails and squinted, as though having difficulty locating the break. "Just a surface crack in the mortar. Don't mean a thing."

"I know. But how long has it been there?" Vail said impatiently.

The handyman shifted his weight from one foot to the other and opened his lips to speak.

"Dun!" Standing behind them, Kay spoke sharply. She intimidated the old man a little, Harry was aware. "It's always been there. You know that."

The handyman gave Kay a hesitant sidelong glance. "Reckon that's right," he said.

But Dun was absentminded and might have forgotten. "You don't have to put words in his mouth," Harry snapped at her.

Kay's face filled with surprise. He saw that she held a manila envelope. "The photos. I found them in a box in the basement. I wanted to show you." She removed a photograph from the envelope and handed it to him. Dated three years earlier in his own writing, it showed a thin series of *W*'s on the outer stone wall. "Now are you satisfied?"

"I'm sorry, Kay," he said humbly.

That afternoon Vail found still another crack in the stone house.

He had gone to the basement on some errand or other and discovered water on the floor. Considering the amount of rainfall, this was not unusual, though he wondered how the water had gotten in. Mopping up the puddle, he realized that the water seemed to come from below a pile of cartons that stood against one wall. Kept in the storeroom before Dun converted it to Kay's studio, the cartons held photos, tax records, outgrown toys and clothes, an ancient Hitachi tape recorder and the like, most of which would be thrown away when he finally got round to culling the contents. He decided to move the boxes to the other side of the cellar where it was dry.

As Vail picked up the last carton, he saw what his mind insisted was a shadow or a defect in the concrete. He approached slowly, praying his eyes were deceived in the dim light, and placed his fingers on the wall. Up from the floor ran a thin crack about a foot long.

Since when? his mind's voice screamed. The crack had not been there a few months before, when he had moved the boxes from the barn, of that he was sure. What could have caused it? But maybe he was wrong about this crack too, just as he had been wrong about the one on the outside wall. Suddenly his mind began to whirl. What was real and what wasn't?

Vail told Kay he was headed for the beach, and soon he sat in his rock chair overlooking the waves. The ocean was flat, almost motionless. The fading sun lurked behind thin clouds, spreading a half-light over the seascape.

He would try to come to terms with himself, to penetrate the

49

layers of his own experience, which until then he had been extremely unwilling to do because the past held pain and terror.

He began by asking himself how many of his actions during the past decade had been taken to escape anxiety or ward it off. Abandoning a seismological career and moving from California were clearly two of them; locating the office on a lower floor of the office building might be included, and so, for that matter, might be the choice of an imposing old car that he associated with stability. His love for Old Brompton? Perhaps, subtly, yes: protected from the outside society, operating according to a strict set of rules and standards, the miniworld of Old Brompton was as unchanging a place as might be found.

But more to the point was his recent obsessive worry about tremors. What had happened, he believed, was that the fall from the ladder and the hearing of an earthsound had triggered off a neurosis he thought to have buried for good.

He had never consulted a psychiatrist for two reasons which seemed to him perfectly good: considering what he had once undergone in Alaska, his condition did not appear remarkable; and in time he thought the problem would simply go away. And so it had seemed until after the fall from the ladder. Its clinical name, if it had one, he did not know. *Seismophobia*, the fear of shaking, would be close, he imagined. Harry Vail was terrified of earthquakes.

He was still convinced that the tremors he thought to have felt were extremely unlikely. Rather, he supposed, his mind had tricked him into finding earthquake clues, made him feel shakings when there were none. He believed his old demon was possessing him, and he would try to exorcise it, no matter how shattering the experience. Carefully, he entered the cave of himself.

Vail recalled himself as a big, quiet, affable youngster who liked to backpack, climb mountains, fish. Secretly, he had been more impressed with natural than with man-made surroundings.

50

He delighted in the contour of a hill, the curve of a river, the sweep of a vista, the texture of soil, the strata in canyon walls. When first he cracked open a rock with a hammer, he had been amazed at the complexity hidden beneath the drab exterior. In sparkling layers, the rock explained the enormous scope of its life.

Without articulating it, Vail had formed an idea of the earth as awesomely ancient and, if not quite friendly, at least a reliable platform. This attitude changed. Vail lived with his parents—his father had been a doctor—in Arvin, California, a small town not far from Bakersfield. In 1952, when Vail was fourteen, the area was hit by an earthquake strong enough to earn a name for the records—the Tehachapi Earthquake, after the nearest town. Like any Californian living near the San Andreas Fault, Vail was accustomed to earthquakes, but not one of this awful power. The world tilted, becoming a heaving place in which the usual bearings disappeared and nothing stable existed.

He could recall his excitement as the ground rippled beneath him. "I'm alive, I'm alive," the earth seemed to say, and he responded to the earth's vitality. The quake seemed almost playful and caused little damage. Then, a few days later, the fickle monster turned dangerous. An aftershock may be worse than the main one, and such was the case at Arvin. Buildings collapsed; a boy Vail knew was crushed beneath a falling water tower.

For nights afterward he woke up shaking in anticipation of a new blow. Later, when he studied geology at Stanford, where he played football, and went on to seismology at the California Institute of Technology in Pasadena for his Ph.D., he would sometimes wonder whether scientific interest was the goad or whether, in some complicated, subterranean way, he was not trying to pit himself against the earth in order to prove that it held no terror. But he liked the work and displayed an instinctive feel for earth mechanics.

51

Besides, seismology took its adepts away from the lab and out into the field with backpacks and equipment. One such chance came to Vail in 1964 when . . . on his rock seat by the ocean his memory again balked, would not proceed in the recollection without instructions on how to handle the pain, how to relieve traumatic suffering. If he could avoid thinking her name . . . if he could objectify, depersonalize her just *that* much, into a nameless wraith, a shadow . . .

She was an undergraduate student and he, the big professor, married her. She had looked something like Wende Demming, he remembered, tall, blonde, thin, but rounder of face, sweeter. He had taken a leave of absence from Cal Tech, and she a semester off. An oil company had hired him to come to Anchorage, Alaska, to study seismic refraction records. Closely analyzing the geological structure as revealed by seismic waves sent off by underwater explosions in Cook Inlet, he might be able to help predict the location of oil there. When summer came and his work was complete, they would travel the Alaska Railway north to the Denali Fault, carrying a mercury tiltmeter that would record the most minute changes in ground level. Only the ground tilted earlier. . . .

They arrived in Anchorage mid-March. On Good Friday, March 27, the library where Vail pored over the seismic records closed early, and he came home to the house the oil company had found for them in an Anchorage suburb called Turnagain-Bluff-by-the-Sea. They strolled to the edge of the bluff in the windless dusk, in light flurries of snow. Sea and sky curved into each other, blending into smooth nothingness, a gray void. The face she turned to him lacked all expression. "It's like a hole to nowhere," she said, or had she said that? His memory was unreliable, because at that gray instant the ground shuddered.

"Earthquake!" he shouted, understanding at once. He seized her arm and they scrambled away from the swaying bluff. Trees rocked, the car creaked on its springs, the white picket fence danced like a chorus line. The churning subsided.

"You're safe here," he told her. "Wait. I'm going inside for the tiltmeter. It's too valuable to lose, just in case . . ."

"In case what?"

"In case there's a second shock. I'll be right back."

She clutched his hand so tightly he had to wrench it free. He took the flagstones at a run, leaving the front door open behind him. The instrument, which he had been testing, lay on the living room floor. He started toward it. Then the front door shut with a bang. The house shook as though in the grip of a monstrous animal. Walls weaved and stretched. Books and dishes flew across the room. The cuckoo emerged from the carved clock ludicrously, said "Cuckoo!" and dropped to the floor. The hands recorded 5:38.

"Hurry, Harry, hurry!" He heard her thin cry through the broken windows. He wanted to go to her but the tremendous shaking immobilized him, made him weak, dizzy, powerless to move. Distant at first, the roar grew, until it resembled a train, a jet aircraft overhead. The house groaned in mortal agony.

"Hurry, Harry, hurry, Harry, hurry, Harry!"

Above him in the room was a wooden chandelier made from a ship's wheel. He watched it, hypnotized, as the wheel on its chain began to spin, faster and faster and faster, shooting pieces in every direction as it disintegrated. Struck on the head, Vail fell.

It was too late to retrieve the instrument. The opening floorboards seemed to snap at him. Fountains of sand spewed into the room. He crawled, lurching this way and that like a steel pellet in a pinball machine. Moving furniture lunged at him. He did not know, and would never know, whether he escaped by door or window. Dazed and terrified, he squatted on the ground, raising his eyes to the deterioration of the world.

In thunderous jerking jolts the land shattered. The flat stones

53

heaved. Trees fell in crazy patterns and the earth cracked into a jigsaw puzzle. In the uproar he heard her cry of monotonous terror, *"Hurry-Harry-Hurry-Harry-Hurry-Harry-HUUAAARY!"*

"Hang on!" he screeched as the picket fence behind her simply disappeared. The foolish, futile words came back to mock him. Hang on to what? To spouts of sand, flying debris, mushroom-shaped promontories rising around her? The ground leaped, split, broke into smaller pieces until she knelt, alone, on a small rocking island in a stormy sea of earth.

"HUUUAAARRRREEEEE."

Paralyzed by the paroxysm, unable to move, much less stand, he watched as the tree fell on her silently, deadly as a guillotine. The ground began to slide toward the edge of the bluff, taking the house with it. The earth opened brutal brown lips, swallowed her body, and moved on.

Whimpering, he crawled away. He woke in a hospital. Diagnosis: shock.

The Alaska Earthquake of Good Friday, 1964, was the largest ever recorded in North America.* In the Turnagain section alone seventy-five homes were lost. Somewhere down the bluff lay her body, a permanent part of the earth's displacement.

Numbly, Vail returned to California, where he found that the slightest rumble, jar or vibration made him jump, caused nausea, trembling, fear. He was constantly anticipating earthquakes in a region prone to them. To remain in California or even to

---

* "South Central Alaska . . . is one of the world's most active seismic regions. On March 27, 1964, at about 5:36 P.M. local time (0336, or 3:35 A.M. GMT, March 28), an earthquake of unusual severity struck the Prince William Sound area. Seismologists record earthquake occurrences in Greenwich mean time (GMT). . . . Not only was this earthquake of large magnitude (between 8.3 and 8.6 on the Richter scale, on which the greatest known earthquake is 8.9), but its duration (3 to 4 minutes) and the area of its damage zone (50,000 mi.) were extraordinary. Probably twice as much energy was released by the Alaska earthquake as by the one that rocked San Francisco in 1906." *The Great Alaska Earthquake of 1964*, National Academy of Sciences, Washington, D.C., 1970–1973, p. ix.

continue in seismology was out of the question, and he moved to an area if not earthquake-free—no such place existed—where the prospect was at least remote. To those who asked whether the profession of a geologist was not a little dull as compared to seismology, he answered, accurately, "The money is better."

After his old balance returned, the mere thought of an earthquake had no longer upset him. He told Kay about the experience before they were married but had not mentioned it again. And he withheld completely the shame of his failure, which he kept buried deep in himself where the memory slumbered, stirring only fitfully. Now it demanded that he remember the tortured earth, the fear, the startled face, the cry, the terror, the desolation.

PART TWO

FRACTURE

June 17 The gray sky on Monday looked reversible, as though the sun might actually come out. At the end of the driveway Vail stopped and scooped the morning mail from the box without leaving the car. Bills, a copy of *Vogue*, a bulletin for him from the Stanford Alumni Association, another from the Old Brompton Historical Society concerning June activities in the community. It had arrived after half the month was over, as usual. There was a letter to him, addressed by hand. "Lamont-Doherty Geological Observatory, Palisades, N.Y. 10964," the envelope said, with "P. Kelly" scrawled over it. Vail put the rest of the mail back in the box and slipped the envelope into his jacket to read at the office.

A rough spot appeared just past his driveway, and he drove over it slowly, then drove briskly up Point Road, between woods and untilled fields neatly marked by stone fences. Occasionally a large house showed discreetly through the trees. Vail did not wear a wristwatch and looked at the dashboard clock, which said just past nine. He flicked on the radio for the last part of the news. ". . . crippled a gasoline storage facility near Newport. The seventh victim died last night, and two others remain on the critical list. Hundreds of thousands of gallons of gas for fuel-short Rhode Island went up in smoke. The cause of the blast is still being investigated. Donald Brown, chief engineer at the refinery, told WROK: 'It couldn't have happened unless a tank or a pipe burst, and that doesn't seem likely. Our safety precautions are the best. I don't rule out the possibility of sabotage. The police are trying to locate a former employee of the company.' That's the news, folks. Now stay tuned for Morning Rock— spelled WROK—with Kip Smith."

Vail switched off the radio and contemplated the tragedy at the tank farm. He wondered if people were more upset by the loss of gasoline than of human life. Then his mind picked up the bearded visage of Kip Smith, the young entrepreneur who owned WROK. For Vail, Smith was an important figure. He had employed the geologist to do a small profile of the ground where the broadcast tower for the new radio station would be built. One day, with a few hours to spare, Vail had driven to nearby Old Brompton just to have a look, and he had been struck by the sense of rural isolation on the finger of land. He had been living in Boston then and had become tired of the crowds and the tensions of city life; in the village's one general store, where he had stopped for a soft drink, he inquired of the small, narrow-faced woman behind the counter whether there were houses for sale here. Mrs. Wilbore's sister-in-law, he later discovered, was the sole person on the peninsula from whom he could have gotten an affirmative response. No other house but hers was up for sale. She had studied him a moment, asked about his occupation, and said warily, "Mebbe. A stone house." But would he have roused himself to look if she hadn't mentioned stone? Stone! As a geologist he dealt in stone. When he saw the roomy, run-down place with its thick walls, beamed ceilings and jutting cupola he wanted it, though he had had no particular zest for home ownership before.

Old Brompton was too far from Boston to commute. To move there meant shifting the small geological concern to Fall River,

60

where Vail's partner already lived. Kay had been harder to convince than Jim Lechine. She, too, adored the old stone house, but she worried about being marooned in the winter when the summer people left. He cajoled her. The house was a real bargain, though it needed plenty of work. When the renovation was done and they could afford it, he would make a studio for her in the barn; Old Brompton with its pastoral vistas was the perfect place to pursue her hobby, painting. Kay had always wanted a saddle horse, and on the peninsula she could have one. "It'll work out fine, you'll see," he argued, and it had, except that now he had worries.

Just outside Old Brompton, Vail pulled into the filling station he always used, pointed to the flat tire in the trunk, and asked, "The gash—could that have been done with a knife?"

Yesterday, when he had returned from the beach, Dun had showed him the X in chalk near the hole in the tire. It was like the ones made at filling stations to mark a leak. Dun wanted to know if Vail had had a flat fixed recently, for maybe it was the same one. Harry said that he'd had a flat, but on a rear tire. He examined the X, and suddenly remembered Cy Wilbore's "Fuck you," his gesture on the hood of the car, the tussle, the moving figure seen through the picture window. It occurred to him that the gash could have been made with a knife, and he suggested this to Dun, who nodded reluctantly. Vail swore. "The village kids!"

Dun's weathered hand rested briefly on Vail's arm. "Possible. I'll look into it. But think of it this way, son. Only a tire. Forget about it. Been trouble enough already."

"Can you fix it?" Vail now asked the attendant.

"Do for a spare. And the spare's practically new. Stop by on your way home, Dr. Vail."

After his handling of the Wilbore boys Vail felt some complicity. In any case, he could see no advantage in making the quarrel worse, even if it did turn out that a teenager's knife had

61

been responsible. He decided to heed Dun and forget about it.

The contrast between Old Brompton's solitude and the press of the real world always surprised him; suddenly he drove on a crowded road between housing developments, bowling alleys, laundromats, cheap motels, used-car lots, filling stations, ramshackle diners, restaurants whose names changed every year. . . . Outside Fall River the Rolls passed abandoned textile factories whose glassless windows stared like sockets without eyes, and entered the downtown section and stopped before the old Academy building. The elevator took him to the third floor, where dark wood doors carried the inscription:

VAIL AND LECHINE, INC.
GEOLOGICAL SYSTEMS

Besides the two partners, the firm consisted of a secretary and a draftsman. It performed typical geological functions—developing water supplies, finding sand and gravel deposits, testing soils for the foundations of buildings and bridges and the like. The job was honest and useful, if to Vail a bit routine.

The secretary, Mrs. Conner, was already at her desk drinking coffee. He said good morning and went to his office with the morning mail. Then he remembered the letter from Paul Kelly and opened it. Paul Kelly had been Vail's professor at Cal Tech. At forty-five, eight years older than Vail, he was a leading seismologist. Something of a traditionalist, he still wrote letters instead of communicating entirely by phone like most scientists. To Vail's regret, he wrote with a pen, not a typewriter, in a wiggly script that resembled a seismograph after a tremor.

Kelly's infrequent missives were really reports on his own scientific progress, and Vail translated as best he could. ". . . understanding earthquakes better . . . time . . . model almost complete . . . dilatancy hardening idea proving . . . experiment continues at Blue Mountain Lake . . . time not far off when . . . have capability to predict earthquakes (dream come true!) and even defuse impending major . . . by triggering small preemptive quakes . . . exciting period for all of us. . . ."

Vail's seismology was rusty, a fact brought home to him when he realized he did not know what "dilatancy hardening" meant, and he felt mildly depressed by Kelly's unending professional enthusiasm. Kelly had strongly opposed Vail's decision to abandon seismology, though he understood the reason. "The trouble with escape," Kelly had warned his younger colleague, "is that you can never escape far enough." But Vail had made up his mind. The two men had kept in touch and seen each other again in New York after Kelly joined the staff of Lamont, the most sophisticated seismological research center in the East. Kelly had given up trying to persuade Vail to return to the fold, but he always referred to "breakthroughs" and "discoveries" almost as if to maintain Vail's interest in science and subtly tempt him. And it worked: Vail found himself remembering the days when he had been part of the select group of pure seismologists—no more than a few hundred in the whole country—who, lugging their equipment over the world, searched out earthquakes with the excitement others display toward prospecting for gold. At his desk he shrugged and sighed. There was no turning back; he was a plain geologist now.

Vail looked up at the sound of a cough to see Jim Lechine standing in the doorway. "You sure can concentrate, Harry," Lechine said with admiration. "We have to talk. My room or yours?"

"You've got the scenery." Vail put down the letter and followed his partner. The two had contrasting strengths and temperaments and handled different sides of the business. Lechine, thirty-nine, had been an engineer. Finding himself too much at a desk, he had returned to college, taken a course in geology and gotten a degree. But he lacked Vail's intensive training and handled the simpler jobs. His real talent was public relations.

63

Open and friendly, Lechine operated as front man, dealing with clients, soliciting business, arguing fees with tightfisted town councils. Vail liked his partner with minor reservations. Lechine could be opinionated at times. Also, Jim, of French-Canadian extraction, had a large family to support, which made him a little greedy as far as Vail was concerned. He was always soliciting new business—more than the little firm could really handle.

Vail settled his big frame into a chair in Lechine's office and let his gaze rove about the room with mild disfavor. Along with degrees and memberships in professional societies, Lechine's office walls housed flashy color photographs of rocks and mountains and a big calendar from a drill bit company, decorated with an artist's nudes. This month's had a white telephone to her mouth and a fuzzy white dog between her feet. Vail's own walls held only cross-sections of rock formations and detailed geological maps.

Wearing a bow tie and red suspenders, Lechine put his feet on the desk, studied his partner and said, "Hey, Harry, you look a little pale. Too many parties down there on the peninsula?"

Vail smiled wryly. "It's not that. Like a damn fool I slipped from a ladder and hit my head. I'm still not quite myself."

"Ouch. You didn't break anything, did you?"

"No, luckily. That's one thing to thank the rain for—the ground's soft." Vail looked moodily out the window at sky damp as soggy tissue. "What's this—the third year of record rain?"

"I forget. Anyway, these clouds have silver linings. The rain's bringing us plenty of work. I just hope we don't drown on the way to the bank. Speaking of which, did you hear about the explosion at the tank farm?"

"Yes. Terrible. I don't get the connection with the bank, though."

"Just that it struck me the explosion might be related to a defect in a tank foundation. I hate to sound like an ambulance chaser but maybe we ought to offer our services."

Vail said, "I don't think so. Foundation problems would be extremely unlikely, and in any case the oil company would have its own geologists. Besides, we have more work than we can handle as it is. Let's get to it."

The two began to discuss their various jobs, among them Vail's new project: how to save an old abandoned Fall River textile factory that was on the verge of collapse. A section of floor had buckled. The building rested on wood pilings immersed in water, which should preserve them. Suddenly, for unknown reasons, the pilings began to fail. Friday, sloshing around in the basement with a chemical analyzer, Vail had determined that the water had a pH reading of 4, far below normal, indicating the presence of acid that ate at the wood.

Lechine's face showed surprise when Vail finished his explanation. "How did that happen?"

"When it was in operation, the factory used chlorine dioxide as bleach," Vail said. "Next to the building they dug a well, and when they'd finished with the chlorine dioxide they dumped it. There it would have stayed, too, except this goddam rain has raised the level of ground water, bringing up the chlorine dioxide again. The ecological sins of the past are haunting us." He outlined his plan of action—drain out the existing water, adding fresh water at an equal rate so that the piles remained preserved.

Finally Lechine said, "Friday when you were out I got a call from a contractor in Eastport, Mass. There's an old people's home called Summerset House or something like that, which has developed cracks in the walls. He thinks the foundation might be settling because the hill is saturated. It's a relatively new building. The contractor asked me to take over the job."

Vail waited and said, "So?"

"So I have one hell of a day today. I just wondered if you could do it. It's not far from your place, as the crow flies."

"I'm not a crow," Vail said. He had plenty to do himself. But buried in Lechine's voice lay a certain urgency Vail had learned to understand. Lechine wouldn't say so, but he worried whether his geology was up to the problem. Vail said, "Any immediate danger?"

Lechine frowned. "The contractor doesn't seem to think so. Still, there are people living in the building."

"Did the builder ever do a soil study?" Vail asked, knowing the answer.

"No."

Vail said fretfully, "People just build things without understanding the ground. We've lived in New England four hundred years, and half the time we don't even know what's underneath it. Nothing would surprise me. Not even a big earthquake," he blurted out.

"Earthquake? Why did you say that?"

"I don't know." Vail looked at his partner with round eyes. "Tell me, Jim, have there been many earthquakes in this area?"

"Doubt it. Seems to me the U.S. Geological Survey did a seismic study of the Northeast Corridor six or seven years back, when the government was first considering a new high-speed railway between Boston and Washington. I may have it."

Lechine went to his files and returned with a manila envelope. The cover said:

ENGINEERING GEOLOGY OF THE NORTHEAST CORRIDOR
WASHINGTON, D.C., TO BOSTON, MASSACHUSETTS
EARTHQUAKE EPICENTERS RECORDED IN OR NEAR
THE NORTHEAST CORRIDOR FROM 1534 TO 1965
prepared by the
United States Geological Survey
at the request of the
United States Department of Transportation
1967

66

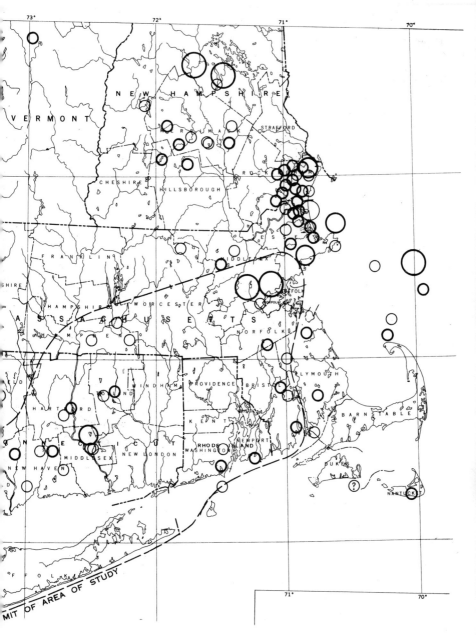

Detail of Survey

67

Vail opened it and stared at a map covered with circles. "Those government geologists are thorough, you've got to give them that," he muttered. "Yes, there have been earthquakes in this area."

"I don't understand why you care."

Vail muttered something about writing a paper. "May I keep this?"

"Too much crap in my files already."

Vail felt embarrassed by the turn the talk had taken. He looked out the window again. Water dripped on the panes. "I'll take on the old people's home," he said. He added casually, "Oh, speaking of cracks, I found one in the concrete wall of my basement. I keep wondering why it's there."

"How big is it?"

"About a foot long."

Lechine shrugged. "The building settled, that's all. It's not like the old people's home, which sits on the side of a hill, apparently."

"The stone house is old and would have settled long ago."

"Water pressure then. The crack's small—nothing to worry about."

"I hope not," Vail said, fighting a vision of falling stones.

The sign said "Summerset Villa." The building stood on the side of a hill, facing the water. With strong field glasses Vail might have been able to see the roof of his own house across the bay.

It was a large brick building with white pseudo-colonial trim. Vail parked and entered the lobby. Old people lolled in chairs and on benches, doing nothing. Summerset seemed to be a place in which you dumped ancient relatives, informed them of the joys of Golden Age and forgot them for good.

Vail's size and comparative youth made him momentarily self-conscious. He stood uncertainly in the center of the room, wondering how to find the manager. An old lady looked up from her knitting and smiled. Vail walked across the linoleum tile.

"May I be of assistance?" she asked in a strong, clear voice.

Vail bent toward her. "I'm looking for Mr. Robinson, the manager. Would you know where he is?"

"No need to shout, young man. My hearing's quite as good as yours," she said. "Of course I know where he is—in his room. Mr. Robinson is always in his room." She stared at him, her wrinkled face bright and friendly.

"What does he do in his room?" Vail asked.

"He has a book of photographs. He looks at it. He dreams, I suspect. Certainly, he pays very little attention to his work."

"What are the photographs of?"

"They show Mr. Robinson, of course. Our undistinguished manager is a former actor. Didn't you ever wonder what happened to former actors when the last show closed? Now you know. They manage old people's homes."

"There must be worse fates."

"Not for Mr. Robinson. He hates old people. We remind him of what he'll become. He avoids us as much as he can. As I said, he stays in his room." She hesitated. "I will get him for you. What is your name, young man?"

"Vail." He glanced at the gold band on her finger. "But Mrs. . . . ."

"Alma Benjamin. I need the exercise. Besides, I enjoy disturbing Mr. Robinson's foolish reveries."

Mrs. Benjamin, he saw when she rose, was a tiny woman, probably no more than five feet tall and weighing a hundred pounds. Her hair was tied in a bun. She walked youthfully.

A few minutes later Robinson emerged, a gauntly handsome, nattily dressed man in his fifties. "Ah, Vail. I was told to expect you."

Vail said, "Are you the owner as well as the manager, Mr. Robinson?"

"Gracious, no," Robinson grumbled. "I wish I were. It's plenty profitable. No, I'm afraid I'm only the manager. The owner is Mr. Summerset, who lives in Florida."

"Does Summerset come here often?"

"Once a year, during the Newport regatta. Mr. Summerset sails a good bit." Envy greased Robinson's voice. "He comes up in his yacht."

"You make all the decisions, then?"

"The buck stops here," Robinson said bravely. He added, "Of course, when it comes to spending money I have to get authorization—when I can find Mr. Summerset."

It was becoming brighter outside as the sun struggled to take off its mask, but no one sat on the benches or walked on the paths. "Your old people like it indoors, it seems," Vail observed.

"Mature citizens," Robinson corrected.

"Dampness bother them?"

"That isn't it," Robinson snapped. "They'd love to go outside, but I won't permit it in this weather. I don't want them tracking mud all over the place."

Vail wondered when the mature citizens had last seen the great outdoors, considering how much rain there had been. As they turned the corner of the building he said, "I understand you're a former actor."

The manager's face creased in anger. "Former?" he said in a sharp, high voice. "I *am* an actor. I'm just waiting for things to pick up in New York. Who's been talking to you? Of course—that horrid Mrs. Benjamin."

They reached the back of the building. Part of the hillside had been cleared for a lawn which had never been planted—probably because the space didn't show from the front. The glistening mud looked like icing on a chocolate cake. Robinson examined his polished shoes with obvious distaste—they bore splotches of mud. He pointed. "What you want to see is there. I'll wait here, if you don't mind."

In the car, Vail had put on his boots. The mud sucked them as he moved toward the wall. Then he saw the cracks, four harmless-looking squiggles that ran up the cement base into the brick.

He walked up the hillside, through the mud and returned to Robinson. "When were the cracks discovered?" he asked.

"Middle of last week. The maintenance man noticed them on the inside of the cellar wall."

"How old is the building?"

"Eight or ten years. It was built before I came."

"How long ago was that?"

Robinson hesitated. "You sound like a detective. Five years, I think."

"How deep are the footings?"

"What is a footing?"

"The foundation. What the building sits on. I'm trying to find out how good the construction is."

"I don't know anything about construction."

Vail frowned. His head turned toward the hillside. "See those ridges?"

Robinson squinted. "Sure. So what?"

"Those are hummocks. The earth has slipped. Behind the ridges is a depression called a slump. It's a miniature landslide, meaning that the soil is saturated with water."

"So?"

"In the West, when you get a condition like that, whole hillsides begin to creep sometimes. The mud carries buildings with it."

"This isn't the West," Robinson insisted, his thin jaw turning stubborn.

Vail replied, "Just the same, something of the sort could happen. The hill could be unstable, the foundation could shift and the building could collapse without much warning."

"Oh, come now," Robinson cried. "That's pretty farfetched."

"Probably. Just the same, we'd better drill some holes and

get a reading on the soil." He stared toward the cracks in the building again. "It ought to be done right away."

"How much will it cost?"

"Not much—to bore the holes. After that, we'll see."

Robinson's face turned angry. "You contractors are all alike —always gouging. It better not be anything expensive. Mr. Summerset wouldn't like that. He'd blame it on me."

"I'm not a contractor, I'm a geologist," Vail answered. "In any case, I wouldn't recommend anything that doesn't have to be done."

"Well, all right," Robinson conceded, his expression indicating that it was fine with him if the building collapsed, just so he wasn't inside at the time. "Anything else? I have to get back to work."

"That's all for the moment. I'm going up the hill again."

Robinson departed, and Vail climbed the slope, inspecting the slump and the nearby trees. The hill on one side had a steep drop that ended in the bay, and he stared down. He retraced his steps to the front of the building. About to get in his car, he saw a small figure standing just inside the entranceway. He went over and poked his head inside.

"Just wanted to say goodbye, Mrs. Benjamin," he said. "You better watch out for Robinson. He's on the warpath because . . ."

"I know. The former actor bit. Or should I say former bit actor? Don't worry about me, Mr.—or is it *Dr.* Vail? Robinson said you're a geologist."

"Dr. Vail," he agreed. "Tell me, Mrs. Benjamin. Is the construction of the building shoddy?"

"Shoddy!" the old woman exclaimed in her clear voice. "Let's just say it's lucky most of the residents are deaf. The walls are *that* thick." She made a narrow gap between her thumb and forefinger. "You can hear everything that happens. And the plumbing is unmentionable."

72

"Why do you stay?" he asked her.

She shrugged. "The obvious reason. Where else to go?"

Vail hoisted the dog by its bushy tail and said, "Shut up, Punch. It's only me."

Kay, running from the studio, gasped, "Harry!" Something strange just happened. There's a rumble in the basement. The house is shaking!"

He could feel the vibration through the balls of his feet. From the dining room the crystal teardrop chandelier tinkled as though in a breeze. He had to force the basement door: because of the humidity, every joint seemed to be swelling as though the house had arthritis. The sound reverberated off the cement walls, and his ears focused on a machine protruding from a square well in the cement floor. He eyed the pump with anger and kicked it. The noise stopped.

"What was it?" she asked anxiously when he came upstairs.

"Sump pump."

"Funny name." She sounded relieved. "What does it do?"

"Pumps water accumulated beneath the house into the septic tank. It's on the blink. Didn't you notice when you looked in the cellar?"

Her nose pointed away. "I didn't go down. Oh, and the grandfather clock is running slow."

"Everything happens at once. If the pump acts up again, unscrew the fuse—if you're brave enough to enter the basement," he said with a grin. "In the morning I'll get Dun to come look at it."

That evening Kay was scheduled to play bridge at the Demmings'; she asked him again if he wanted to come—Mark wouldn't be a problem. They'd take him along and put him in a bedroom. Harry shook his head and Kay looked relieved, he thought; his bridge was not of the best, and undoubtedly Jeff was a good player.

73

Conversation at supper was desultory. He told of his day, she of hers: "Went for a ride on Brioche. Took Mark to the beach. Played doubles at the club with Wende, Jeff and somebody else. Washed clothes. Shopped. Piano's out of whack just like Big Ben. I called the repair people, who said they'd come tomorrow. They won't, of course. Oh, did you call me today?"

"Too busy. Why?"

"Phone rang a couple of times when I was in the backyard, but time I got there, nobody was on the line. I thought you'd gotten impatient and hung up."

"Not me."

"Mark! Use your napkin."

Kay put Mark in his pajamas while Harry cleaned up. She kissed the boy good night and her station wagon disappeared down the drive in the rain. He liked evenings spent alone with his child. They wrestled on the living room floor, fending off affectionate lunges from the dog and cat. "Read to me, Daddy!" Mark cried finally. The boy trudged upstairs and returned with a book called *At Paddy the Beaver's Pond*.

"We've read that three times," Harry said.

"I know. Read it again."

Harry lay on his back on the floor, holding the book over his head, with Mark and the animals curled up beside him. He read: " '. . . Down from the mountainside on the still air came the sound of deep grunts. They didn't sound exactly the same and they came from places some distance apart. They were angry grunts. There was no doubt whatever about that. What is more, each grunt sounded angrier, more threatening than the previous grunts.' " Harry cleared his throat and continued, " ' "They are coming this way. There is no doubt about it," declared Uncle Paddy. He sounded as if he were getting excited.' "

"Go on, Daddy!" Mark cried.

Harry sat up. "Did you hear anything, Mark?"

Mark's eyes, blue like his mother's, and mouth, round like his father's, had opened wide. "What?"

"Did you hear anything just then, son?"

"Yes. The grunts. I heard the grunts. Go on, read!"

He read on for a few moments and closed the book. "Time for bed, honey," he said.

After the usual protests Mark agreed, and Harry carried him up the stairway. Mark's room lay at the opposite end of the carpeted hall from his parents' bedroom. On the wall was a circus poster with lions, tigers and clowns. A mobile of blue plastic fish hung from the ceiling. Mark favored the top of the double-decker bunk, and Harry threw him into it, firmly resisting the boy's demand that he get into bed, too. Harry went downstairs and he pulled the hard chair to the light. He was rereading Kelly's letter and pondering the mention of a preemptive earthquake when he felt a vibration crawl up the chair legs. The shaking was slight; reading to Mark, he had experienced it as sound, he realized. Vibrations could be audible or inaudible, depending on frequency and the medium they traveled in; they could affect inanimate objects without being detected by the human ear.

He returned to the basement. The pump grumbled, but not so vehemently as before. When he kicked it the machine fell obediently silent. Of themselves, his eyes turned to the crack. Vail froze: the crack, he was convinced, had grown longer.

The steps creaked as he clambered up, returning with a tape measure, pad and pencil. He put the tape on the crack and measured up the wall from the floor. He was about to record the result on the pad when, upstairs, the phone rang. He ascended hurriedly, but the caller had hung up. In the basement again, he searched his pockets in vain for the pencil. He had left it by the phone.

To hell with it! He stepped quickly to the far end of the basement and opened a door. Inside was an exercise room he had installed at the time of the renovation and which, predictably, he generally ignored. He kept a robe, slippers and shorts there, and he worked himself to the limit on the bicycle and rowing machine. Then he sat in the burning sauna.

Few of the villagers had phones, and Dun was no exception. The next morning Vail drove to the village, passed the church, turned left at the square and continued on a rutted road that led along the shore. About halfway to the high red cliffs at Shonkawa Point stood a row of one-room shacks with stovepipes protruding from the roofs. Dun's old truck was gone, and Vail left a note in the mailbox marked "D. Sowles."

As he headed for the office, Vail considered the anomaly of shanties occupying some of the best beach front in Old Brompton. Vail wondered why Dun went along with the villagers' pact not to sell, when he could probably get enough to retire to a warmer climate. The old man was different from the others, after all.

Among other things, Dun had traveled. While the other villagers rarely left the peninsula—some hadn't gotten as far as Fall River, it was said—he had lived all over the Northeast and even been a logger, farmer, miner, carpenter, that much Vail knew. Unlike the others, too, Dun was hard-working, reliable, punctual. A genius at all kinds of repairs, he was in demand throughout the peninsula, though he seemed choosy about whom he worked for. Like the rest of the villagers, however, Dun looked to be poor, and Vail wondered why. He had no family to support, there was plenty for him, and surely he had Social Security. Perhaps he salted his money away; but then the season was short, and the rich summer people were notoriously ungenerous—when they bothered to pay their bills at all.

Toward Harry Vail, Dun always displayed a special partiality, coming as quickly as asked and often calling him "son." Kay rather thought he meant it, too. Spending most of his life on the move, he had never married. Asked if he had children, he would say with a sly wink, "None I know of," as if to imply that his bastard progeny were strewn all over the Northeast. But that was just an old man's idle boast, they felt sure. "I bet he wanted a son like you," Kay said to Harry, not quite kiddingly. "Big, smart, educated, a scientist yet. Nice but tough down deep, like he is. Maybe you're what Dun would like to have been."

Vail respected the old man and would have been flattered if that were true, yet Kay's notion seemed too simple. Between Vail and himself Dun maintained a wall of habitual restraint and reserve, never offering personal information. True, Dun might consider himself an employee and keep a certain distance. True also that he *was* a villager, and the locals were eccentric. But, though perhaps he imagined it, Vail sometimes had the sensation that behind the wall Dun was on guard.

When Vail returned home that evening, the old man came out of the barn to announce, "Your missus is horseback riding. Asked me to keep an eye on the boy. He's in the backyard." He hitched up his dungarees with his thumbs, shuffled his feet and said suddenly, "You was right about the tire. Not a rock but a knife."

"I knew it!" He wondered quickly why Dun had told him. "How did you find out?"

"Everything here is known sooner or later. Reckon the boys felt they had a score to settle, and settled it. As I said, if you'll let be, that'll be the end of it."

"People just don't go around hacking up tires," Vail said. But he had already decided against taking action. "Okay, let's forget it. Don't tell Mrs. Vail about it, all right? It'll just make her nervous." The old man nodded.

Vail took a piece of paper from his pocket. "So many things I had to write them down. Doors stick." He told Dun which ones. "The leaf in the dining room table is fouled up. I raised it but can't get it back. Sump pump is out of whack. Upstairs toilet doesn't work."

Dun said, "Afraid there's also a leaking pipe in the upstairs bathroom—one the kid uses. Missus showed it to me. Have to replaster the wall after I've fixed the leak."

Vail said, "What caused that?"

"Things happen in an old house."

"Too many things around this one."

"Been lucky so far, Mr. Vail."

Vail reminded himself that everything had functioned perfectly at the stone house until Saturday, the day he fell from the ladder.

The two men descended to the basement. Again water stood on the cement floor, and Vail told of the noise the now-silent pump had made. Dun said, "Too much ground water, I reckon, for that old pump to handle."

"That account for the puddle?" Dun nodded, and Vail went on, "Unless water leaks through the wall. Look." He pointed to the crack. "That, I'm sure, is new."

Dun squinted in the dim light and moved closer to the wall. He had put in the concrete lining himself. His silence affirmed that the crack was new. His keen eyes searched the surface. He scratched his whiskers with yellow nails. "Hard to say if the crack leaks. Wall's discolored, but that could be the concrete. Anyhow, crack don't mean nothing—cement most likely just dried out on the inside, even with the rain. Get a new pump and see what happens."

A folding rule stuck from Dun's back pocket. Vail said, "Measure it, will you?"

Dun bent and measured. "Fourteen and five-eighths," he announced as he straightened up.

"Are you sure?"

"Measure it again?"

"No. I'll take your word for it." He was confused as to

78

whether, the evening before, the crack had measured 14⅜ inches or 14⅝ inches. He remembered ⅜ inches, but perhaps he was wrong.

"Harry?" he heard Kay call. Dun folded up the rule, and Vail went upstairs.

On the kitchen wall hung a blackboard where Kay listed, in chalk, shopping lists, doctors' appointments, things to do. The board read, "Tues. Pollidors, 6:30." She pointed at it and said, "We'll be late if we don't get going."

It was almost dark as they drove home, with Mark silent in the back seat. "Ugh!" Harry exclaimed. "What an awful evening." He had drunk more than he ought and felt cross with himself and the others.

"It wasn't all that bad," Kay said, "though I can see how *you'd* think so. You really got Pollidor angry when you told him cement was falling from between the fireplace bricks and that nailheads were working out of the wood. You made it sound as though his house was about to fall down. He was angry enough to have taken a poke at you. He might have if you weren't so big."

"I didn't say his house was about to fall down. I just said that there were signs of stress," Harry muttered sullenly.

"And the business about how the ball veered when you were playing croquet by yourself. Nobody felt the ground shake but you. The fall from the ladder did something to your balance. You *must* see Dr. Bjerling."

"You were all so busy at the goddam computer bar you couldn't have felt anything," he said defensively. "Still, maybe I ought to pay Bjerling a visit if this keeps up."

"That's better. I thought the bar was kind of fun. Imagine putting a card in a slot and out pours the drink you ordered. I must have tried ten of them."

"I had too many too," he said, turning onto Point Road. "And

79

Pollidor, that stupid lush! I was sore when he scared Mark with the burglar alarm."

"It wasn't nice of him," Kay agreed quickly. "I wish they wouldn't talk so much about crime. You'd think we're having a crime wave in Old Brompton. Maybe they're right. I keep wondering if we shouldn't have a burglar alarm, too. I'd feel safer. I'm having trouble sleeping."

"For Christ's sake!" he exploded. "Who's going to break in? What would they steal—a five-year-old TV set?"

"Thanks a bunch. How about my paintings?" She smiled briefly. "Seriously, what about the china, silver, my Toby jugs? The collection's worth two thousand easily, and I couldn't replace it."

"A thief wouldn't know what a Toby jug is," he reassured her.

"Well, I feel nervous is the point, I guess." She shifted in her seat. "And Jeff with his game about predicting how we'll all die. He really wants to play it."

"What's he, a necrophiliac or something? I can't believe Fred Demming will do it."

"Oh, he'll do just about anything Wende wants, you know that. And she loves games, any game at all. Including the one she's playing with Jeff."

Vail swerved as he reached the broken place in the road. "I thought they fixed that," he remarked.

"It washed out again, I guess. Jeff and Wende are really having a thing. Fred must be blind not to notice."

"I'm tired of talking about all those people," he said as he turned into their driveway. "What else is new?"

"New? Did I tell you that both the piano tuner and the clock man came today? A minor miracle."

"What was wrong with Big Ben?"

"Something rubbing against something. How should I know?"

Punch barked from inside the house as they drove up. Already fed at the Pollidors', Mark went reluctantly to bed. They had a pickup supper from the refrigerator. "Will you clean up?" she asked as she made instant coffee and started for the living room. When she turned on the light, she screamed softly, "Harry!"

The Toby jug lay on the floor, its only unbroken part being the grin. Her gaze was shocked. "One of my best jugs. How could that have happened, Harry?"

"I'm . . . not sure."

"Vandals. Somebody's broken in. Or . . ."

Kay seemed greatly agitated, and he wanted an explanation reasonable enough to calm her down. Punch and Judy stood near the bar cart, staring up at them solemnly, like conspirators. "Did you do that, Judy?" he asked.

"Judy doesn't walk on furniture."

"But she does sometimes. I've caught her at it." He thought carefully. "You remember when Pollidor staggered against the bar the other night? He must have jarred the shelves and the jug got moved to the edge. Judy, prowling around, dislodged it."

Kay's face was hard with disbelief. "She wouldn't go up on a glass shelf."

"She wouldn't have to," he insisted. "She jumped on the cart and nudged the jug with her tail. It fell, hit the corner of the bar, and broke." He showed her a mark on the bar.

"I guess so. Well, it's only a two-hundred-year-old beer mug." As she picked up the pieces, tears flashed in her eyes.

Kay seemed satisfied with the explanation, but he wasn't—not quite. He began to prowl. On the mantel stood some of the arrowheads he had found in the cornfield; they leaned against the chimney, but a few were down. He picked them up. The bar cart on its sturdy wheels was an inch away from the wall and he pushed it back. She watched him carefully. "Stop that," she said suddenly. "Stop pacing."

81

He stopped. "Kay, why did you leave the record cabinet open?"

"Haven't been near it. Must be Mark. He can play the record machine by himself now." She sucked in her cheeks. "Any cigarettes in the house?"

"No! You're not going to start smoking again, not with the hell I went through when you quit."

"All right, all right." She pulled on her index finger until it popped. "We're both in a funny mood, aren't we? Maybe it's because the sun never shines. I read somewhere about a valley in the Northwest which has a fantastic rate of suicides. There's always rain or fog and people get depressed." Kay sat down abruptly at the piano, played a few bars, rose, hit the tuning fork that stood on the piano, then a note. She frowned. "The piano is still out of tune. The man must have done a lousy job." She went to the birdcage, drumming the brass with her nails. "Bird, bird, why won't you sing?" She whirled to face him. "It's too much! Nothing works right around here. Look! The clock is *still* slow. I want a cigarette. Just one."

"There aren't any."

"You're lying. I'll drive to the bar in the village and buy some."

"You win," he said coldly. "Cigarettes somebody left are in my desk."

She returned at once. "Harry, did you throw books on the floor?"

His mouth opened. "Me?"

He raced to the study. Books were strewn over the desk top and the floor. She found the cigarettes, lit one quickly and coughed. "Somebody's been in the house. I want a burglar alarm," she shouted.

"Nobody's been in the house. Calm yourself." He inspected the debris and pointed to the empty shelf supports over the desk.

"I had books on one end of the shelf and a light on the other. The whole thing came down. The shelf must have been unbalanced." He found the shelf and the clip light on the far side of the desk and returned them to the wall, holding the shelf with his hand until the books balanced it again. He switched on the light. "The bulb isn't even broken." He took the last book from the floor and glanced at it—Charles F. Richter's famous *Elementary Seismology.*

"It's enough to make you believe in a poltergeist," she muttered.

"A what?" he asked sharply.

"Poltergeist—an evil spirit that moves things, throws them, sets fires. Poltergeists haunt people."

Something in her voice caused him to look at her carefully. "You make it sound like you believe in such things."

"Of course I don't," Kay said defensively. "It's just that so many things are happening at once."

"I'm going to the basement," he announced, "and check for water."

Kay gripped his arm insistently. "No! I don't know why, but I'm all upset. I need you."

Anxiety seemed to make her erotic. She led him up the elliptical staircase without releasing his arm, and he could sense a certain desperation in the haste with which she undressed herself and helped to undress him as well, unbuttoning his shirt, pulling off his shoes, tugging at his trouser legs. She writhed and moaned and crumpled in a heap on top of him. "What are you waiting for?" she whispered.

He had been waiting, he realized, anticipating that the bed would shake. When finished, she rolled on her side, her back to his chest. He cradled her until convinced she slept. Then, gently, he withdrew his arm, rose, put on a robe and slippers, and went downstairs to the basement. The floor was dry—today it had only drizzled. He remembered now where he had left the tape—in the pocket of the old robe he kept by the sauna. He knelt in front of the crack.

It measured exactly 14¾ inches—he placed the tape upon it three times. What had been its length the first time he measured it? Had Dun's measurement been wrong? Or had the wound in the wall grown since the day before yesterday? That, he understood suddenly, was how he regarded it, as a wound in the body of his house.

He stood still in the center of the cellar studying the crack. What, exactly, was happening? You really only have two ways to go. You either decide that the whole goddam problem is a lot of small things happening at the same time, by chance—blow on the head, dizziness, clock stops—or you take a different position. You conclude an earthquake is underway. If true, it's one event no matter how many ways you experience it—like God, if He exists. Just one thing, with various manifestations, concrete proof of which is the crack: ground shakes, crack grows. But suppose you tell people a slow earthquake is in progress? They would laugh if you said it—wouldn't believe you. Or maybe you really did injure your head. No, don't say anything until you have more. But try to be a scientist for a change. Look for evidence and keep your emotions out of it. If there really is a big quake coming, it'll surface and you'll know, you'll *know*. Watch and wait.

The stairs squeaked, and, whirling, he saw the small figure in pajamas. "Mark! What . . ."

"I woke up, Daddy. I'm hungry."

"Okay," he sighed. In the kitchen he poured the boy a glass of milk and sent him back to bed. His eye fell on the blackboard and, seizing the chalk, he returned to the basement. At the tip of the crack he placed a small white dot.

Marjorie Conner, the secretary, had been with the firm only a few months. With her employers she was still in the formal stage.

Divorced, in her late thirties, she wore bright clothes that showed off her copious figure, and she was always fully made up, with bright red lipstick, jewelry and even, sometimes, false eyelashes, so she seemed a little out of place in the simple surroundings.

"Can I get you some coffee, Dr. Vail?" she asked when he entered. "You don't look quite yourself."

"I'm not," he admitted. "I'd love some coffee. Lechine in?"

"I'll get him."

Vail's desk calendar said *Wednesday, July 19.*

Vail hadn't talked to Lechine yet about Summerset Villa. He motioned his partner to a chair and said, "I'm worried about the old people's home. The ground it stands on is like wet dough. There's been some creep on the hillside already—I'm willing to bet some of the trees are angled, though it's hard to be sure."

Born in the region, Lechine knew it like his own skin. "The hill must be made of Mother Nature's Irish stew—till,* sand, gravel, boulders and anything you can think of. It ought to be stable."

"But it's saturated. Till doesn't absorb water easily. And the hill edges on a bluff."

Lechine blinked. "What do you plan to do?"

"After screaming like hell for speed, I got Charley to take his rig over there yesterday and drill some holes. If the ground is as wet as I think, we could try digging a well and pumping out the water. If that doesn't work . . . well, let's worry about that when we come to it."

Lechine said uneasily, "We don't have a contract with the owner, do we?"

"No. The manager's trying to find him."

"Suppose he won't pay for it?" Lechine demanded. "Aren't you a little premature?"

_____

* A dry, hard, unproductive clay subsoil—old glacial debris.

Vail's mind saw the wrinkled face of Alma Benjamin. "I'm supposed to anticipate things," he snapped. "The construction of that building is cruddy. You want it to go down?"

Lechine looked hurt. "I'm only saying we ought to have a contract. That way we don't get blamed if anything happens."

"It's too risky to wait, contract or no contract," Vail said stubbornly.

"I still don't like it," Lechine said. He hated uncertainty about being paid.

There was no change in the crack with the white dot riding on top of it, like the head of a long insect. Kay now seemed constantly positioned so as to preclude unobserved access to the cellar, and made remarks like "Planning on moving to the basement? Hunting for buried treasure? Got a body stashed down there?"

In the office, he asked Mrs. Conner whether the test results had come.

"I'm afraid not, Dr. Vail."

"Jesus! I marked the job 'rush.' Words like that have no meaning nowadays except when it comes to paychecks."

Mrs. Conner's plucked eyebrows arched and retracted. "No sense getting agitated. Life's too short. Besides, they only did the job on Tuesday," she said in a soothing voice.

"This is Friday," he complained. "I'll call Charley myself."

He dialed the number on Mrs. Conner's phone and said, "Charley, it's Vail. I want those test-drilling results today and no maybes. . . . I know you've got a lot of jobs. . . . I know the weather is lousy. . . . Yes . . . Listen, Charley, this is top priority."

Lechine wandered out of his office and said, "By the way, apropos of nothing, looks like they've located the guy who blew up the gasoline storage tanks. He's in Florida. Only a matter of

86

time before they nab him. Son of a bitch. I hope they throw the book at him. I hate kooks."

"What's supposed to be his motive?" Vail asked.

"Some crap about being in an industrial accident and not getting compensated, he's told people."

"Maybe he didn't do it," Vail said.

"Sure he did," Lechine said impatiently. "How else could it have happened?"

Late that afternoon Mrs. Conner handed him an envelope which had come by messenger. "The report you've been asking about."

"It's about time."

He went to his dripping office window and read the report standing up, made two telephone calls, and walked quickly to his partner's office.

Vail said, "I've got the Summerset drilling results, and I don't like them at all." .

"Water saturation?"

"That's part of it. The hill the old people's home stands on is like molasses. The water table has risen twenty feet."

"That's enormous!"

"But not unheard of. Don't forget, we've had a huge amount of rain. The bedrock won't let the water seep out. I put in a call to Robinson, the so-called manager, to get authorization to dig a well and try to drain the water, but he's away for the weekend, nobody knows where. I've gone out on a limb and ordered Charley to start digging the well on Monday."

Lechine said worriedly, "I still think you should talk to the owner first."

"I haven't given you the whole story. Something in the report surprised me. There are limey layers."

"Not much limestone around here." Lechine's gaze faltered. Sometimes the deficiencies of his geological training showed like an outcropping of rock. "I'm afraid I . . ."

"Limestone might be significant," Vail said. His tone turned monotonous as though he were thinking out loud. "Water passing through vegetation becomes acidic. Limestone contains calcium carbonate and magnesium carbonate. They're soluble in acid. When water reaches limestone it turns basic, but solution openings occur in the stone. If you have a crack or a fissure the process is accelerated. You could get a cave."

"That would take centuries," Lechine scoffed.

"True. But an existing cave could have grown larger because of the excessive rainfall during these last years. Especially if there's a fault line there. Water would collect along the fault. It would have to."

"What makes you think there's a fault?"

"I don't. I just say it's possible. I wish I had a better idea of the geology."

Back in his office, he paced thoughtfully, then went to his desk and removed the manila envelope with the survey reports. In addition to the chart depicting earthquakes in the region, he found one that said:

ENGINEERING GEOLOGY OF THE NORTHEAST CORRIDOR
WASHINGTON, D.C., TO BOSTON, MASSACHUSETTS
BEDROCK GEOLOGY

No fault was shown in the area of Summerset Villa, but one did exist at the mouth of the Sakonnet River, not far away. He drew a black square around the area and was still examining it when, minutes later, the phone rang.

"Anything new?" Kay asked.

"The supply store called. The sump pump came. I'll pick it up on my way home."

"Have you forgotten there's a picnic at the club beach? Also, we're invited to the Demmings' on Sunday."

"I think I'll pass up the club party," he told her. "Anyway, it's raining."

88

"Weatherman says it's due to stop. Good weather's on the way!"

"Oh sure."

But the rain had stopped when Vail steered the Rolls around a puddle and turned down the beach road which led to the cliffs at Shonkawa Point. Seeing Dun's old pickup truck parked outside the shack, Vail climbed the stairs and knocked. He heard the scuffle of slippers. Dun squinted from behind the screen.

"Oh, Mr. Vail." He seemed surprised.

"I've got the new pump, Dun. It's in the back of the car. Could you come tomorrow?"

The old man nodded and said cheerfully, "Okay." Vail was turning to leave when Dun added, "Care to come inside?"

Perhaps Dun was merely being polite. Yet Vail wanted to understand the man better; besides, he had something to ask.

"I didn't know you were eating," Vail apologized, seeing a sturdy table upon which were a glass of milk and a plate with food.

Dun took the plate into the alcove kitchen. "Wasn't hungry anyway. How about a drink, Mr. Vail?"

The back windows faced the sea. The horizon was touched with pink for a change. Kay and Mark would be at the picnic. "Well . . ."

"Rum do? All I have." Vail nodded.

Dun went to the cupboard and returned with a bottle and cheese glasses, scrupulously clean like everything else in the room. As they sat down, Dun poured hookers of rum.

On the table, open and face down, lay a soft-cover book. When Vail glanced at it, Dun carefully closed the book and placed it under his hand. Vail leaned back in his chair, raised his glass and said, "Luck."

Vail observed that the cabin's principal decor consisted of stones. Stones of various colors and shapes lined the windowsills, and on the coffee table and the chest stood large glass jars, each filled with stones.

"Nice rocks," he said.

"Red ones from the cliff, white ones from the beach down by the pier." There was a silence and then Dun said, "Don't get much company."

"It must get lonely, especially in winter," Vail responded.

"Oh, don't mind that. Work. Walk. Fish. Read a lot. Every Sunday, church."

"Funny about your church. The whole village attends, doesn't it?"

"Just about."

"Yet your people don't strike me as especially religious, in any conventional sense."

Dun's laugh showed his stubby brown teeth. "All kinds of religion. Some show it, some don't. You religious, Mr. Vail?"

Vail shifted in his chair. This was the closest thing to a personal question Dun had ever asked, and he wanted to answer truthfully without offending the old man. "I'm a scientist, Dun. Ultimate questions aren't my affair."

"I guess you mean answers, not questions," Dun said. "All of us got the same questions. It's our answers that ain't the same."

"Except maybe we have different ideas about what an answer is."

"Maybe there ain't answers for some things—not your kind of answers."

"There are answers. We just don't know them yet."

Dun scratched his cheek with yellow nails and asked, "How can you *know* there are answers when you ain't got them?"

"Faith, I guess."

"Well, Mr. Vail, that's religion."

"You'll make a convert of me yet," Vail said with a laugh. "What denomination are you?" he asked.

The old man hesitated before answering. "Well, ain't exactly connected with any church. Got our own ways. Sort of . . . earthy in our views."

"Fundamentalist?"

"That's right." He looked at their glasses and said, "Have another, Mr. Vail?"

"Just one."

The bottle was empty. Dun went to the alcove kitchen and returned almost at once, picking up the glasses and the book. The charade became even more absurd when he returned with a new bottle of rum and the same empty glasses. He poured their drinks and said jocularly, "Trouble at the church. Pipe organ's ailin'. Gives some bad notes."

"Can't you repair it, Dun? You can fix anything, it seems to me."

Dun grinned at the flattery. "Got to admit that this one stumps me. Know anything about pipe organs, Mr. Vail?"

"I'm afraid not." It occurred to Vail that he did know a pertinent fact about pipe organs but could not recall it. His mind switched to the book Dun had removed. In the second Dun had left the book on the table Vail's eyes glanced at the title. He had not wanted to pry, but curiosity overwhelmed his reticence. Anyway, the question was harmless. "I noticed the book you were reading when I came. I've heard the name Cayce but can't place it."

Dun's face gave nothing away. *"Kay-See*, not *Case*, Mr. Vail. He was a clairvoyant. Predicted things."

"My God, of course! I remember hearing about him in California. Cayce's the one who claimed he could predict disasters —stock market crash of '29, World War II." He paused. "Earthquakes."

"That's him." The gray eyes opened wide. "Something to wonder at, if he could do the things they say he could, like diagnose sickness at long range or predict earthquakes."

Vail grunted. He waved his hand as Dun raised the bottle, but the old man poured anyway. "For where did he predict earth-quakes?"

"California, Japan."

"Hard to miss with those predictions. Tremendous amount of seismic disturbance in both areas. Dun, do you know how many earthquakes there are every year over the world, little and big?" Dun shook his head. "A hundred thousand, at least," Vail said.

"You studied earthquakes once, didn't you, Mr. Vail?"

"Yes, Dun. How did you know?"

"Your missus told me."

"Yes, I was a seismologist once. Where else did Cayce claim earthquakes would happen?"

"The Bahama Islands."

"None yet, that I know of."

"Alabama."

Vail smiled. "That was last century."

"Major earthquake in Alaska."

Vail scowled. "When?"

"Between 1959 and 1998," Dun said. "Made the prediction in 1934."

Dun seemed to know his Cayce. Vail said, "That's a forty-year period, and the area is earthquake-prone. There's been a big one already." He chewed his lip. "Where else?"

Dun said slowly, "Here."

"*Here?*"

"Here in New England," Dun said in an ominous tone. "He believes that everything will fall apart."

"Cataclysm," Vail said after a moment. "Is that what you believe, too? Do you teach that in church?"

His guess had been impetuous, but the hesitancy in the face of the other caused him to believe that the hunch in some sense was accurate. Dun said, "No. But respect nature."

Dun would not elaborate—as though, having given Vail a peek inside, he pulled down a blind. Loosened by the rum, Vail asked one more question as he rose to go. Waving toward the darkening sea through the windows, he said, "Dun, you live on this lovely stretch of beach. It must be worth a fortune. Why don't you sell and retire to a warm climate?"

"Think about it. Can't. Now you, you could sell and go. Someone might make you a good offer. Take it? Why don't you?"

"Me? Sell?" Vail cried. "Of course I won't sell. Who told you to ask?"

"Didn't exactly say anybody did. Just that they might. Who knows?" Vail had reached the front door. Dun added, "Been thinking about the crack in your basement. Weak spot there, simple break in the masonry because water pressure built up. We ought to dig her out, reinforce, waterproof, when the rain stops. Nothing to worry about."

Out on the stoop Vail heard a noise. Seeming to emanate from beneath the shack, it sounded like a deep, guttural moan or a loud flatulation. "What is that?"

"What?"

"That sound. Didn't you hear it?"

"Wind's coming up, that's all," Dun said impassively. "Come back again. Pleasure to have you."

He drove carefully on the narrow, pitted pavement, worried by the sound. But he was a lousy drinker, and Dun was right about the breeze.

He turned and speeded up as he reached the square. His tires, finding a puddle, sent up a sheet of spray. He heard a yell. The voice was familiar and so was the face he could barely discern in the semi-darkness: one of the Wilbore boys. Of all the goddam fool places to be standing. He pretended not to have heard the outraged cry.

The clay bell in the elm tree clanked in the breeze. He brought the pump inside and left it by the kitchen door. He nibbled on cheese and gulped a glass of milk, then wandered the house dis-

93

consolately. Then he heard the pump and went downstairs to kick it into silence.

The white dot had vanished from the crack. He raced upstairs to his study. The tape measure was not in the drawer where he had put it. Frantically he began to search the house for a measure of some kind, returning at last to the basement with Mark's one-foot ruler. He pressed it to the crack. This time he got a reading of 15 inches on the nose.

There has been another tremor. . . .

Wait a minute, he cautioned. Where the crack was there was also a slight bulge in the concrete, which would throw the reading off since the wooden rule could not lie flat on the wall.

He visualized Kay's lipstick on her dressing table and ran upstairs sweating and panting. He had to know, beyond the vagaries of measurements and memory: down the length of the crack he drew a thick red line and, dropping the lipstick on the floor, stood up to look. Now the crack resembled a real wound, and he left the cellar hastily.

Upstairs, unlike him, he poured himself a drink at the bar, then another, and another. The shaking, if it occurred at all, came simultaneously with the great upheaval in his stomach.

"You smell like a brewery," she said to him in the morning.

He smiled weakly. "Feel like one. What time is it?"

"Nine. You didn't stir when we came in. Where did you get drunk?"

"Had a couple with Dun."

"Dun? How odd. Well, he's here. He's fine."

A cup of coffee woke him. The pump, he saw, was gone from the kitchen—the old man had carried it downstairs, where Vail found him installing it. Kay and Mark stood facing the wall where the crack was, and Kay held a rag in her hand. She said, "If I've told you once I've told you a hundred times *not* to come down to the basement alone, Mark. And this . . ."

94

Harry stepped forward. "What did he do?"

"He smeared the wall with one of my lipsticks." The crack had been wiped clean.

"But I didn't," Mark protested. "I just put Daddy's tape there like Daddy does." The boy showed her the tape in his hand.

"Liar!" Kay said angrily. "I found the lipstick on the floor. How did it get there, Mark? Answer me!"

"I did it," Harry said.

She looked at him with a kind of horror. "What? Why, for God's sake?"

"There's a crack there. I marked it."

"Crack?" She peered at the wall and then at her husband. "I didn't even notice it. What's the big deal?"

After Kay and Mark had gone upstairs he said, "Dun?"

The old man seemed to have been waiting. Wordlessly, he took the folding rule from his pocket and placed it on the crack. "Fifteen inches," he announced.

"That's bigger than you measured before."

"Well, wasn't being careful then. Finger might have slipped."

Harry said bitterly, "Oh, come on, Dun. The crack has grown, and you know it."

"Doubt it," Dun insisted.

On Sunday Vail discovered that the stone house had sprung another leak.

Mark entered the bedroom in his pajamas and said, "Daddy, the circus is wet."

Harry sat up with a start. "What are you talking about?" he asked softly.

"The circus! The circus! On the wall!"

"What is it?" Kay said sleepily.

"He says the poster on his bedroom wall is wet."

The circus poster was damp to the touch. On the wall behind, brown watermarks ran from ceiling to floor. "Why?" Kay asked as he started to dress.

"It poured last night. Either a shingle's loose or that old crack—the one you painted—has opened up. I'll try waterproofing compound. There's some in the barn."

"You won't get up on a ladder, will you? Let Dun handle it."

"I shouldn't become totally dependent on Dun. It's bad enough as it is."

On summer Sundays Kay went riding, with Mark sitting side-saddle in front of her. With others from the club they rode through the woods and along the beach. Mark had a riding habit as did Kay, and, though he looked natty at breakfast, his face underneath the little cap was pale.

"How's m'lord this morning?" Harry asked him.

"Fine, Daddy," Mark said in a subdued voice.

"He seems tired. Maybe with all this dampness he's catching a cold," Harry said, glancing through the window at the oyster-colored sky. "It might rain. Should he go?"

"The weatherman said it would clear up."

"He's been saying that for two days now."

The phone rang and Vail picked it up. There was no one on the line. "Damn," Vail said.

"I want to ride with Mommy," Mark was yelling. "I don't want to stay in the house."

Kay went to the barn and saddled Brioche. She rode the horse to the house. Old, swaybacked, gentle, the sorrel's patience was infinite. Harry hoisted Mark to her back.

"Promise you won't use the ladder when I'm gone?" He nodded. "Okay, giddyup. Harry, look!" She pulled on the reins.

He turned and saw the long narrow ridges on the lawn. "Mole traces, I guess," he muttered. "They weren't there yesterday. Ground's soft. I guess moles dig fast."

"What'll we do? They'll ruin the yard in no time at all."

"Poison," he decided. "The stuff was used on the mice."

96

"But won't Punch get into it?"

"I'll put it where he can't. The dead moles may stink for a few days," Harry warned.

Kay sniffed the air. "Talk about the power of suggestion! I can smell them already."

He sniffed too. "There's a stink, but it's not dead moles. The septic tank is backing up, I'm afraid."

"Let's get out of here, Mark, before anything else happens," she said in desperation. The mare ambled down the drive. "We'll be back in plenty of time for Mark to take a nap before we go to the Demmings'."

How unsystematic moles are, he thought. Some put their holes at the ends of the ridges and some on top of them. But moles know their business, he had to suppose. He inserted the pellets of poison with his bare hand, reaching in until the earth seemed to grab at his arm.

He flirted with the question of whether the earthsound could have been caused by a mole. No, he decided, not likely, not likely at all. . . . He went to the barn, where he put the poison away and found the blackened can of waterproofing compound and a long brush. He returned to the house, climbed to the small attic on a narrow ladder in the upstairs hall closet, opened a trapdoor and emerged on the roof.

Examining the shingles near the edge, Vail looked at the yard. Something he had been unable to see on the ground was clearly discernible from the roof. The mole traces were not irregularly placed, as he must have assumed. Instead, all ran across the lawn in a north-south pattern. Earthquake activity could leave traces like this—running in a definite direction.

Nothing seemed wrong with the roof—there was no loose shingle nor open place through which water might seep. On his hands and knees, he went down the gentle slope of the roof until his head hung over the cornice and he could see the crack

97

directly below. A piece of mortar had fallen out, and rain blown in a certain direction could enter this hole.

Vail crawled back up the slope, opened the can and smeared the brush with the compound. Lying on his stomach at the edge of the roof, he began smearing the crack. He had just completed the job when he felt the shaking.

Careful! You'll fall off!

Warily, he crawled up the roof, returned to the trapdoor and entered the house. He found the tape and quickly went to the basement, to find the crack, his primitive seismometer, unchanged.

This time the blackboard said "Demmings."

If it was late or raining somebody would drop them off afterward, so they decided to walk through the woods, under sky that was pasty but bright.

She said, "You're not very talkative this evening."

"I'm not quite myself, I guess," he replied.

Kay peered at him thoughfully and said, "When did you fall off the ladder?"

"A week ago."

"That's when you started acting funny, talking about cracks and buildings falling down. I worry about you. When was the last time you felt shaky?"

"Today," he confessed.

"It's dizziness, that's all. Harry, you must promise me something. If it happens one more time, you go to the doctor. All right?"

"Okay."

The shelty barked and they turned. Punch was on top of the boulder and Mark was trying to scale the side.

"Mark!" Kay shouted. "You come right down. You'll get yourself filthy."

They crossed Torturous Creek on the stepping-stones, with Punch wading. Halfway over, Mark bent and dipped his finger in the stream. "Warm water!" he cried.

Harry put his finger in the water, too. "It does feel warm," he agreed.

"Maybe summer's coming at last," Kay said.

Mark ran ahead on the leaf-slick path. Suddenly he vanished. Kay glanced around. "Mark?" The boy was not to be seen, nor did he answer. "Mark?" she called again into the bushes.

"The playhouse," Harry said.

The side trail was obscured by a branch that he pulled aside, revealing a small clearing and the playhouse with a shingled roof. Harry bent and knocked on the door, calling "Anyone home?"

A giggle. "Come in."

He poked his head inside without trying to squeeze his shoulders through the narrow doorway. The room contained a table, chairs and a mock kitchen, and was large enough for a grown-up to lie outstretched but not to stand up straight, emphasizing that the house was intended for children. He noticed an air mattress rolled in the corner. Mark, on his knees by the little couch, held something in his hand. "Come on out, honey," Harry said, backing out. "Be sure to close the door behind you."

The boy emerged, holding out a glittering object. "See what I found?"

It was a gold cigarette lighter with *WBD* engraved on the side. He took it.

"WBD—Wende Baldwin Demming. Where did you get it?" Kay asked, grabbing the lighter.

"Mark found it in the playhouse." Their eyes made questions when he told her about the air mattress.

"Playing around in the playhouse."

"Well, we don't know for certain. Anyway, it's their business.

But what'll I do with the lighter? I can't hand it to her and say, 'See what I found in the playhouse.' "

Kay said, "Keep it out of sight so that Mark won't remember." She glanced at the boy, who ran ahead. "Put it under a chair cushion so that Wende will be sure to find it. She'll think she dropped it there." She gave him back the lighter, which he placed in his pocket.

The path opened on an expanse of emerald lawn the size of a football field, passed manicured bushes and trees and a formal garden. Farther on was the house, three stories high, with a carved wood exterior, a widow's walk, turrets and an untold number of bedrooms, mostly unoccupied. By the forty-foot pool a white-jacketed manservant served drinks from an outdoor bar.

The usual faces cried, "Hello, hello," to kisses and handshakes. Wende said with a self-deprecating smile, "It's just us folks again."

"We're practically a family," Kay said cheerfully.

"I was afraid to ask anybody else, in case we decide to play Jeff's game," Wende went on. "It could be, well, revealing."

"It *has* to be revealing or it's no fun," Jeff exclaimed with a jerk of his mustache. "You find out exactly what other people think of you."

Harry surreptitiously slid the lighter beneath the cushion of his chair as Demming snapped. "Out with it, man. What is this fool game of yours?"

"The game's called 'Inquest,'" Jeff continued, ignoring the interruption, "and it's more fun if everybody's a little liquored up. We're the coroners and we have to determine the cause of death. The death of each of us, that is."

"What's a coroner?" Mark asked.

"Sort of a doctor," Wende said hastily. "Mark, go to the kitchen and ask the cook to give you something to eat."

Fred said loudly, "I don't get the point of it."

"Doesn't the manner of a person's death often explain how he lived? What kind of person he was? That's our job—to figure out how each of us died by how we lived. But we must talk frankly."

"One doesn't go to an inquest for amusement exactly," Bill warned.

Wende said, as if to stop discussion before too many negative ballots were cast, "It's getting chilly. Shall we go inside?"

Yellow plaster, dark wood paneling, mahogany cabinets with glass doors, bulky furniture, harsh ancestral faces in wood frames with oval mats. Wende had wanted to repaint, install bright lights, buy new furniture, give the glowering visages of Demming's early American forebears to a museum; but Fred, compliant to most of her wishes, refused. The house had been in his family for generations and must remain intact, he decreed.

Nobody mentioned the game at supper, as though judgment were being reserved, but over brandy Wende said carefully, "I like to try new things."

Jeff replied artfully, glancing at Polly, "Well, I suppose we shouldn't do it, after all. I'm just a newcomer here, and I don't know you all that well."

Polly seemed wounded. "Jeff! We're like a family, just as Kay said."

"Explain the rules," Wende said firmly.

"We each die in turn. As we file around the bier, we give our verdict on how the person died, from what we understand about their lives."

"What happens if the corpse doesn't like what's said and talks back?" Wende inquired.

Jeff threw up his hands. "That's against the rules! Half the fun of it is saying what you've always wanted to tell someone, and the corpse is forbidden to answer, because it's dead."

"Some fun," Demming grumbled. "Where'd you get this game? Did you make it up?"

"Everybody's playing it in New York," Carmichael answered.

Polly's expression was perplexed. "But why should people know so much about how we lived?" Her frown line deepened.

Mark appeared in the doorway and Bill pointed. "Is he going to play 'Inquest' too?"

"Of course not!" Kay said, hugging the boy.

"I don't like the idea of dying before my time even in sport," said Demming.

"I'm dead against it," Bill roared.

Jeff turned to Wende. "We have a rebellion on our hands."

Wende's pale blue eyes were cold as Arctic water: she liked to get her way. "Listen! We need some shaking up. It would be good to try something different. Let's play, it won't hurt. It would be fun to hear what we think about each other."

"Who wants to hear that?" Bill said.

"Cowards! You're scared of a harmless little game!" Wende was angry; capsules of red broke beneath the pearly skin of her cheeks.

Kay had a hooded look. "I'll play," she muttered.

"It's only a game, I suppose," Fred said deferentially.

"Okay?" Wende, victorious, glanced at each. "You'll have to give me a moment to set the stage. I always wanted to be a director, and now I am—a funeral director." She rang for the servants and pushed the company out of the dining room, sliding shut the dark doors.

With Mark on his shoulders, Harry climbed the stairway, and Kay followed behind.

"Grown-ups scare me," Mark confessed.

"Me too, sometimes," his father answered. He found an empty room and put Mark in bed. "Will you go to sleep now?"

"Yes," Mark said grudgingly.

102

In the hall Kay popped a knuckle and said listlessly, "Listen to how quiet it is. Even the sea is still."

"You don't really want to play. Why don't we just forget it?" he suggested.

"We'll ruin the game, and Wende's determined to do it."

They returned to the living room. Soon a servant entered quietly and put a record on the machine. At the same instant the dining room doors opened, and Wende appeared in a long black dress and gold jewelry that brought out the light in her hair. The heavy chairs had been pushed back to the walls and the thick draperies shut. A sheet lay on the long oak table, on both ends of which candles burned. Sorrowful music sounded.

"Come in, come in," Wende called gleefully.

They entered slowly, as if unwilling to cross the threshold. "It's so realistic," Kay muttered.

"It's supposed to put you in the right mood."

"There are seven candles and seven of us."

"How observant you are, Kay. Each of our candles has to go out. Who's first?" Wende asked.

Polly pointed at her husband. "Him. He deserves it."

"Me?" Pollidor took stumbling steps backward.

The women grabbed his thin arms and pulled him protesting to the table. "Lie down," Polly commanded. Bill did, as Kay removed his white loafers.

Wende folded Bill's hands across his chest, closed his eyes with the tips of her long, thin fingers, and wrapped him in the sheet. "His winding sheet," she giggled.

Sipping her Scotch, Polly began to walk around the table, the others in train. "What am I supposed to say?" she asked. "I've never been to a funeral, much less a wake."

"Tell what you thought of him," Jeff laughed.

"A fine, upstanding man, a leading New York lawyer, a credit to his profession."

"Come on, needle him a little," Wende said gaily.

103

"Well . . ." Polly seemed fearful as she stared at her husband's still face, yellowed by candlelight. "He looks sort of small and pathetic."

Bill opened baleful eyes, but Wende shut them with her fingers. "You're dead," she warned.

Jeff's mustache turned. "You can do better than that, Polly. Tell us more about him so we can try to guess the cause of death. Did he have any bad qualities?"

"I wouldn't know where to start." A smirk played briefly on her features. "For instance, the poor man believed he had a fine sense of humor, but can a person be witty who doesn't know a good joke from bad?"

"Go on," Jeff said.

For once Polly appeared to grope for words. "Should I? I mean, he is . . . was my husband, after all, but, oh well, he's dead now, isn't he? Take his pride. He wouldn't listen when Harry said the contractor was gypping us, and now we've a house that trembles in the wind. Bill would deny it, but it's so. And extravagant—when it came to himself. How he loved to show off, but he was an absolute Scrooge where others were concerned. I think the real reason he didn't want children was that he would have had to share with them."

Pollidor made a strangled cry, and Wende put her hand on his mouth. "More," she commanded.

"I guess money was his real passion—how he envied Fred Demming for his wealth. For money Bill would do just about anything. He saw himself as a man of action, but what he did mostly was bend his arm. I could have put up with his drinking except for his rages. He could be violent, and don't think he wasn't capable of slugging his own wife, his own sweet wife." Tears came to her eyes, but after she had blown into her handkerchief her face brightened. "They did an autopsy on him, and guess what they found! The man was a freak, a biological monstrosity. He was all liver. No heart, stomach, anything but liver. That's what he died of—cirrhosis."

"I thought he was poisoned by the computer bar," Wende said.

"Judging by what you've told us, it seems to me Pollidor must have died violently," Jeff put in.

Shuffling slowly, Kay extended her hand and ran it gently across the hollows and ridges of Pollidor's polished skull, gleaming in the candlelight. "He was shot," she announced with authority. "Shot in the head, I think."

Pollidor rose and pointed at his wife. "I'll get you, bitch. You're next."

Wende blew out one candle.

Holding a fresh drink, Bill circled the table on which Polly lay wrapped in the sheet, face passive, forehead smooth. "Poor Pol. I believe the Lord silenced her out of desperation, as the only way to make her stop talking."

"Did she die of lockjaw?" Wende asked in a stage whisper.

Pollidor scowled. "You're got to know a couple of things about Pol. She worried terribly about growing old. I wouldn't want to accuse a woman cold on her bier—ahem, a cold bier— of lying about her age, but I wouldn't be completely surprised if her birth certificate showed that she was older than she admitted. A certain plastic surgeon knows about that."

"Bastard," said Polly's hoarse voice.

"Her age wasn't all she lied about, either," Pollidor continued, seeming to enjoy himself. "For instance, she made out that her husband—that's me—didn't want kids, but the truth was that *she* couldn't have any. Well, on second thought, maybe that wasn't lying, for can you call a person a liar if he can't distinguish between fact and fancy? Polly was like that. When it got bad enough she'd go to a place in Connecticut and rest."

Polly struggled to disentangle herself from the sheet. "Bill

Pollidor, you're a son of a bitch. You're hinting I was in a loony bin, and you know that isn't true. The real liar around here is you. As for children . . ."

"No squabbling!" Wende shouted. "Polly, don't you want to know how you died?"

"All right." Polly sank back on the table.

"Of premature old age," Pollidor said mercilessly.

"Maybe she died of boredom from having to listen to you," Kay chuckled, and then her face grew serious. "I believe she died a natural death."

Nobody appeared to want to argue with Kay's verdict. Polly rose looking sheepish but relieved. "Your turn," she said to Jeff as Wende blew out a second candle. Jeff wound the sheet about himself and lay down, his arms crossed on his chest, the light flickering on his profile. "The darling!" Polly babbled. "The dear boy, he had almost no faults at all—charming, handsome, intelligent, friendly."

"The girls will miss him," Wende joshed. "I wonder how he died?"

Fred Demming said softly, as though no one were supposed to hear, "Perhaps a jealous husband murdered him."

"What an awful thing to say," Wende cried.

Polly said quickly, "I'm sure he died doing something heroic, like covering a war for television."

Harry, unable to resist, put in, "He was something of a thrill-seeker, wasn't he? I bet he died doing something foolhardy."

Kay mumbled, "Drowned."

"What?" Wende asked.

"He drowned." Her voice was almost mechanical.

"You really sound like you know what you're talking about, Kay," Wende told her, but Kay said nothing.

Wende blew out Jeff's candle and swung her long legs up on the table as Jeff, smiling, came down. She closed her eyes and murmured, "Be nice to me when I'm gone."

Jeff's words were careful and cool. "She was a lovely woman in all respects. Everyone will miss her very much."

Kay walked behind him. "She's beautiful even in death, and she must have died young. How?" she asked no one in particular.

Fred paced slowly, gazing at his wife's oval face, smooth as a mask. "I loved her," he said somberly, "and I hope she hears that, wherever she is. But she was not perfect except in appearance. She was a willful woman who wanted her way and always got it. Whatever impulse she had she indulged, no matter what the effect on others. She was a child, essentially, and had to be treated like one. Like a child's, her universe was herself."

"But how did she die? You haven't told us!" Polly called.

Demming seemed surprised by the query. "I . . . haven't the vaguest idea."

"Next witness," Jeff urged.

"In a nice way, I'm sure," Polly simpered. "In her sleep."

"Maybe she lost her looks and killed herself. Wasn't vanity her middle name?" Bill Pollidor offered.

"It was shock," Kay said decisively.

"Shock?" Harry said, looking at her closely.

"Yes," Kay said in the same authoritative manner that seemed to preclude further offerings. "A shock." Kay's lips were slack, her eyes dull. Occasionally she popped a joint in her finger. "I know."

"Know?" Harry studied her. "This is a game, remember?"

"Game? Oh yes."

Wende blinked but lay quite still for a moment, eyes clear and depthless, hands folded across the waist of her black dress. Sitting up, she said in an even voice, "Your turn, Fred."

Demming mounted the table with effort and evident reluctance. "No sheet for me," he said bossily, pushing it away, "for I intend to be cremated." His hands shook a little as he closed his eyes behind the thick glasses.

"Now that's a man who didn't die from worrying about money," Pollidor said brusquely.

"Grief?" Polly suggested to Wende. "Grief over you?"

Wende asked Kay, "Well?"

"I'm . . . not sure." Kay bent and studied Demming's face, gray in the ever darker room. "Yes, that's a part of it, but not all. Fred fell into a hole."

"This dame's got some imagination," Bill roared. "Why, for Christ's sake, a hole?"

"That's how it appears to me. I'm just guessing, just like everyone else."

Wende said, "So I'm the widow Demming." She bent and kissed Fred's brow. "I wish I'd had the courage to tell him what I'm able to now that he's dead. That he lived too much for power. He had to dominate everything around him, including me. He was too stiff, too unfeeling, too ungiving, and if he'd been different I might not have done some things I did. It's too bad you can't hear me, Fred. Things might have changed if you were alive to hear me."

Fred snorted slightly and his body shook. Pollidor said, "He's fallen asleep!"

"Yes. Come on, Fred, get up," Wende said with deep impatience. Demming rose sheepishly, and his wife blew out a candle and said coldly, "Only two left. Kay?"

Kay took a step back. "Well . . ."

"What's the matter, Kay? Come on, Kay. . . ." "You have to, Kay. . . ." "Whatcha scared of? Being a corpse won't hurt you. . . ." "Don't do it, darling, if you don't want to. . . ." Kay's head twisted helplessly toward each speaker in turn before she went to the table, wrapped herself in the sheet, and lay down, fists crossed on her breast.

"Another stiff," Pollidor was saying. "What happened to this one, you think?"

"Nice-looking woman," said Jeff, "but a nervous type, I bet."

"Something in her face says she didn't die peacefully," Wende offered.

"Maybe we ought to perform an autopsy," Bill said loudly.

"Not necessary," Jeff objected. "She died of fright."

Kay's thin frame shuddered slightly, and Harry glared at them, saying, "Come on, she died peacefully in bed, of old age. Didn't you, Kay? Come on, darling," he coaxed, "join the living."

A single candle burned and it was Harry's turn. He reclined on the table, hands outstretched, palms flat. Words floated down to him: "Funny about him . . . seemed like a nice feller but had this *thing* about the ground . . . thought the earth was alive . . . screw loose somewhere . . . something in his past . . . feels shaking when nobody else does . . . unstable person . . . imagines things . . . be telling us there'll be an earthquake . . . wonder how he died. . . ." Then the table shook; he could sense it through his hands, his back, a faint vibration, barely perceptible. In his mind a crevasse opened and he glimpsed the shape of his anxiety, which was insupportable, and he opened his eyes. In the dim light their faces hovered above, and he blew out the candle as though to extinguish the sight.

The Pollidors with Jeff in the car dropped them off at the stone house. Harry carried the sleeping boy up the staircase on his shoulder while Kay made coffee in the kitchen. When he returned, he found Kay walking back and forth. "That's a game I can live without," she said.

"Me too. But what scared you so?"

"I don't know. It was, well . . ."

"Go on."

Her eyes would not look at him. ". . . like there was someone else in the room."

"Is that where you got your predictions about how people would die?"

"I hardly remember what I said."

"So you do believe something talked to you?"

"I didn't say that, Harry." She popped a knuckle.

"That's a brand-new habit, Kay. Where did you get it?"

"What?"

"The noise you make with your finger."

"Oh. You've got a funny habit, too—telling people things shake when nobody else feels it. Tomorrow you'll see a doctor. You promised, remember?"

They went to bed, turning away from each other as they searched uselessly for sleep.

PART THREE

SLIP

Monday, June 24 At the office that morning, Vail made a number of calls: to Dr. Bjerling's office, asking to be squeezed in during the next few hours; to Robinson, learning that the manager was not expected back until later on; to the outfit that drained septic tanks; to the phone company about the false rings. Through his doorway he called, "Mrs. Conner, send Walter in, please."

Walter Johnson was the company draftsman. When the partners worked up a report or a proposal Johnson took their notes and data and turned them into drawings, diagrams or graphs, whether of a geological cross section, the construction of a well, or the long-term trend of a water table.

Johnson entered the office. In his middle fifties, his expression customarily a little bewildered, Johnson was a highly competent draftsman once the task had been explained to him.

Vail said, "Morning, Walter. Can you take on a new job?"

"Do I get to say no?"

Vail laughed. "I guess not." He handed Johnson the data the drilling outfit had sent over. "I'd like drawings of the hill of the old people's home—a cross section and a topographical sketch

113

too. You'll have to drive over and have a look at the building and the topography."

"Tomorrow do?"

"I'd prefer you went today."

With the doctor's visit impending, Vail found it hard to concentrate. He prowled the office impatiently, eager to get the examination over with. He was oddly unconcerned about his own physiology: what seemed to matter more than whether he suffered from a mild concussion or a fractured skull was to establish the reason for his shakiness. For if nothing were wrong with him—as he suspected—then he was that much nearer to proving the existence of an earthquake.

Bjerling's office was only a few blocks away, and Vail walked rapidly under the first sun in what seemed like weeks. The receptionist waved him in at once, and Vail seated himself before a crisp, white-coated man his own age.

Bjerling had been their family physician ever since they moved from Boston. He gazed at his patient thoughtfully and said, "How are you, Harry? You look a little pale."

"I'd think anybody who *wasn't* pale in this weather would have something wrong with him," Vail observed. He added, "I've been working hard."

"Then slow down. What's the trouble?"

"About a week ago . . ." Vail explained his fall from the ladder, the continuing dizziness and sense of imbalance.

"Can you tell me what it's like?"

"Well, being on a rolling sea. Or in an earthquake."

"Never been in an earthquake and never expect to be," Bjerling said.

"Most Americans haven't." Vail paused. "Or if they have, it was a small quake and they didn't recognize the clues. In a big earthquake you really feel disoriented."

"Frightened?"

"Depends on how strong it is."

114

"Let's think about a concussion first. After you fell off the ladder were you unconscious?"

He remembered the earthsound. "I'm not sure. Maybe for a second or two. It's hard to say."

"Headaches?" Bjerling sounded serious.

"No."

"Feel sleepy a lot?"

"No."

Dr. Bjerling rose from his chair, walked behind Vail, and probed the back of his head with deft fingers. "Hurt?"

"No."

"There?"

"No."

"Nothing wrong with the occipital, it seems. Take off your shoes and socks." Vail did. "Walk on the balls of your feet." Vail complied. "Walk on your toes." He did this as well. "Squeeze my hand." Vail squeezed. "Ouch. Let up. You're strong as an ox." Vail sat down, and Bjerling went back to his desk and returned with an ophthalmoscope with which he examined Vail's eyes. He clicked off the light and returned to his desk. "No sign of papilledema. I'll take some X rays before you go to make sure. But I think we have to rule out a concussion. For one thing, you'd be constantly sleepy. That leaves the vertigo. You say you've experienced nausea, light-headedness, disturbed orientation. Often?"

"Often enough to bring me here."

"Any particular time of day?"

"No."

"That's not important. Buzzing in your ears? Ringing?"

"No."

"Happen when you sit up or move suddenly?"

"No."

"Ever had problems with your blood pressure? Have a cold? Taking medication?"

115

"No, no, no."

Bjerling checked his blood pressure. "Normal. All right, stand up. Leave your shoes off. Put your feet together tightly. Close your eyes. If you fall I'll catch you." The doctor hovered anxiously near. Vail smiled and closed his eyes. He outweighed the doctor by fifty pounds. He did not fall. "Sit down," Bjerling said, sounding happier by the second. "Follow my finger with your eyes. Keep your head still." Vail did so. "No nystagmus—jumping of the eye, part of the vertigo syndrome. Not a trace of it. I'm going to put some warm water in your ear." He used a rubber bulb. Then he had Vail's eyes follow his finger again. "Let's try it with cold water this time." If Bjerling had found anything the matter, he gave no sign of it. "I want to test your hearing," he went on. He removed his wristwatch and held it to Vail's ear. "Can you hear it tick?"

"No," Vail said, "because I have water in my ear." He tipped his head until fluid ran out on the tissue Bjerling handed him. "Now I can hear fine." The watch moved farther and farther away. "Yes. Yes."

Bjerling said, "Normal hearing. Hyperacusis in fact—better than normal." He poked instruments into Vail's nose and ears, returning at last to his desk. "I can't find anything the matter with you. My bet is a mild case of labyrinthitis—disturbance of the inner ear. We don't know what causes it—virus, most likely. Probably what made you fall off the ladder in the first place. I'll give you a prescription for Dramamine. I'm sure it will go away in a few days, a week or two at most. No, it's not catching. The nurse will take skull X rays just to be sure there's no fracture. I'll call you this afternoon or this evening with the results. I'm sure they'll be negative. I wish all my patients were as healthy as you." He extended his hand, then quickly withdrew it. "Take it easy, Harry. You're fine," he bubbled.

Vail frowned. He had wanted a clean bill of health or a clear

116

diagnosis. Labyrinthitis sounded like neither one, and the ambiguity of the shaking, maddeningly, remained.

A bump appeared in the road just before Summerset Villa, and Vail slowed sharply. The bay glittered in the noonday sun like something shiny and new.

Down the slope Vail saw the drilling rig with a truck beside it. Two men lolled under a tree. He descended and said to the foreman, "Isn't it early for lunch, Charley?"

"Just waiting for you," the man said. "That Robinson character won't let us work. He came in about an hour ago and started to scream."

"I'll talk to him."

Vail climbed back up the hill. Evidently the sun had made Robinson relent: old people sat on the benches and strolled along the paths. Among them he saw a familiar face.

"Ah, Dr. Vail. Now nice to see you. I thought you would be here today."

"Any special reason, Mrs. Benjamin?"

"You're interested in cracks, aren't you? Everybody knows that. The cracks have gotten bigger. The janitor says you can see daylight through one of them. The building is safe, isn't it, Dr. Vail?"

"There's nothing to worry about," Vail said, feigning confidence.

"Well, if you say so. You seem like such a nice, dependable young man," Alma Benjamin said in her clear voice. "Intelligent, too." She made a wrinkled smile. "You'd better go talk to Mr. Robinson. He's waiting for you."

This time the discussion took place in the manager's office, and he was angry. "I gave you permission to drill some holes, and now you're back again. What is it this time?"

"This hill is too wet. I want to dig a well and dewater it."

"The machinery is ugly. You're driving a heavy truck over my lawn."

"It won't be here more than a couple of days."

"It'll cost a fortune, no doubt. I'll need Mr. Summerset's permission."

"There's no time. The cracks must be sealed. You can see daylight through one. Also, I want to dig a hole on top of the hill."

"All right, dig your fool holes. But that is absolutely *all* I authorize without Mr. Summerset's consent. I wish I could reach him." Robinson wrung his small hands. "Vail, I hope you don't cause any more trouble."

Vail laughed bitterly. "Me? It's the rain, Mr. Robinson, the way this place is built, the ground."

Punch's inevitable bark sounded hollow and far away. Vail walked to the back of the house where the shelty was scratching vainly at a mole hole. The dog greeted him with another bark and resumed scratching.

Kay appeared wearing a flowered apron. "Hello, you're early."

"I decided to quit at five like normal people because Bjerling said I work too hard." He pecked her cheek.

"Oh, he called. He said you don't have a concussion or anything. All you suffer from is a little virus I can't pronounce."

"Labyrinthitis—I think that's how you say it. A mild infection of the inner ear. He's given me Dramamine—seasick medicine —and says it will go away in a week or so. *If* that's what I've got."

"What do you mean 'if'?"

"Well, doctors say 'virus' when they don't know what else to say."

"Bjerling's a good doctor. If he says you've got something, you've got it."

118

"I guess so. What's for dinner?"

"I'm tired of hamburger. Let's have something festive. How would you feel about a cheese soufflé?" He nodded. "And we'll eat in the dining room for a change, without Mark. I'll feed him early and put him to bed. We haven't had a nice evening alone for a while. Make a fire."

She reappeared later in pearls and a long skirt. She looked nice, he told her, without mentioning that she seemed wan. He fixed gin and tonics. Kay sat in the rocker, he in his straight-backed chair. Outside, the wind had started to gust. "Storm's coming," he remarked.

"Windstorm, the radio said. What a summer. I hope we have good weather for the holidays. When is the Fourth?"

"A week from Thursday." He listened to the windows rattle.

"I hate the Fourth of July," Kay said suddenly. "Firecrackers make me jumpy. Did you call about the septic tank?"

"Yes. They'll come as soon as they can. Did you call about the clock?"

"I forgot," she said guiltily. "Forgot to call the piano tuner too. When you have as little to do on some days as I do, you forget to do anything. Harry, think I should become an honest woman and find a job?" Kay rose and straightened the painting over the sofa.

"Well, it's a thought. The trouble is there's no work on the peninsula, and you can't very well commute to Fall River and get back in time to pick up Mark at school."

"That's a problem," Kay agreed with a helpless frown. She began to chatter. "There's a lot of news. Polly called—oh, she had trouble getting through; you did call the phone company?" He grunted. "—to say that Jeff is returning to New York. He leaves Wednesday and hopes to be back by the Fourth. I saw Jeff and Wende in the Wilbore store this afternoon. Wende bought a six-pack of beer and put down a fifty-dollar bill. It was all she had, she said, and Mrs. Wilbore couldn't make change.

119

Jeff didn't have any money, so I ended up paying for it. Think Mrs. Wilbore would let Wende charge it? Not her. Wende and Jeff were off to play tennis, they said, but I didn't believe them. Why would they want beer? There was a blanket in the back seat of Wende's convertible. They were heading for the beach, I think. You know, those two are together constantly now. It's the talk of the club, but Wende doesn't seem to care."

"You don't think she'd leave Fred for Jeff, do you?" he asked with a kind of bored fascination.

"I don't think so. She's too practical to abandon her nest for a TV reporter in the middle of a divorce, our Wende is," Kay said. She pondered a moment and continued, "Still, she did say she was going away for a few days and didn't tell where."

"Anybody mention the game last night?"

"Nobody said a word. It's like they all want to forget it. I do too."

"Amen," he said.

There was a loud rap on the door and Kay whirled in her chair. "What in God's name is that?"

Harry opened the door to find Fred Demming leaning on a cane. His Cadillac loomed behind him in the dark. "Come in," said Harry. "What brings you out on a night like this?"

Demming entered and stood hesitantly, his heavy face slack. "Wende went out hours ago. I thought she might be here and called, but your phone is on the blink."

"Yes. It ought to be fixed soon. Maybe she's at the Pollidors'."

"No. I called."

"How about a drink, Fred? Maybe she'll show up here."

"Couldn't hurt. Bourbon, please," he said aimlessly.

The phone rang, and Kay, with a startled expression, picked it up and put it down again. "Nobody there."

"What?" Fred asked.

"Nobody on the line," she said in a loud voice.

"My phone's been acting funny, too," Demming said. "It

rings, and there's nobody there. Happened just before I came over. Kind of spooky, with the wind whistling and Wende not home and a dead phone in your hand. I wonder if it's a prank."

"Prank?" Kay asked sharply.

"The village kids, dialing and hanging up."

"They don't have phones," Harry reminded him.

"There's a phone in the bar. They could use that."

"Fred," Harry said in a slightly embarrassed voice, "strangest goddam thing. Dun Sowles said somebody was interested in buying *my* house. Have any idea who?"

Demming seemed surprised. "No idea at all. Somebody up the peninsula, I imagine—interested in selling?"

"*Me?* Definitely not."

"You didn't tell me about it," Kay said.

"I forgot."

Another rattle sounded, which Harry took to be the wind, but after it happened twice he went to the door, to find the Pollidors. "Hello, hello," he greeted them. "What are you doing out there?"

Polly answered, "We didn't want to just *barge* in. What took you so long? I was practically blown off the porch. My poor hair . . ."

Harry, considering why he had not gone to the door at once, realized that he would have expected Punch to bark had there been people outside. "Where's the dog?" he asked Kay.

She shrugged. "Up in Mark's room, I guess. Make our friends a drink, Harry."

"Just a bitty one," Bill said. "We only popped over to look for Jeff, who evidently isn't here." He toured the room with his gaze.

Polly said rapidly, "Jeff still must be at the club. He was going to have a few drinks after tennis and get a ride back. I figured maybe he came with you, Kay. Gracious, what a terrible night! It's absolutely scary. The wind's making our whole house

121

shake." The frown line bisected her forehead. "I feel so much safer here in the stone house."

"Stop it about the house," Bill yelled at her, glaring at Harry.

The phone rang and Kay went to it hastily, raising it to her ear but saying nothing. "Jeff," she gasped. "I'm sorry. The phone's been ringing and there's nobody at the other end. I thought it would be the same this time, but I guess they've fixed it. . . . Yes . . . Well, I'll ask them. . . ." She said to the Pollidors, "Jeff's back from the club. He wants to know if he should come over, or whether you're going home. He's hungry, he says."

"Tell him we'll be right home," Polly said.

"They're coming home, Jeff."

"Well, see you tomorrow," Polly said, following her husband out.

"Can I use the phone? Maybe Wende's shown up." Fred picked it up and dialed. "Nobody." He licked his pale lips. "I guess she's walking on the beach. Walks a lot lately." His voice trailed off.

"I hope there's nothing wrong," Kay said.

"Of course there's nothing wrong. Why should anything be wrong?" Demming asked huffily.

"No reason. It's just that when Harry takes to the beach it usually means trouble. He uses the ocean the way others use tranquilizers."

Several sharp raps sounded. Kay said in a strained voice, "What's that?"

Harry ran to the door and opened it. There was no one outside. "Punch?" he said, knowing the answer.

"Punch is in Mark's room, I told you," she said sharply. "Anyway, since when does Punch bang on doors?"

"The wind then." He closed the door and switched on the porch light.

"What's going on?" Fred asked.

"That's what I'd like to know," Kay said.

The rapping sounded again. Harry ran to the door and jerked the knob quickly. "What's the matter, Harry?" Wende Demming said in a startled voice.

He felt foolish. "I didn't mean to frighten you, Wende. Come in. Fred's here. Did you just knock, seconds ago?"

"Me? Why would I do that?"

"It must have been the wind."

Wende advanced into the room, blonde hair tousled, cheeks flushed as though from the open air—or contact with a mustache. She wore a sweater and tennis shorts which had a black mark on the seat, as though from tar. "Fred, darling," Wende breathed, "how long have you been here?"

"A while. Where were you?"

"After tennis, I took the longest, most wonderful walk on the beach. The big surf is marvelous. I went farther than I meant to go. I figured Fred would either be here or at the Pollidors', but your line seems out of order so I came over." She blinked at her husband. "Poor Fred, how I neglect you. You haven't even had dinner." Kay started to speak, and Wende said rapidly, "Don't even suggest it, dear. We'll eat at home. Come along, dear."

"Wasn't she in a hurry to get out of here," Harry remarked when the front door closed.

"She was afraid I'd blab something about seeing her at the store, which I wouldn't have, of course." Kay looked dejected and said, "Well, I guess we ought to eat."

"Dinner isn't spoiled, is it?"

"No. The soufflé should just be ready, but I don't feel so hungry as before."

Just as she was removing the soufflé from the oven he felt a shake.

"I don't know what happened," she said, arriving in the dining room. "The soufflé fell, dammit!"

"It'll taste fine anyway."

They finished and carried the dishes into the kitchen. In the living room he took the tongs from the brass plate on the wall and stoked the fire, adding logs. Kay entered carrying the coffee and said, when they were seated, "Polly was afraid to stay in her house. Could it really fall?"

"If a storm were big enough, yes, or if . . ."

"If what?"

"Well, in a place like California the Pollidors' house wouldn't have a chance of surviving. It's too fragile."

"Survive what? Oh, I get it, an earthquake."

"Neither would ours, probably. Stone houses don't fare well in earthquakes."

She sighed. "Everybody has at least one irrational fear, I guess." The wind spluttered. "Mine comes out on nights like this. Thank God there aren't many of them."

He chuckled. "Don't say it. Ghosts again. Next thing you'll tell me you really believe in them."

"Maybe I did once," she said through a tiny mouth.

"You mean it's true?" His voice was perforated by surprise. "You never told me."

"Because you're a scientist. You would have laughed at me."

"With you," he corrected her. His big hand rested on her knee. "When did you stop being a believer?"

"Oh, years ago!"

"How many?"

"When I got to college."

"*When you got to college!* You mean you believed in ghosts as late as that?"

The gale ricocheted off the building, and Kay said, "You don't have to really believe in something to wonder about it, do you? And I read things. Like those two women in upper New York State last century. A ghost sent messages by knocking, and told them his name, where he was from, that he'd been murdered, and that his body was buried in the basement. They found the body, too, and the story checked out," she said.

"Oh, for Christ's sake."

"No, it's true! It happened! Nobody knows the explanation. Harry, give me a brandy, please."

He went to the bar and poured Cognac into a snifter. He noticed that one of the Toby jugs lay too close to the edge of the shelf, and glancing over his shoulder to be sure Kay was looking elsewhere, he pushed it back in place. "So," he said, returning, "you really believe in ghosts."

"In a way. It was strongest when I started to menstruate. Teenage girls—all teenagers, I guess—have wild imaginations. Almost anything's believable."

"Ghosts wearing bloody sheets—it fits."

She smiled faintly into the fire. "Shouldn't we use the screen, Harry?"

"The fire's small. Go on."

"Well, more subtle than ghosts in sheets. Nasty spirits who can read your mind and know just what frightens you."

"What . . ." he started to say when he heard the pounding.

"What's that?" Kay shrieked.

"A loose shutter," he said, isolating the sound from the general turbulence of the night. "In the laundry room, I think." He marched down the hall, opened the window, reached out and latched the shutter closed on the inside, and came back. "That must have been the noise we heard before."

"I'm positive that noise was at the front door," she said.

"There's a big draft in here," he said. "Is there anything open?"

"Not that I know of."

"Well, when you were a girl, what frightened you that ghosts would know about?"

Kay said absently, "Unexpected things. Things you couldn't prepare for. I don't mean I ever thought I saw a ghost—it was

125

more like sensing a presence that was jealous you were alive and wanted to make you pay for it."

His smile revealed his big teeth. "If the Virgin Mary had felt that way about spirits there would never have been a Jesus Christ."

Her face showed resentment. "Don't kid me. It isn't fair."

"Okay. Go on."

From upstairs came the hollow crack of a door slammed shut. "Oh, Harry," she moaned.

He took the stairs two at a time. Mark's door was shut. The boy lay on his back, breathing deeply, the light sweat of childish sleep on his forehead. Harry propped the door open and went downstairs.

"Mark's door. It swung shut."

"Why did it swing shut."

"Draft, I guess. What did the ghosts do?"

"They didn't actually *do* anything," she said, sipping her drink and lighting a cigarette from what he saw was a new pack. "It was just the sensation that they *could*, if they chose."

"And what was your reaction?"

"You honestly want to know?" He nodded vigorously. "I tried never to be alone. I slept in my sister's room whenever I could, hung around with my parents or friends as much as possible. Believe me, I stuck like glue." She smiled sadly. "My poor father. Anyway, I figured when I got old enough the ghosts would understand I wasn't vulnerable and go away for good. And they did."

"You're sure you don't still believe in them?"

"Absolutely not."

There was an interval of silence as they examined the fire, and then Harry said, "Kay, I thought you said that Punch was in Mark's room. He isn't there now."

"Where can he be? Punch? Punch? He's not in the house," she said in a worried voice. "How could he have gotten out?"

"Maybe the screen fell off the window in the study again. No, I closed the window because of the storm."

"Go look."

He thought he had left the study door open, but now it was shut. He felt resistance when he pushed it, and as the door opened the teardrop chandelier in the dining room tinkled like tiny bells as a wind whipped through the house. He switched on the light. "Kay," he called. "The window is broken."

She entered the room hesitantly, shutting the door behind her. The floor was strewn with papers and glass. "How . . ."

He inspected the shattered pane, raising the sash, and put his head into the howling wind. "Broken branch down there. It knocked off the screen and broke the window. Punch must have been trapped in here when the door shut and jumped outside."

"Why didn't we hear the glass break?"

"Maybe it happened during the knocking."

"Which we still can't account for, if you ask me." Examining the floor, her eyes seemed to fasten on something. She knelt and rose, holding out a flat white stone. "What's this doing here?"

"Mark bring it in?"

"I don't know. I don't think so."

He secured the papers on his desk and closed the door behind him. "I'm going to have another drink," she said, moving to the bar, "and then let's go to bed. You want one?"

He shook his head and listened to the groaning trees. "What a wind! The surf must be over the bluffs. I hope the studio's all right. Dun hasn't quite finished caulking the picture window. I better go look."

"Not on your life. You stay with me. Where do you suppose that fool dog is? I hope he hasn't gotten hurt from a falling branch or something."

"I bet he's out checking the mole holes, wind and all. I'll call him."

The wind roared as he opened the kitchen door, stepped out

in the yard and called "Punch! Here, Punch!" into the uproar. There was no response. "Punch!" He closed the door and went to the living room.

Kay sat in the rocker, back to him, and only after he had passed her, stoked the fire and turned did it come to him that she sat stiffly, hands clutched to the rocker's arms, as if encased in a block of glass, her eyes set on some point behind him—whom she did not seem to see—and which with several examinations of her stare's direction he was able to identify as the bronze birdcage. "Kay! What's the matter? Have you gone to sleep? Why are you sitting there like that? Say something!"

She did, in a very small voice: "Bird."

"I can barely hear you. Bird?"

"Song."

"Come on, honey," he said impatiently. "What gives?"

She opened her mouth. "Harry, something quite horrible just happened. I tried to call, but I choked up. I had this funny feeling, like somebody was shaking me, and the rocker began to rock without me rocking it and I looked around and there was nobody and then all of a sudden those fireplace tools began to rattle together and then, you won't believe it, the bird sang, the green singing finch actually sang, only it wasn't a pretty song, not a nice little trill like you'd expect but this awful croak, after all this time, and I can see why it wouldn't sing before because it's embarrassed about how it sounds. Harry, that bird was scared to death." She began to sob.

The lights went out. "Fuck," he said. The fire seemed to burn brighter in the darkness, flickering in the burst of wind down the chimney. "Storm's knocked out the power. Or is it just our house. I'll go upstairs and see if the Pollidors' lights are out. Will you get candles from the dining room?"

He took the flashlight from the closet, illuminated her way to the dining room, and watched her light the candles. Then he went upstairs, peered through the tossing branches toward the

128

Pollidors', and returned. The candelabra burned on the coffee table. Kay sat in her chair, rocking slowly, eyes closed. "I thought maybe we'd blown a fuse, but the Pollidors' house is dark, too."

"Harry," she said in a detached voice, "something's burning. I smell it."

"Nonsense, honey, you . . . Christ, the rug's on fire!" He stamped the burning ember with his foot. "You were right about the grate."

She said dreamily, "Is the rug ruined?"

He pointed the flashlight. "Well, there's a small hole."

"*They* start fires."

He brought her out of the chair and into his arms, telling her that it was all in her imagination—that a down draft caused the fire, that the bird hadn't sung, that the tools hadn't rattled, that she herself had rocked the rocker—that once they were in bed it would be all right. She seemed to listen, allowing herself to be led up the elliptical staircase as he held the candelabra. Then, deep and guttural, a creak like that of a huge hinge filled the house.

"Harry, what was that?" she said, her voice pathetically controlled.

He tried to think carefully. "That was the old elm swaying in the wind."

He watched her undress, then walked down the corridor to check again on Mark, who still slept soundly. She had gone from the bedroom to the bathroom, and he arrived to see her shake two pills from a bottle into her palm.

"What's that?" he demanded.

"Seconal."

"Don't. That stuff's rotten for you. I'll calm you down."

She swallowed the pills. "I'm too tense to make love."

Dramamine, Seconal, a fine pair we are, he thought. He returned to the living room. He stared at the silent birdcage gleaming in the candlelight, and he said out loud, "Come on, sing! Sing your goddam heart out." The bird stayed silent.

He got the flashlight, fetched the tape from the windy study, went to the basement and laid it on the crack, which was unchanged. Then he went outside. The wind had abated. The flashlight revealed the trunk of the elm, at any rate, to be sound, nor could he detect any big broken branches.

After checking the studio, his keen eyes detected movement by the barn, and he shone the torch. Shielding his eyes, Dun emerged from the darkness, and Vail lowered the light. "Dun! You scared me."

" 'Fraid I'd do that. Parked the truck on the road and walked in so I wouldn't disturb you people. Wanted to be sure the picture window was okay. Looks to be. Everything else all right?"

Did Vail imagine a timbre of worry in Dun's voice? "Seems to be. Hear that noise a while back?"

Dun nodded. "Elm tree creaked."

"I thought so. Oh, Dun, there's a broken window in the study if you could come by and fix it tomorrow."

"How'd that happen?" Dun asked.

"Branch fell down, I think. Well, good night, Dun."

" 'Night, Mr. Vail."

There was one more task, Vail thought as he entered the house—what was it? Yes, the rappings. He switched on the porch light and began examining the stone stoop on his hands and knees, slowly extending the radius of his search. He was about to give up when he found what he was looking for. He examined them under the flashlight: two flat white stones, identical with the one Kay had found in the study.

On Tuesday morning Kay and Mark overslept as if exhausted. The electricity was on again, and the phone worked normally. Vail called the operator to see what time it was. He set the electric clock in the kitchen, made himself fresh orange juice, a soft-boiled egg and instant coffee, and swallowed a Dramamine tablet. Upstairs, he shaved with the bathroom door closed and tiptoed about as he dressed. In the silence of the darkened bedroom, Kay snored softly.

He backed the Rolls from the barn and drove away. Near Point Road he remembered Punch. Where could the rascal be? Once before Punch had run off, and it had been days before he returned, wet, muddy, covered with sores and ticks. If the dog wasn't back by evening, he would search for him.

The broken place on Point Road seemed to resist every effort at repair. He sighed, glancing up. A school of clouds hurried along like fish in an upside-down ocean. Later, undoubtedly, it would rain; by then the road crew would probably have finished, and the pavement would begin to wash out again. He wondered if the problem was not more complicated than it seemed. Perhaps an underground stream weakened the road, a swollen tributary of Torturous Creek, whose source had never been properly established. So much about the ground they lived on remained obscure.

As he headed toward Summerset Villa his thoughts turned to Kay. He wished now that there had been a place in his college curriculum for psychology courses. Kay's statement that she didn't believe in ghosts, poltergeists, evil spirits, whatever one chose to call them, was, he felt sure, perfectly true. Just the same, she might harbor secret, irrational fears and not be fully aware of them—she had acted in such a way last night. He could understand more clearly than before the pangs of her hunger for human companionship. He could see how desperately long and lonely the winter months in Old Brompton must be for her, with the summer people gone and himself at the office and frequently away on business trips for two or three nights at a time. The winter for Kay must be a real test of endurance, with the cold wind shrieking and those ghosts of hers rattling around in the closet of her subconscious.

He switched on WROK. ". . . Williams contends that he was in Florida at the time of the Newport gasoline blast and so could not have perpetrated the crime even if he had a grudge against the oil company, which he claims he does not. Florida officials, however, have been unable to locate persons said by Williams to have known he was in Florida on June 15, the date of the explosion, and in the absense of corroboration of Williams' story Rhode Island authorities are moving for immediate extradition of the suspect. . . . In baseball, Boston defeated . . ."

A football fan, Vail found baseball a bore. He turned off the radio and reflected on Williams. Imagine choosing to commit a crime which would be seen as an act of terrorism against Rhode Island itself. Of course, maybe Williams' alibi would stand up.

Vail maneuvered the Rolls around the bad spot in the road near Summerset Villa and drove up the hill. On the crest behind the building the rig was in place, the outline of its pyramidal scaffolding against the sky suggesting a guillotine. Charley and his helper stood in front of the home, holding coffee mugs.

"Good morning, Charley," Vail said.

"I wouldn't call it a *good* morning, Mr. Vail," Charley said, eyeing a crab-shaped cloud that was devouring the sun. "Just a morning."

Vail looked toward the entranceway, crowded with old people. The drilling operation was probably the most exciting thing to happen at Summerset Villa all year. "Give me a report."

Charley said, "The well is in. Got hoses down there."

A medical image formed in Vail's mind: a hole in the body of the earth, tubes draining excess fluid from the tissues. "And?"

"The hill's dewatering, but not as much as I'd like. The till don't carry water so good."

"I know. But let's give it some time. What about the top of the hill?"

"All set. We'll take a split-spoon sample."

The door opened, and a frail figure appeared bearing a cup.

132

"Good morning, Dr. Vail," Mrs. Benjamin said effusively. "I brought you some coffee."

"Good morning, Mrs. Benjamin!" Vail took the cup with a genial smile.

"We'll leave you lovebirds and get going," Charley said wryly. "See you on top of the hill."

Vail nodded. "Did you have a good night, Mrs. Benjamin?"

"You mean, I suppose, what happened to the building during the storm? It was ghastly, Dr. Vail. The building shook as though a terrier had hold of it. I hate to think what might have happened had the storm been worse. Well, most of us here have lived long enough."

"Don't talk like that, Mrs. Benjamin. You've a lot of good years left."

Vail made his way up the muddy hill. The rig was twelve feet high. Within its confines, a 350-pound steel weight hammered the drill head into the ground. The work had already started, and Vail could hear the steady sound of the hammer, *pum pum pum pum.*

"What are you getting?" Vail asked Charley.

Charley watched the drill shaft entering the ground.

"About fifty, I guess." Vail understood what this meant. If it took the hammer three hundred blows to drive the drill a distance into the ground, the drill bit was encountering solid rock. The fewer blows it took, the softer the ground. Fifty blows for the same distance meant soft ground, but not quite as soft as Vail had expected. He waited.

The workman stood by the rig, keeping an eye on the machinery. He said suddenly, "It's going down faster."

Pum pum pum pum, went the monotonous beat.

"Twenty, I'd say now," Charley said, a little anxiously. Twenty meant silty, clayey soil, very wet. It was like driving a pin through gauze. "Slower now," Charley said. "Looks like we're hitting rock."

Vail felt relieved—bedrock, if it was bedrock, this close to the surface meant that the ground was more stable than he had supposed. His optimism abated as Charley shouted, "Faster, much faster."

The two rigmen were staring down at the drill shaft rising and falling in the sod, but Vail's gaze shot to the top of the rig which had begun to move back and forth against the leaden sky. "Watch out!" he bellowed. He lunged and, seizing the man by the rig, dragged him away. At the same moment there came a hollow pop. The ground buckled, and the rig crashed into the hole. Only the top appeared above the ground.

The rigman dusted himself off. "Son of a bitch! Thanks, Dr. Vail."

"You may have saved his life," Charley gasped.

Vail said, "What happened?"

Charley examined the opening. Water sloshed below. "There's a cave down there. The drill went through the roof."

"Must be limestone. We've got to find out how big it is," Vail said. "And how far down the hill it extends. You've got to drill some more, Charley, farther down the slope."

"Do our best," Charley said glumly. "This ground is dangerous."

Silence greeted him at the stone house. When he entered the kitchen Mark ran up to him. "How's my little darling?" Harry said.

"I miss Punch."

"Daddy will look for him."

He circled the house, whistling and calling Punch's name at the trees, the sedges, the paddling swans, until he found himself at the house again.

"I'm going to the village and see if he's there," he told Kay.

On the end of the pier, Sam Wilbore was throwing stones

over the water. Vail called, "Sam?" The boy turned. "Sam, did you see my dog? Shetland sheepdog. Wears a collar. Missing since last night."

Wilbore's head responded negatively while he bent and picked a flat white stone from the pile beside him. He launched it over the bay.

Vail went home. "There's nothing much we can do but wait. He'll turn up," he said in a comforting voice. "Well, what happened today? Septic tank people come? The yard stinks."

"No. Not the piano tuner nor the clock man nor the phone company nor Dun. Nobody came," she replied mournfully.

A hand pulled at his sleeve, and he stared down at the small, pale face. "What is it, Mark?"

"Daddy, I want to show you something."

"Can't it wait? Daddy's talking to Mommy."

"No. Come." Mark tugged at his hand.

He followed his child. "What is it?" he repeated.

"I found a funny plant. A really funny plant," Mark said in a hollow whisper. "Over there." He pointed to the far side of the giant boulder. Vail walked faster, with the boy hanging behind.

Vail stopped abruptly. A brown growth of some kind stuck up straight from the ground—or was it a stick? He put his hand on his stomach and said tensely, "Go back to the house, Mark. Tell your mother to stay where she is." Mark ran.

He approached reluctantly, forcing his legs to move. He reached down, pulled, and looked away from the dead shelty.

"Harry!" said her broken voice behind him. "Oh, Jesus God."

"I don't get it," he said softly, staring at the stiff corpse of the dog hanging from his hand by its tail.

"I warned you about poison!" she shrieked.

"I don't see how he got to it. I don't remember putting poison

135

on this side of the boulder." He examined the dog carefully. "Punch's head looks crushed."

"Crushed? By what? By *whom?*" Kay fainted.

She was not very heavy, he reflected as he carried her to the house. She must have lost weight. As he thought of it, he could not recall Kay eating a decent meal in days.

He placed her on the couch and rubbed her temples with cold water. Her eyes opened. "What are you going to do?"

"Bury him."

"Get it over with, will you? Mark, stay here with me."

"Yes, Mommy." Mark began sucking his thumb and Kay pulled it from his mouth. From the barn Vail took a shovel and, holding the dog by its stiff tail, looked for a suitable place. Up the small hill, at the foot of the giant boulder seemed right: the slab bore a resemblance to a giant gravestone, as Kay's painting recorded. The ground here was soft. There were gentle ridges he hadn't noticed before. He dug a pit quickly and laid the shelty under the sod. He marked the grave with a rock.

Inside the house, Kay rested in the bedroom while in the living room Mark turned the pages of a children's book, now and then stifling a sob. Harry decided to give the boy his dinner. He was in the kitchen when Dun appeared at the back door. Harry went outside.

Vail noticed at once that the old man was agitated. "Came by after another job to repair the broken window," he began almost apologetically. He shuffled quickly from one foot to the other and blurted, "Mr. Vail, somebody been digging on the hill?"

Vail said slowly. "The dog's dead. I buried him."

"Oh." His weathered face could not control relief. "That's too bad. Nice little doggie."

"Yes." Vail studied him suspiciously.

Dun scraped the ground with his toe as if searching for something to say. "Well, one thing about dogs is that if one dies you can get another. Not like people dying. Look at it that way, Mr. Vail."

"I suppose so," Vail said. "How did you find the grave?"

"How did I find it?" Dun faltered. "Well, you know, often take a look around the property to see if everything's all right. Saw the shovel marks. How did the little dog die?"

"Well, he got into some poison. Either that or . . ."

"Or?" the old man asked, glancing up with his gray eyes.

"Or he was killed somehow and put in the mole hole where I found him."

"Ain't nobody around here who'd do that."

"The head was crushed," Vail replied. He glanced up at the elm, black against the twilight. It seemed to him that the tree looked different in some way. He heard something. "Hear anything, Dun?"

"Nope. What'd it sound like?"

"A crash. Like a small tree came down."

"Could be. Lots of trees weakened by the windstorm," Dun explained. "Sorry about the dog."

Poison, acting instantly, was bad enough; that Punch might have suffered a violent death affected Kay even more, and he was sorry to have raised the question. Several times after Mark went to bed she referred to it.

"But I've told you already," he said, "on thinking it through, I'm sure that the condition of the head is due to rigor mortis."

She faced him. "Do you mean that or are you telling me a story?" She lit a cigarette, inhaling deeply. "I wish I believed you."

"You must believe me," he insisted.

She picked up the cat and stroked it. "If anything happens to you . . ." She strode around nervously, then said, "I've got to

137

stop thinking. Crazy ideas are running about my head. I'll go to the studio and try to work."

"Yes, do."

He fed the cat and the silent finch in the brass cage, then went to his study. He looked thoughtfully at the books on the shelf above his desk and took down *Elementary Seismology*, flipped through the pages, stopped at a table dealing with earthquake effects and read it carefully.

"Macroseismic Effects"—that was the rub. Richter referred to the big quakes, the ones that caused tremendous convulsions, usually over a big area, and which, on the scale the seismologist had devised, would measure in the upper magnitudes. The Richter scale was divided into ten segments, with each segment again divided by ten, but the difference from one magnitude to the next was exponential, so that an earthquake with a magnitude of 8.4—like the Alaska quake—would be 20,000,000 times as powerful as a quake of mag 3.5, itself large enough to be perceptible to humans. Vail wondered if a quake of magnitude five, enough to cause considerable damage, could occur in a small geographical area as an earthquake of low magnitude and low intensity would. It seemed to him that there had been a quake like that in Agadir, Morocco, which had killed thousands of people and yet been only 10 miles long.

He was studying the page again when he heard the knocks. There were three of them this time, one sounding as though it had struck the front door, the others the wall of the house. Racing to the front door he flung it open, finding only night outside. He bent and rose with a flat white stone that had lain in the doorway. "You!" he shouted into the darkness. "That's enough."

Kay stood beside him. "Who are you yelling at?"

"The village idiots. Those kids are stopping their car and throwing stones at the house."

"They couldn't throw that far."

138

Table 7–1   Principal Macroseismic Effects of Tectonic Earthquakes*

Effects on	Primary	Secondary Permanent	Secondary Transient
Terrain	Regional warping, etc. Scarps Offsets Fissures, mole tracks, other trace phenomena Elevation or depression of coasts; changes in coast line	Landslides (slumps, flows, avalanches, lurches) [1, 2, 3, 4] Secondary fissures [3] Sand craters [5] Raising of posts and piles	Visible waves? Perceptible shaking
Water (ground and surface)	Damming; waterfalls; diversion Sag ponds Changes in wells, springs		Changes in well levels Earthquake fountains [5] Water over stream banks Seiches Tsunamis Seaquakes
Works of construction	Offsets, and destruction or damage by rending or crushing; buildings, bridges, pipe lines, railways, fences, roads, ditches	Most ordinary damage to buildings, chimneys, windows, plaster	Creaking of frame Swaying of bridges and tall structures

* From *Elementary Seismology* by Charles F. Richter; W. H. Freeman and Company. Copyright © 1958 by W. H. Freeman and Company.
[1] Earth flows properly belong with water phenomena.
[2] Landslides may produce damage to works of construction.
[3] Landslides and secondary fissures may produce the effects on terrain and on surface water listed as primary.
[4] Classification of landslides from California Earthquake Commission, vol. 1, pt. 2, p. 385.
[5] Production of sand craters and fountains is a single phenomenon.

139

Effects on	Primary	Secondary Permanent	Secondary Transient
Loose objects		Displacement (including apparent rotation) Overturning, fall, projection (horizontal or vertical)	Rocking Swinging Shaking Rattling
Miscellaneous		Clocks stop, change rate, etc. Glaciers affected Fishes killed Cable breaks	Nausea Fright, panic Sleepers wakened Animals disturbed Birds disturbed Trees shaken Bells rung Automobiles, standing or in motion, disturbed Audible sound Flashes of light?

"Sam Wilbore could. The kid has an arm like Hank Aaron. Listen. Hear it?"

"Hear what?"

"Their car starting up."

"No." Kay turned and he closed the door. "Why would they do it?" she asked.

"Revenge because I dressed them down."

"Maybe. If it was them."

"Of course it was them."

"Did they kill the dog, too?"

He hesitated. "I don't think so."

"What did, then? It wasn't poison, you said." Her eyes showed white around the irises.

He said slowly, "The ground did it, I've decided. Somehow the earth crushed him."

"Lord, Harry, is that what you believe? Isn't it clear that . . ."

He put his hands on her shoulders and shook them. "Kay, snap out of it. Punch's death has driven you over the line. Come back."

"What?"

"I said come back—come back to normal."

"What's normal?" she asked bitterly.

He would consider later how differently they experienced the same event. For him the floor leaped upward slightly, accompanied by the sounds of rattling pots from the rack in the kitchen, the jiggling mugs on the glass shelf, the jingling fireplace tools, the arrowheads falling from the mantel to the floor. The phone rang once and stopped. "They're all over the house!" Kay cried.

"Kay, it's not . . ."

From above came a thump and a scream. Vail ran up the elliptical staircase and down the hall and found the boy on the floor, whimpering. Suspended from the ceiling, the fishes on the mobile swung slowly, like live aquatic creatures.

"He's all right. He fell out of bed," he said to Kay, whose white face flashed in the doorway and vanished. "Come on, honey, it's all right. Get in the lower bunk this time."

"Lie down with me, Daddy."

"Yes."

He covered the boy with a blanket and squeezed in next to him, cradling the small body with his own until Mark stopped trembling and his breathing fell into a sleep rhythm.

The door to his own bedroom was closed. He entered to find Kay in bed, completely covered by blankets and pillows. The Seconal bottle stood open on the bed table.

"Come on, Kay," he said.

"There's nothing to do. Better leave me alone," she said in a muffled voice.

He seized the tape from his desk, went to the basement, and measured the crack. It was now 18 inches long.

141

Old Brompton, Vail now felt certain, was experiencing a certain kind of earthquake—spasmodic, slow, but it might be building up. This earthquake had killed his dog. There could be further victims, not necessarily animal.

PART FOUR

FAULT

Wednesday, June 26 Rising early, Vail trotted to the beach and sat in his rock chair, watching the waves and the gulls. It was clear overhead, but clouds spotted the horizon like warning flags.

Having identified the adversary as real, Vail felt a certain relief; at least he faced an actual thing and not his fantasies. Still, though convinced that an earthquake was underway, what should he do? The slow quake might remain at its present magnitude and intensity, causing no real harm; but it could also grow from a baby into a monster, and that worried him, because people ought to be warned. How? The newspapers if he went to them would take him for a freak—a self-appointed seer of natural disasters like those predicting that half of California would fall into the sea. It would be dreadful for his professional reputation if the little earthquake just died away after he'd cried doom. In any case they wouldn't believe him. Kip Smith at WROK would make a joke of it. Kelly at Lamont was the natural recipient of his information, but Paul would want proof—especially in view of Vail's history, which the seismologist would invoke in judging the credibility of his story. If only reliable, corroborating witnesses existed or if only proof existed . . .

Perhaps there was such evidence, and sifting his mind Vail remembered the elm tree in the backyard. What he had per-

145

ceived in the twilight, he now believed, was a slight list to the tree. Such a thing could happen if the earth had crept during the tremors. Prove it, he thought, and maybe you'll at least convince Kay.

Jogging back to the house, he went to the studio and removed the painting of the black elm from the wall. Out in the yard, he changed positions, glancing at the picture as he tried to find the exact vantage from which she had painted it. At last he found the spot on the bank of Torturous Creek, but in trying to compare the picture with reality he realized that the work had been accomplished in the winter, when there was no foliage in the way, and so the change was hard to discern.

Her voice startled him. "What are you doing?"

"I was comparing the elm with your picture of it. Look—the tree leans now."

"Why should the tree lean?"

"It might have happened in the windstorm, but I doubt it. The tree's too big. There's been a change in the ground."

Kay seized the picture. "It looks the same to me."

"There's a difference."

"I remember my own backyard. You're imagining things."

"You should talk," he said coldly. "Where did you put those before-and-after photos of the place? Maybe there's one of the backyard."

The pinched look of her face was new to him. "I don't remember. Maybe in the hall closet. Look for yourself."

But the photograph he found was really too small to permit him to make a judgment. He placed it in his jacket and drove off.

On the street level of the building was a shop that did photocopying and enlargements. Vail took the photograph there, then rode the elevator to the third floor.

Johnson entered, saying, "Here's what you wanted."

146

"Already? Good." Johnson handed him a geological profile of the Summerset area, mounted on cardboard with surface features—the home, the road in front of it, the hill—depicted on a sheet of acetate. "Nice job. Something else, Walter. I'd like you to extend the area of coverage to include the end of Old Brompton peninsula. There are three houses, one of which is mine, a road called Point Road, a fishing village and finally some cliffs. Be sure to get all the salient features, like the town square, the church, the pier. Why don't you drive down this morning? Oh, yes—" He went to the filing cabinet and returned with the map covered with circles. "These represent earthquake epicenters in this region." A confused look appeared on Johnson's face and Vail went on, "That's the point on the surface above an earthquake. What I'd like you to do is to give me the direction and distance of every recorded earthquake in a radius of, say, a hundred miles from here. Put them on the acetate around the sides."

Lechine appeared in the doorway, holding a newspaper. Johnson looked at him quickly, and Vail guessed that his partner had given the draftsman trouble about the time already spent on the Summerset Villa job.

"What's this?" Lechine demanded.

"Thanks, Walter," Vail said, and stood. Johnson left.

Lechine said in a despairing tone, "Why do you want new information?"

"If there's a fault around here I want to find out where it runs."

"For heaven's sake, what makes you think there's a fault?"

"There's a cave in the hill at Summerset. It could indicate a fault," Vail replied.

"First a crack in your cellar and you think your house is in trouble. Now a cave and you detect an earthquake or something." Lechine snapped his red suspenders in irritation. "In the meantime, how do we get paid?"

"Robinson's still trying to locate Summerset, who's on his yacht."

"Yacht-schmat. This is a business, not charity. We've spent too much time on the place already. How are you coming with the abandoned factory?"

"Well, I haven't done much about it recently. I'll get over there today."

"See! You neglect paying customers for that building—it will surely be standing longer than you!" Lechine retorted. He looked sorry. "I didn't mean to shout. It's just that we've got to pay the bills around here or we'll be on the street even without that earthquake of yours. Vail's earthquake!" He laughed and socked Harry playfully on the arm. "Say, did you read the paper? They let that bastard loose."

"Which one?"

"The one who blew up the tank farm. Son of a bitch, they believe his alibi. It's all the fault of the goddam Supreme Court for tying the hands of the cops and letting everybody free, including nuts with dynamite." Lechine exhausted his invective, of which he had a large supply.

When Vail came home he removed a large sheet of posterboard from the back seat. Facing the elm, he held the board in his hands and studied it.

Kay emerged from the studio. "What's that?"

He showed her the five-by-three-foot photograph mounted on the board, of the tree and the boulder. "It's a blow-up of the photo I took with me this morning. I had to bribe a guy to get it done this fast. Look, it proves my point. If you study the photo carefully you can see that the tree *does* lean."

Kay covered her eyes with her thin hands. "Harry, I don't want to encourage you in any way. What you're into is nuts." She turned and ran to the kitchen.

He stood still, trying to capture the meaning of the tree's list,

148

ignoring her disbelief. If he was right about the creep, the tree would eventually fall and crush the barn.

He went inside, where Kay talked excitedly into the telephone. "That was Polly," she said when she hung up. "Wende has been missing since last night. Polly's coming over."

Harry took Polly by the arm and led her to the couch. "Calm down, Polly. What happened exactly?"

"Fred went to Boston on business yesterday. He called around five to say he'd be late—she was home. He got back around ten and Wende wasn't there. Neither was her Mercedes. He thought she must have gone to a party and waited up, but she never came back."

"Wouldn't the servants have known where she was?" Kay asked.

"The servants know nothing."

"Did he report her disappearance to the police?" Harry said.

Polly answered, "I learned only because I went over there. He hasn't told anyone else, much less the police."

"But why?" Harry asked in surprise.

"Because he's afraid Wende's run off with Jeff Carmichael."

He stared at his wife. "Do you believe it?"

"They've been carrying on openly, it's true," Kay said, tugging her finger. "Still, I would have thought Wende was more practical than that."

"It all fits," Polly insisted. "They spent the day together and Jeff came back for an early supper. Then he left for New York in his car. That must have been about the time she disappeared."

"What did she do with her Mercedes?"

"Put it someplace so Fred would believe she'd gone off on one of her spontaneous little trips. No, I'm certain she left with Jeff for New York. I feel so guilty for letting it happen. Poor Fred, he's really suffering," Polly wailed.

"Shouldn't you call and make sure?" Kay asked.

"Me? I never want to speak to Jeffrey Carmichael again, the bastard. Well, the first scandal of the season. I'd better go check on Bill. He says he misses Wende already, but at least it gives him the excuse to work the computer bar overtime. . . ."

She left, chattering. Kay turned a bleak face to Harry. "I hope she's all right. I have a terrible feeling."

"But she planned to go away for a few days. She told you that."

"I wish I knew for sure that she was with Jeff. I'd call him, but I don't have any right to poke into her business."

"I'm going to the village," he said.

He stopped, got out, and wandered through the village square, mentally cataloging the various kinds of junk that had accumulated—abandoned cars and boats, torn netting, pieces of scrap. In particular, he noted a pile of creosote-covered boards. Climbing back in the Rolls he heard the clatter of stone on metal and saw Sam Wilbore on the pier. He was winding up for another throw into the square, like a warning shot. Vail ignored it.

Dun was at home. "Good evening," Vail said, stepping into the shack.

"Rum, Mr. Vail?"

"Some other time, Dun. A couple of things, sort of important. I believe the village kids—the Wilbores, Bill Pabodie, maybe—are throwing rocks at my house." He took from his pocket a flat white stone that matched those in the glass jar. "I found that on the porch."

"Lots of stones around like that."

"Not ones that fly through the air and hit doors and windows."

Dun stared at his toes. "Guess it's possible. Told you those kids was mean."

"If they don't stop I'll call the police." He sighed inwardly, thinking of Old Brompton's one ancient policeman.

He followed an agenda now. "Crack in my basement, sump pump that failed, coupling that broke, leaking pipe in the upstairs bathroom, other things you don't know about—they add up to the possibility of small earthquakes happening more or less continually around here during the past few weeks. Maybe I'm wrong, but can you think of anything that would support that idea, Dun? Anything cracked, broken, bent?"

Dun's weathered face underwent an immediate change. It seemed to contract to reduce itself like a military parameter on the defensive. The voice turned cold. "Don't believe I have, no."

"Nothing?"

"No," said the old man.

"Well, maybe not, then," he said. He began to think out loud. "Still, it might be smart to take precautions in case I'm right. Stone houses aren't worth a damn in an earthquake. I'd like to brace the cellar, Dun. I went to the square—there's plenty of wood and metal lying around for the job. Can you do it?"

" 'Fraid not this week. Too busy."

"Too busy for *me?*"

Dun said with stiff lips, "Yes. Mr. Vail, you were right. Awful lot happening to that house of yours. Maybe you should sell and move away. Get your mind off this earthquake of yours."

Vail turned angrily to the door. *They're all alike, the villagers,* he found himself thinking. *Can't rely on any of them, not even Dun.* Hand on the knob, he heard several loud pops.

"What's that noise?" he asked sharply.

"Firecrackers," Dun said quickly. "Kids impatient for the Fourth of July."

Slowing down for his driveway, he heard the rush from behind and pulled in sharply, twisting his neck to see the oversize tires and raised rear end of Cy Wilbore's souped-up blue car receding down the road. Catcalls. A finger. Bastards, he thought, it's a war of nerves. But why?

151

Entering the house, he found Kay hunched in front of the TV. "Come here," she said excitedly. She was watching the six-thirty news. "Look."

On the screen bobbed a thin mustache. The television face said, "Jeff Carmichael, filling in for Bill Ducksworth, who is on vacation."

"The son of a bitch," Kay said when the show was over. "I'm going to call him after all."

Harry listened while she placed the call to New York. At once the switchboard connected her to Carmichael. They chatted a second, and then Kay asked if Wende were with him. Her face turned, startled. "You're telling the truth, Jeff, honest? Where can she be?"

"Where can she be?" Kay said to Harry. "She's not with Jeff, and I don't think he's lying."

"We'd better tell Fred," he said.

"Not yet. The fact that she's really disappeared might worry him even more. This way he's got only his ego to contend with." She sounded alarmed.

They look terrible, he said to himself at supper, Kay with her pallor, Mark with blue rings about his eyes. He keeps sucking his thumb like a two-year-old.

"Harry," she informed him, "the tap water has started to run brown again. And Mark has a little diarrhea. Is there a connection?"

"The septic tank could be draining into the well." He hesitated. "No. I don't think so. We'd be sick, too. It's just brackish water getting into the well from the pond because the water table's so high. Nothing to worry about."

"There are little cracks in the ceiling of Mark's room."

"Because of the leak in the pipe, probably."

She poured coffee. "Harry, we must leave the house."

"Abandon it?"

152

"Yes, for a while. Let's go stay in a motel at Fall River and see what happens. I don't think this atmosphere is good at all for Mark—or for me."

"Why don't you go to your mother's until the Fourth of July? You could leave today. It would give you a whole week in Boston."

Immediately, Kay began examining the reasons why she should stay. "Too long to stay at Mother's. She'd drive me crazy —crazier than I am already. Day camp has just started and I hate to pull Mark out so soon. There are so many good parties coming up next week. I don't like to leave you alone here."

"Think it over," he muttered.

In the cellar he measured the crack—now almost two feet long.

As he parked the car in front of Summerset Villa he could hear Charley's drill pummeling the hill. He walked through mud which hadn't dried after three long days of sunshine. "Morning, Dr. Vail," Charley said. "We're getting there. A few more holes to drill, but looks to me like that's a small cave, extending to about there." He pointed to an imaginary spot some distance up from the building.

"How's the draining going?"

"Pretty good. Water is coming out."

"Call me at the office when you're finished."

"Yes. Dr. Vail, there's something I want to show you." Vail followed Charley to the hilltop. From the hole through which the drill had fallen, water burbled and flowed down the hillside. "And look." Charley pointed. Following his finger, Vail saw a series of small cones on the hillside, running down in a straight line past the building toward the road. The cones were about a foot high, and each was capped by a hole, like a miniature volcano. "I think those are caused by water, but I don't know the name for them."

Surprised, Vail said, "Earthspouts. You get them in California, if that's what they are."

"Never seen nothing like that around here."

"Me neither."

He went back down the hill. As he entered the reception room, Alma Benjamin sprang at him. "Just the person I want to see."

"Any trouble, Mrs. Benjamin?"

"There's always trouble these days. The clothes dryers won't spin, basement's flooded, lights have gone off several times. There's no end to it. Mr. Robinson doesn't work either, but that's not new."

"Where is he?"

She looked at her watch. "Nine-thirty. I doubt he's yet out of bed."

"I must talk to him."

"I'll try to get him."

Fifteen minutes later Robinson appeared, cheeks cut by sleep lines. "Really, Vail, I wish you'd arrange your visits later in the day."

Vail ignored him. "Did you reach Summerset?"

"No. Something must be wrong with his radio. He usually returns my calls quicker than this."

"Usually?" Vail asked.

Robinson looked down at his yellow shoes. "Well, there are times when it takes weeks to get hold of him."

"I hope this isn't one of them. Look, Mr. Robinson, there's a decision to be made. By draining the hill, we've managed to stabilize the ground to some extent. Of course, if the rains start again all bets are off."

"It won't rain again. The sky hasn't got that much water."

"Don't count on it. And if there were seismic activity . . ."

"Seismic activity?"

"Tremors. Little earthquakes. Or even a big one."

154

"Nonsense. What are you getting at?"

"Well, there's a procedure available for strengthening unstable ground. It's called pressure grouting. I won't bore you with the details, but it amounts to digging holes and inserting liquefied cement."

Robinson blinked rapidly. "It sounds expensive."

"It is."

"I think you're trying to high-pressure me, Vail," Robinson said with contempt. "It won't work. Think how silly I'd look if I told Mr. Summerset that he had to shell out a bundle because some local geologist said there was going to be an earthquake. Like a complete fool. He'd fire me."

"You're not even going to suggest it?"

"No. It'll be hard enough to get him to pay for what you've already done."

"Perhaps you'll change your mind. I'll stop by early next week—there are a couple of things I want to keep my eye on. Oh, Mr. Robinson?"

The manager had already started to leave. "What now?"

"If I were you, I'd put scaffolding around the building."

Robinson's small eyes stared accusingly. "Vail, are you insane?" His yellow shoes departed with quick, birdlike steps.

"Morning, Dr. Vail," Mrs. Conner said effusively.

"Place a call for me, will you? To Dr. Paul Kelly at the Lamont-Doherty Geological Observatory in Palisades, New York." Lechine was nowhere to be seen. Vail poked his head into Johnson's office. "How's it coming?"

"Jim threw a load at me, all of it rush," Johnson complained. "I went to the peninsula yesterday, but I don't see how I can get to the drawing until tomorrow."

"I'd like it this afternoon, please. Lechine's stuff can wait if it has to."

155

"Your party's on the line," Mrs. Conner called.

He went to his office and picked up the phone. "Hello, Paul?"

"Talk a little louder, will you, Harry? I can hardly hear." Kelly's brisk voice was clear.

"I'll try. That better?"

"Fine. How's the geology?"

"It has its ups and downs," he laughed briefly. "Thanks for your letter. Glad to hear everything's going so well." The two men chatted for a few moments and then Vail said, "I have a question for you. Have your seismic stations picked up any unusual activity recently up my way?"

Kelly sounded surprised. "No, I don't think so. I would have heard about it. Why?" Vail's silence lasted a long moment and Kelly asked, "Are you there?"

Vail said abruptly, "I believe there's an earthquake underway here."

"Earthquake? Why do you think so?"

Vail laid out his evidence of shakings and cracks; of the north-south direction of what he had perceived as mole ridges but which were, he felt reasonably sure, earthquake manifestations; of the waterspouts at Summerset that could be regarded as a sign of a fault, along with the limestone cave. He failed to mention the dog.

Kelly plainly found the information less than conclusive, as Vail feared—his tone was doubtful. "The nearest seismic activity to you at present is at Moodus, Connecticut. We have a team there now, studying it, but the earthquake swarm is not new. The noises have been going on a long time."

"Noises?"

"Ground noises. We're getting them on tape. Harry, are you all right? Is it possible your . . . er . . . past experience is making you imagine things?"

Vail said stiffly, "I'm sure that isn't the case. I thought so for

156

a while, but there's too much indication of seismic stuff, as far as I'm concerned."

"All right, I'll tell you what. I've been meaning to pay you a visit anyway. I'll come up there with a portable seismometer and check out the action—if any."

He sounded as though he were trying to placate Vail, who said, "When?"

"Not till after the Fourth. Maybe not till August," Kelly replied vaguely.

Vail said quickly, "That might be too late. Suppose I come down and borrow a seismometer. Will you be in on Saturday?"

Kelly laughed bitterly. "I'm always in the shop on Saturday. You've forgotten what seismology is like. All right, I'll dig up a machine," he said casually, as though people borrowed seismometers all the time.

Vail saw Lechine in the doorway.

"You heard all that?"

"We all did. You were shouting. Portable seismometer. Nuttier and nuttier." He tugged his suspenders and shook his head.

Johnson's drawing was ready by late afternoon, and Vail took it home with him. The new survey covered both sides of the body of water separating Old Brompton peninsula and Massachusetts. On the acetate sheet were buildings and roads at the tip of the peninsula. Arrows around the edges indicated the location of previous earthquakes within the ordered radius. There had been dozens, the map showed, none major. Of course, the records were not reliable. Others might have happened.

Using a felt-tipped pen, Vail marked the location of the cones he had seen that morning on the hillside. On the acetate, he made another dot close by that represented the break in the pavement below Summerset Villa, and still a third on Point Road where the pavement was broken also. But the location of

157

the fault (if there was one) remained too speculative for his purpose—the pocked roads didn't necessarily mean a thing. He needed more evidence.

Vail marched down to the basement and glared at the crack. It looked thicker as well as longer. He drove to the village.

Sam Wilbore stood on the pier with his cache of stones which he flipped at the water. He watched as Vail prowled the square. Vail found what he wanted in a pile of rusty machinery—a long, thin metal strip with holes around the edges. Under the weight he struggled, carrying the piece to the car.

From the side of his eye he saw Wilbore bend and throw. The stone bounced and clanked among the machinery close to where he walked. Then came another stone and another. Vail moved faster, put the metal plate in the trunk, and gazed accusingly at Wilbore.

The boy, he thought, had been trying to frighten but not hit him. He suppressed an instinct to run to the pier and confront him; the crack, he decided regretfully, had priority—he'd settle with Wilbore later. Looking through the rearview mirror, Vail decided that was just as well. Cy Wilbore and Bill Pabodie had emerged from behind the corner of the store. It had been a trap: the three youths would have ganged up on him.

At home, he removed the metal piece from the trunk and lugged it to the basement. He found the electric drill in the tool section of the barn, and an extension cord which he plugged into a socket in the light fixture. He held the plate to the wall and made marks through the holes with a pencil. Inserting a bit, he began to drill into the hard face.

The racket fetched Kay at once. "Harry!" she yelled from the top of the stairs.

Stopping the drill, he asked, "Yes?"

Kay descended a few steps slowly. "Now what?"

"The crack. I'm trying to reinforce the wall."

"The crack!" she said bitterly. "You worry about a little crack at a time like this."

An hour was needed to bolt the plate to the wall. The metal covered the crack completely, hiding it from view. Perhaps he hoped in vain that the break could be contained, but at least he was fighting back, and it felt good.

Upstairs Kay murmured dejectedly, "We'd better give Fred the bad news. I called and said we'd come over. Wende hasn't shown up yet. Where can she be?"

"Where can she be?" asked Fred Demming. In the last few days he seemed to have aged; his jowls hung slackly and the hand holding the cane head trembled. Kay had told him that Jeff denied Wende was with him. "I was certain she was with Carmichael—counted on it, I guess, in terms of her safety." His eyes turned inward. "She thought I didn't notice what was going on, but I did. I tried to ignore it, told myself that sooner or later Carmichael would go away and that would be that. Now look what's happened."

"Wende's taken little trips before, hasn't she?" Harry pointed out. "Just hopped in the car and gone off?"

"Yes, she has," Demming confessed. "She likes to do spontaneous things, but she's always left a note."

"Did she take a suitcase? Clothes?" Kay asked.

"I checked, or tried to. She's got so many suitcases and clothes that it's impossible to say."

"Makeup?" Kay quizzed him. Demming didn't know about makeup either. "Money?"

"That would be no problem. She always carries a lot of cash."

"Where would she go?"

"Cape Cod. Watch Hill. Newport. Bar Harbor. Anywhere."

"At least she's not with Jeff, Fred. You ought to be relieved. She'll be back in a day or two," Kay said with an enormously false smile.

"Maybe you should call the state police," Harry suggested.

Demming looked horrified. "Police? It would get in the newspapers. Better to wait."

The house and grounds seemed oddly silent. Harry asked, "Where is the staff?"

Demming's thin lips barely moved. "They quit today, the whole lot of them. They didn't like it here, complained the atmosphere made them nervous. I'm all alone."

Kay was subdued that evening to the point of utter silence, and he asked her whether she was preoccupied with Wende's whereabouts. "I was thinking of Fred just then. I saw something in his face that I don't want to talk about." She took a drag on her cigarette.

"Tell me," he insisted. "You'll feel better if you do."

She shook her head. "Listen!" The hum was like a bee's. It faded and rose again. Kay crept across the room almost stealthily in the direction of the piano, hand to her ear. She seized the tuning fork and the sound stopped. "What caused that? Tell me!" She brandished the tuning fork like a weapon.

"Vibrations passing up through the floor, through the piano, to the tuning fork. The house shook."

"Did you feel it? I didn't!"

"No," he tried to explain, "but that doesn't necessarily mean anything. Kay, listen." Vail gave his wife the same information he had presented to Kelly about a probable fault, about the existence of an earthquake swarm shaking the house with increasing frequency, about the visit he planned to the Lamont Observatory on Saturday. "There are tremors so small a human can't feel them. We're in the middle of an earthquake."

"You're just saying that. No, you believe it, don't you?" she said. "Well, though an earthquake would be bad enough, I wish it were true." The tendons in her neck stood out. "Make me a whiskey, will you? I've got to relax."

160

"Won't you believe me, Kay?" he sighed from the bar cart.

"I want to, but I can't."

"Goddammit, Kay, what is this? Can't I make you see?" She turned her face away, convincing him that further discussion would be useless.

"Let's do something to take our minds off this. Gin rummy?"

"No. I couldn't concentrate."

"Backgammon?"

"All right."

Harry went to the hall closet and opened the door; the leather case of the backgammon set seemed to leap from the shelf above as though aimed for his head. Stepping back, throwing up both hands, he managed to catch it. He muttered, "Christ."

"What did you say?" Kay called.

"Nothing." They laid out the pieces and began to play in silence.

"Harry? Would you give me some more Scotch?" She handed him her glass.

"You just finished one. You'll be another Bill Pollidor," he said over his shoulder.

"Watch out!"

He stepped back quickly, and a Toby jug crashed just where he'd stood, spreading its grin on the floor. "Christ."

"They're turning dangerous, Harry. Before, they only wanted to frighten us. Now they'd like to hurt—to kill. We can't stay in this house, Harry. We have to leave."

"Get hold of yourself," he said as he eyed the row of mocking faces. "The jugs have been shaken too close to the edge of the shelf. It's the fault of the tremors. That's the reasonable explanation."

"You and your reasonable explanations. Can't I make *you* see, Harry? There are spirits of some sort in our house. They follow us. They went with us to the Demmings' the night we played Inquest. They—it—talked to me in some weird way, inside my

161

head, kept telling me how everyone was going to die. I could almost visualize . . ."

A sharp rap sounded against the wall of the house, followed by another at the front door. He ran outside and bellowed, "You rotten jerks! I'll get you!" From the darkness a stone struck the wall near his head. Inside, locking the door, he opened and closed his big fists in fury. Kay kneeled on the floor, sobbing. He pressed her to him, stroking her hair. "Those goddam kids! One more stone and I'm going after them."

"Not the kids," she said with a sharp intake of breath. "It's them. They're everywhere. I started to tell you what they're saying: Wende is dead. Demming is dying. Something about the Pollidors. And we're being warned. I'm leaving, Harry. *I want you to come,*" she shrieked.

"I'm staying," he said severely. "Kay, there are no such things as spirits, you know that. Use your smarts. What about the crack? No spirit could cause *that*, could it?" He grasped her arm.

"No," she said in a small voice, "I guess not. But . . ."

"No buts. There aren't any spirits. There are tremors and bad kids. Will you believe me?"

"I'll try. It's no fun to get hung up on ghosts."

Simultaneous with the peal of the telephone, a scream sounded from far out in the night, louder and louder, and as Kay switched on the bedlight Vail realized he had never heard a siren on the peninsula before. It advanced on them like something alien.

"Hello . . . yes . . . Oh, my God . . . You poor dear . . . yes . . . St. Vincent's . . . I pray so . . . Bill Pollidor shot himself by accident," she said to him as she hung up.

"Jesus Christ. Is he alive?"

"He's breathing." Vail got out of bed and started to dress. "No, don't. She's going to Fall River in the ambulance with him."

Through the window he could see lights flashing through the trees. "Where was he shot?"

She muttered from behind him, "In the head."

The picture of Pollidor's fragile cranium flashed in his mind and refused to disappear. "How?"

"He was loading his shotgun or something and it went off. She said the side of his head was all . . . I can't talk about it. Polly was barely coherent, but she did say she'd call tonight—if he dies. Otherwise we can go to the hospital in the morning and be with her." Kay kept repeating, "In the head. In the head."

On Friday morning Pollidor remained alive but unconscious. The doctors refused a prognosis, but even if Pollidor pulled through, it looked as though he would suffer brain damage, especially as he might be unconscious for days.

The Vails, leaving Mark with a sitter, spent most of the day at the hospital, and it seemed peaceful at home, if deceptively so. They spoke little at dinner, but afterward Kay said carefully, "I've decided to take Mark to Mother's after all. I wish you'd come, but I know you won't. We'll go tomorrow. I can't take any more of this. One more sleepless night and I'll get sick. I just lie there waiting for the noises. You never seem to hear them, do you? I hate to abandon Polly, but I can't help it. If anything happens to Bill I want you to call me at once. She's got relatives arriving tomorrow and Jeff's scheduled to return next week, so I feel a little less guilty."

He said slowly, "It stands to reason that the shooting—I mean the fact that poor Bill got it in the head—that just confirmed your worst fears, didn't it? I mean, what you said at the party . . ."

She answered mutely in the affirmative.

"Kay, Bill was loading or cleaning his shotgun. A tremor came—we were asleep—and the gun fired accidentally. It could have happened in several ways. Couldn't you be satisfied by that explanation?"

She answered mutely in the negative.

"I guess each of us has to see things in his own way," he continued helplessly. "You've got this crazy notion about spirits, and I know there's an earthquake. Well, I think there's one thing we can agree on—we ought to put breakable things in a safe place."

"Where in this house is a safe place?" she cried.

"The cellar, I guess, is the safest." He found a box in the kitchen, and together they packed the Toby jugs. "What else?"

"The glasses and the good china. I'll find another box."

"Can't you? Please."

"I can't. I just can't. I'm too tense and they're watching."

"There's nobody watching, honey."

"Aren't you afraid the bed will shake?"

"Yes," he confessed.

They clung to each other like children.

PART FIVE

CREEP

The Lamont-Doherty Geological Observatory of Columbia University, a cluster of ordinary-looking buildings, stands on the lofty palisades west of the Hudson River, not far from New York City. A student pointed Vail to Kelly's office on the second floor where the seismologist greeted him ebulliently. A short, broad-shouldered man with a snub nose, Kelly had come to Lamont from Cal Tech four years before. He and Vail had met infrequently since then, but never on either one's home ground. Kelly's pursuit of earthquakes had on several occasions caused the cancellation of his always-impending visit to old Brompton, and Vail had never found the time to come to Lamont.

After the preliminaries Kelly asked warily, "You've been experiencing tremors, have you?"

Vail said cautiously, "I think so." He told Kelly some of what he had felt and seen. "It's worth checking anyway. And if I could prove there are tremors, or an earthquake swarm, it might help my wife. She's begun to interpret my seismic events as psychic phenomena."

"You're kidding!" Vail shook his head solemnly. "Harry, where are you located exactly? Show me." Vail went to a large map of the Northeast on the wall and pointed. "Well, that's about the last place you'd expect seismic stuff," Kelly said.

"Earthquakes have occurred in the region before, though," Vail observed. "And we've had a tremendous rainfall. There could be an old fault and water could have collected there, activating it, like what happened in Colorado." At the Rocky Mountain Arsenal near Denver, both men knew, the Army dug deep wells in which to dispose of large quantities of a chemical-warfare agent. Pumped into the ground in a water solution, it had triggered a series of earthquakes that continued until the pumping was stopped.

"Well, anything's possible when it comes to earthquakes," Kelly said dubiously. "Blue Mountain Lake and Moodus aren't so far away, I'll grant that."

"You mentioned Moodus on the telephone. What about it?"

"Seismic activity has been going on there for centuries. The name 'Moodus' itself is an Indian word for 'ground noises,' or something."

"Noises?"

"Yes. You don't feel the occasional Moodus quakes but you can hear them. There hadn't been many such noises in a long while but in the past year or so they've started up again. The tremors are zero magnitude so only instruments can pick them up. We have a team studying the phenomenon, which is one reason I'm short on seismometers."

"The noises happen in just that one area?"

"Just that one small area, near Mount Tom."

"How do local people react?"

"They take the sounds for granted. But in the old days it was different. It seems the noises turned the Indians into devil worshipers of some sort. The early settlers had some quaint ideas, too. Somewhere around here I've got a paper on them. Want it?" Vail nodded and Kelly looked bleakly at the morass on his desk. "I'll dig it up before you leave. Anyway, the noises also happened at Blue Mountain Lake—that's in upstate New York, in the Adirondacks—only there you find bigger tremors. We're doing some interesting work on earthquake prediction there."

"Explain, Paul."

Kelly did happily, and the result was a half-hour lecture on the latest in seismology, to which Vail, interrupting occasionally with questions, listened with care.

Considering the large volume of the earth's crust involved in an earthquake, it had always seemed likely that a signal would be released before the shock itself, and that this telltale sign, if detected and properly interpreted, would provide a warning of when and where a quake was due to occur. Kelly noted that, in the decade or so since Vail had left seismology, the search for such a clue had intensified, and a number of possible precursory earthquake phenomena had been identified. But even if these changes were related to the immanence of earthquakes, there had seemed no way to tie them all together into a unified thory of earthquake prediction.

Then Soviet scientists working in Central Asia made a significant finding. Unlike sound waves in air, vibrations caused by earthquakes travel in two different directions. One, the P, or compressional wave, moves parallel to the direction of wave propagation, as though a spring had been released. The other wave is called the S, or shear wave, and its motion is perpendicular to the direction of earthquake propagation, like the wave in a taut, vibrating string. P waves travel at about 3.75 miles per second, S waves at about 2.25, and the ratio of these two velocities has long been an established fact. The Soviet discovery was that several months before an earthquake occurred, the ratio became smaller. Just prior to the earthquake, the ratio returned to normal.*

* The Soviets have also experimented with driving a current of many millions of kilowatts through the earth, using portable generators. By observing changes in the electrical conductivity of rock, they hope to identify time, place and magnitude of impending earthquakes.

This discovery startled the American seismologists who were studying the earthquake swarm at Blue Mountain Lake. They proceeded to check out the Russian notion, finding it accurate except that the ratio anomaly lasted only a few days, not months as the Soviets claimed.

What was the explanation for the ratio anomaly in the first place? The scientists applied themselves* to the puzzle and eventually found an answer in an obscure property of rock known as "dilatancy." Solid rock, Kelly continued, exhibits dilatancy. Subject a rock to enough pressure and it will break, he said. But shortly before breaking, the rock becomes dilatant. Small cracks spread through it and, as a result, it expands, which dries the pore water that exists in all rocks since the amount of water remains constant while the rock area has increased. P waves travel slower in dry rock than in wet. Therefore, as the rock dries, the P wave speed decreases relative to the S wave speed, which is constant no matter whether the rock is wet or dry.

"In other words," Vail interpreted, "as pressure in the fault zone increases and the rock becomes drier, it seems stronger. That accounts for the ratio anomaly."

"Yes, but it is a temporary phenomenon. Because water is now sucked in from adjacent areas, until there is more water than before, and the increase in pore pressure weakens the rock and triggers the quake. As this is happening, P wave velocity returns to normal, signaling that the quake is about to occur."

Kelly said that the dilatancy theory accounted for nearly all the premonitory earthquake phenomena which had been discovered. Implicit in the hypothesis was the ability to predict almost infallibly the time, place and magnitude of a quake. And the bigger the impending quake, the greater the warning time,

* Kelly here noted that other seismologists had been involved—Drs. Lynn Sykes, Chris Scholz, John Armbruster, Yash Aggaral and Marc Sbar at Lamont and, independently, Amos Nur at Stanford.

because the ratio anomaly would last longer. This was the reason the anomaly observed by the Russians had a longer duration than those observed in the Blue Mountain area—the Blue Mountain quakes were smaller.

"What stands in the way of actually predicting earthquakes then?" Vail inquired.

"Besides the remaining theoretical problems? Money. To predict earthquakes properly we need instrumentation over big areas as well as a large computer system. It'll take hundreds of millions of dollars, which nobody's willing to spend."

"But wouldn't the theory offer possibilities of earthquake control? Couldn't we—you—defuse an earthquake by making the fault area dry? Or pump water to small sections of the fault and set off small harmless quakes which would remove the tension without a major earthquake happening?"

"We're thinking along those lines," Kelly observed. "Let's go to the lab."

In the hall, they passed a large room where banks of seismographs silently recorded action in the Northeast from twenty stations hooked into Lamont-Doherty by telephone line, Kelly said. "Any sizable tremor in your neck of the woods would show up here."

"Where's the nearest station to me?"

Kelly checked a chart on the wall. "New London, Connecticut."

"Too far to pick up tremors as small as the ones I'm getting, I imagine," Vail said.

"Yes."

Kelly's lab downstairs was a maze of machinery. He showed Vail what he called a biaxial loading frame with a hydraulic ram which could produce 200 tons of pressure. A small section of rock was in its grip. Kelly said that the rock had been cut with a diamond saw and the polished faces placed together again under pressure. "It's a simulated earthquake. The rock faces move in

171

tiny jerks, just as happens in a slip-stick fault. If I inject water into the crack the process is accelerated, and when I withdraw the fluid it decelerates again, confirming the dilatancy theory."

Kelly pointed to an aluminum box the size of a large suitcase. "There's your seismometer. Don't lose it, please; it's worth four grand. If you get anything on it—though, frankly, I doubt strenuously that you will—call me right away."

Kay had left that morning, and Vail returned at dusk to an empty house. The kitchen door stuck and he forced it with his shoulder, carrying the seismometer inside. He looked around the kitchen, silently cursing Kay's sloppiness. She had gone to Boston leaving the refrigerator wide open, and a puddle of water stood on the floor. Open as well were the drawers Dun had built, with easy-to-slide hardware, and several pots had fallen from the overhead rack. His mouth contracted.

Judy lunged for his legs, and he plucked the cat from the floor. Holding the frightened animal, he began to explore the house carefully, searching for clues. Several arrowheads had fallen from the mantel. The picture over the couch hung at an angle. A fireplace tool lay on the floor. He saw that the bar cart was several feet from the wall.

Everywhere Vail found evidence of what might have been mischief—screens down, open drawers, angled pictures, books on the floor. But the most spectacular damage he found in their bedroom: a crack ran the length of the mirror on the back of the closet door.

Carrying the 50-pound seismometer, he descended to the basement and opened the instrument. It consisted of a drum covered by smoked paper that rested a delicately balanced stylus. Kelly had given him a week's supply of the paper, which had to be changed every day. To the two geophones—microphones for picking up vibrations—he attached the cords and placed one on

172

either side of the room. The device ran by batteries, and as he switched it on, the drum turned slowly.

He watched a moment, as though the machine would begin immediately to record seismic activity, but nothing happened: the stylus drew a straight line. Upstairs, he fed the cat and put birdseed in the brass cage and made himself a hamburger. Then he went to his study and began to read the paper Kelly had given him.

The "Moodus Noises" are localized, low-intensity earthquakes. They have existed in the Township of East Haddam since the beginning of the recorded history of Connecticut. The superstitions and fantasies that they have created fill many historical texts.

Since the early settling of homesteads, the town of Moodus has always been associated with mysterious noises. The name Moodus itself is taken from the Indian word Matcotmoodus which means in English "place of noises." The Wangunk Indians who lived in the area had obviously been familiar with these noises long before the white man started to penetrate the area. Indeed, the Indians of Moodus were noted for having powwows, sacrifices and religious ceremonies in association with these noises. They would often meet on Mt. Tom, the legendary source of these mysterious sounds, to "drive a prodigious trade at worshipping the devil." (Barber, 1938.)

When the early settlers arrived in the '60s, they were also disturbed by this phenomenon. Within a relatively short time, numerous stories and superstitions grew up about the noises. The Wangunks claimed that the god of evil, Hobomcko, was angry at the white man and caused the noises by the light of a carbuncle* under Mt. Tom, near the Connecticut River. (Skinner, 1896.) The early settlers in return proposed several newer theories that were equally as unusual as the Wangunks' explanation. . . .

[A] Dr. Steele believed that the noises were caused by a giant carbuncle that grew under Mt. Tom and that the removal of the carbuncle would stop the noises. Dr. Steele was reported to have found the carbuncle in a cave on Mt. Tom and removed it at night during a series of unusually loud "Moodus noises." However, the

* A dark-red semiprecious stone.

doctor stated that the piece he left behind would grow for fifteen years and then again produce "noises." This prediction was strikingly fulfilled with a sudden noise and vibration about fifteen years after Dr. Steele left for England with his carbuncle. The doctor, though, never reached England. He and the carbuncle both sank in the middle of the Atlantic, where it was reported that the stone produced a large red glow from the bottom to "strike fear in the hearts of passing sailors." (Parker, 1915.) *

He read on. Over the years in the limited area there had been hundreds of earthquakes. Most were tiny, but there had been exceptions like one in 1791, which had been assigned, on the basis of a written record of its effects, an intensity of VIII on the Modified Mercalli Scale. That would have been a powerful earthquake, capable of knocking down buildings.

Vail finished the thesis and went down to check the seismometer, which had recorded nothing. He got into bed and lay in the dark, listening to the house sounds—the crack of a beam, hum of a pipe, whine of the refrigerator, rumble of the pump. All seemed peaceful, familiar, and yet . . . the old stone house, once so pleasantly grumbling, seemed full of menace.

He reached out to touch her but found only empty sheets. He lay on his stomach and then on his side, turning restlessly, unable to sleep in his wife's absence. The first alien noise he heard resembled a low cry, forlorn and faraway, like a prisoner in a pit. Vail jerked involuntarily, then sagged back on the mattress. He could account for the sound, he decided: ground noises, like the ones at Moodus. How easy it was to slip into unscientific explanations for things, as the Indians, the early settlers, and Kay had done. Spirits, ghosts! How else would you account for a sound like that, if you didn't know . . . ?

The next noise was harder to explain to himself. He heard

* James S. Meyer, *An Investigation of the "Moodus Noises,"* a thesis submitted in partial fulfillment of the requirement for the degree of Master of Science, Central Connecticut State College, New Britain, Connecticut, April 1967, pp. ii, 1, 2.

footsteps, like someone scuffling, the brush of leather (soft moc-casin?) on a hard floor, a foot dragging, as if moving across the stone floor of the cupola, toward the elliptical staircase and the second story . . . scrape, scrape . . . somewhere below, a door slammed. Why? Account for that, a frightened inner voice demanded. He could see why Kay was scared. Finally he got it: the scraping sound must be the rustling of the stones moving slightly in a tremor, the same tremor which would twist a door jamb that small fraction required to make a portal close. Yes, it could happen. . . .

He raced downstairs. A jagged line had been traced on the smoked paper of the seismograph. He stood before the machine, opening and closing his hands. Vail was excited—one wasn't credited for finding an earthquake as one would be for the dis-covery of a new species or a star, and yet he and he alone had detected this one. He felt almost proprietary about the tremors, as if they belonged to him. "Vail's earthquake," he recalled Lechine saying, and smiled mockingly at the ring of it.

The smile vanished. The little tremors might grow. They could be harbingers of a bigger one. It seemed unlikely, and yet at Moodus the earthquake swarm had developed into an VIII intensity quake. Vail had a vision of the crack shooting up the wall, breaking his house in two. In his imagination the red stones fell down. He left the basement hurriedly, his old fear clutching at him.

By morning several tremors had been recorded. Vail made a long distance call to Kelly and learned that the seismologist had gone on a hike. He would not return until evening. At his desk, felt-tipped pen in hand, he studied Johnson's drawing. He felt safe now in drawing a dotted line, representing the fault, from Summerset Villa to the stone house. Next he analyzed the ques-tion of why his immediate neighbors had not noticed the trem-ors. True, all were inexperienced observers; true, also, that all suffered from various disabilities and self-preoccupations which might cause them to overlook the abnormalities. Still, if the shakings at the Demmings' or the Pollidors' had been as hard and sustained as at the stone house, people would have noticed sooner or later. Since the stone house had taken the brunt of the seismic action, the fault must be extremely narrow.

Vail extended the dotted line to the broken pavement on Point Road and beyond to the village, where it arrived at the church. Someone—Dun, was it?—had said something about the church that might have been a clue, but Vail could not remember what. He decided to go there.

Vail, ideally, would have preferred to visit the place at a time when it was empty, but he knew the church was always locked except during services. He decided to arrive late to minimize his presence, and waited until 11:30 before he left the stone house.

No cars were parked outside—with a few exceptions such as Dun and the teenagers, the villagers didn't own cars and trucks. Except for the sound of singing and the pipe organ, he would not have known a service was in progress as he approached the closed white door. He became aware of his own curiosity about the villagers' fundamentalist creed—"earthy," Dun had called it.

He entered quietly. Backs toward him, about a hundred people—the entire population of the village, he believed—stood in the nave singing.

> O safe to the Rock that is higher than I,
> My soul in its conflicts and sorrows would fly;
> So sinful, so weary, Thine own would I be;
> Thou blest "Rock of Ages," I'm hiding in Thee.
> Hiding in Thee,
> Hiding in Thee,
> Thou blest "Rock of Ages,"
> I'm hiding in Thee.

Vail hung back in the doorway, partially concealed, and examined the interior of the early-eighteenth-century church. Except for the pipe organ—added later evidently, when the farming was still good—everything about the church was plain to the point of being drab. The stark simplicity of the interior was emphasized by the lines, all of which were horizontal or vertical without a hint of a curve. The square, six-paned windows were screenless and dirty on the outside; several were propped open with blocks of wood. Crossbeams were overhead on which Vail could see cobwebs and white spots; birds must get into the place. Before him, the straight backs of the pine pews, dark and cracked with age, the tops brightened by the endless grip of hands. In front of the pews, in the center of the church under the pulpit, was a square pit filled with sand. He recalled that churches like these used to be heated by potbellied stoves that rested safely in sandpits. Beside the pulpit—an unadorned box —was a raised platform where the church elders must have sat. On it stood a gray stone cross flanked by two neat pyramids of rocks, the familiar red rock of the stone house. There were no candles or other altar decorations.

Dun, the deacon, led the singing from the altar. He wore a surplice the same color red as the rock, and a large necklace, of the same red rock. Scrutinizing the backs of the parishioners, Vail saw that all clothing was dark red, brown or gray, colors he associated with earth.

> How oft in the conflict, when press'd by the foe,
> I have fled to my refuge and breath'd out my woe;
> How often, when trials like sea billows roll,
> Have I hidden in Thee, O Thou Rock of my soul.
> Hiding in Thee,
> Hiding in Thee,
> Thou blest "Rock of Ages,"
> I'm hiding in Thee.

Dun climbed the small pulpit and turned the pages of the Bible. The congregation sat.

I will love thee, O Lord, my strength.
The Lord is my rock, and my fortress, and my deliverer;
my God, my strength, in whom I will trust my buckler
and the horn of my salvation, and my high tower.
I will call upon the Lord, who is worthy to be praised:
so shall I be saved from my enemies.
The sorrows of death compassed me, and the floods of
ungodly men made me afraid.
The sorrows of hell compassed me about: the snares of
death prevented me.
In my distress I called upon the Lord, and cried out unto
my God: he heard my voice out of his temple, and my
cry came before him, even unto his ears.
Then the earth shook and trembled; the foundations also
of the hills moved and were shaken, because he was wroth.
There went up a smoke out of his nostrils, and fire out of
his mouth devoured: coals were kindled by it.
He bowed the heavens also, and came down: and darkness was
under his feet.
He made darkness his secret place.
As for God, his way is perfect: the word of the Lord is
tried: he is a buckler to all those that trust him.
For who is God save the Lord? Or who is a rock save our God?

Dun closed the Bible and began to speak in a louder voice, clearer and more resonant than Vail had ever heard it. "Friends: we are gathered here as always to celebrate the Lord, the good Lord Who dwells among us, Who hears the words in our hearts, Who speaks to us if we will listen.

"Know you that the earth is the Lord's, with all its spite and sorrow, with all its fighting and wars, with all its jealousies and hatreds, with all its hurting and killing. The Lord's voice can be heard, His ways can be uncovered. And by living according to the Lord, day by day, hour by hour, minute by minute, that rocklike sureness of self that comes from sureness in Him may be thine. That is the meaning of 'He is a buckler to all those that trust in Him.' "

Dun's weathered hands seized the edge of the pulpit as he surveyed the congregation with blank, unseeing eyes. "In recent days the Lord has been raising His voice, as before. He grumbles and He mutters, and in this way tells us of His displeasure at our iniquities. From his secret place in the dark He tells us of His anger. Do we listen?

"For some time the Lord has not chosen to visit us, but has stayed in His hiding place, His dark hole, listening through the rocks, watching through His eye of the waters. And now He has returned, and how else are we to interpret His messages but as His displeasure at our iniquities?

"Our fathers and our grandfathers and their fathers before them knew that the Lord lives in the earth—not in some vacant heaven as others wrongly believe—and from there conducts His surveillance and occasionally sends His word. And now He is back. What does He wish? What are we to understand? How are we to proceed so as to please the Lord once more and make His angry voice fall silent?

"It is time to ask these questions, for the Lord's voice is like the voice of the Last Day. His lips open and His tongue peals the bell of doom. Catastrophe approaches—none can prevent it if the Lord chooses to deliver His final blow." Dun's words seemed to echo from every corner of the church. "We are the chosen ones and to us, in Shonkawa Village, does the Lord speak, and He says, 'Live in peace with your brethren. Cease thy iniquities, O chosen ones, or ye shall be destroyed! I shall lay in thy path the snares of death. I shall make the sea to heave up its waters, for I *am* the sea! I shall cause the earth to shake and tremble to its very foundations. I will crush ye with the rock for I *am* the rock!'" Suddenly a large rock appeared in Dun's hands. He held it high above his head and smashed it into the sandpile. The church seemed to tremble from the blow. "Let us pray. Lord of the Earth, Earthgod, Noisemaker . . ."

"ARCHDEACON OF THE ANCIENT ORDER OF THINGS,

179

WE PRAY. LORD OF THE EARTH, EARTHGOD, NOISE-
MAKER . . ."
"For we have sinned."
"FOR WE HAVE SINNED."
"Shield us with thy darknes. Protect us."
"SHIELD US WITH THY DARKNESS. PROTECT US."
"Be our solid rock."
"BE OUR SOLID ROCK."
"Cause the earth to be silent and still."
"CAUSE THE EARTH TO BE SILENT AND STILL."
"For thou art the Lord, our God."
"FOR THOU ART THE LORD, OUR GOD."
"Amen."
"AMEN."

The pipe organ played. The parishioners began to dance, jiggling their feet, shaking their bodies, holding their arms out and
jabbing their fingers vigorously toward the ground. In the midst
of this ritual, Vail heard the off-key notes and instantly remembered what he had forgotten about pipe organs. He stepped forward to hear better. At the same moment the congregation
kneeled, leaving him exposed. From the pulpit Dun stared at
Vail as if seeing him for the first time, eyes alert and frightened.

The organ died and Dun came rapidly down the aisle.
"Shouldn't have come here, Mr. Vail," he mumbled.

Vail said, "Dun, I know what's wrong with your organ."

The parishioners turned and muttered. Their narrow faces
dark with anger, the Wilbore boys stepped toward him, followed
by Bill Pabodie with his long hair. Dun placed himself in front
of Vail and raised his arms, the loose cloth of the red surplice
making him look far larger than he was. "No, not *here*," he
shouted.

"He has no right . . ."

"Trespassing on the Lord's ground!"

"Blasphemer!"

"The stone! The stone!"

"Listen to me!" Vail cried. He seized Dun's arm and propelled him roughly through the crowd until they stood before the pipe organ. "Pipe organs don't have strings. They don't get out of tune. But yours is, and there has to be a reason." He pointed. "Two of the organ pipes are bent."

At their very tops, two of the longest pipes veered off at slight angles. Dun squinted and said reluctantly, "It's true."

Vail shouted, "Don't you see? You've had an earthquake here! Nothing else could have caused that."

"A sacrilege! A sacrilege!" Mrs. Wilbore's sharp voice shouted.

Dun said dejectedly, "Another sign from the Lord."

"No. Earthquake. Little tremors are shaking the church."

"Better go now, son," Dun frowningly advised as the Wilbore boys came closer. Through the growling throng he escorted Vail to safety.

Returning home, Vail, full of questions, remembered the hate-filled faces he had seen in church. What "iniquities" had Dun commanded them to cease? What had led Dun to predict a cataclysm? Was it apocalyptic mumbo jumbo? Did Dun know something factual that Vail didn't?

He descended to the basement to check the seismometer. There had been a tremor while he was in the village—one large enough, he judged, to be apprehended by human senses. Yet in church he had felt nothing. What was the meaning of that?

At his desk, he stared at Johnson's map. An idea stirred deep in his mind, rose nearer and nearer the surface and finally burst out. With the felt pen, he extended the dotted fault line to the church and then beyond to the bay, where the drawing ended. He pictured Sam Wilbore bending, hurling the flat stones skipping across the water toward the column of dark smoke. Of course, the gas tank farm! A quick alignment of his map with one from the Rhode Island guidebook proved that the extended fault line went there unerringly.

It was not difficult to imagine what had happened. A quick jolt—even a small one could account for the damage—at exactly the same moment he had felt the shaking on the ladder. A leak in a pipe or a connection. (In this area, earthquake precautions might be inadequate.) Contact with fire—the burn-off of fumes? A blast. The few survivors from a small crew working on Saturday morning would have muddled memories of the explosion, which would have been almost simultaneous with the jolt, itself almost imperceptible. Vail felt certain that an earthquake had caused the accident.

He decided to appraise the situation from the beach. Crossing Torturous Creek, he put his hand in the water, which still seemed abnormally warm. Were there thermal springs beneath the ground which, because of the shaking, had begun to feed into the creek? What manner of thing *was* happening down there in the crust? He passed the pond and saw fish jumping straight out, as though they longed to escape the water. The swans appeared to be acting strangely too, darting this way and that across the surface instead of paddling at their usual leisurely pace.

At this moment, Vail became conscious of something new: the pond lay in a low hollow that paralleled what he now presumed to be the fault line. This was not a natural position for the water, according to the direction of ground drainage, and he had always assumed, without particularly thinking, that the pond had been the result of an old earthern dam, raised perhaps by the Indians. Now it occurred to him that the water could be a "sag pond," which often marks a fault. In that case, faulting itself would have created the pond, and further seismic activity could destroy it. The water would simply disappear into the sea.

That could happen as a result of a phenomenon known as a "seiche." When the ground tilts, a body of water on it naturally tilts, too, running to one bank. When the earth's equilibrium is reestablished, the water rushes back in a wave, overflowing the other side.

A seiche wasn't as bad as a tsunami, he thought, associating from one frightening possibility to the next. Caused by a seaquake, a tsunami, or seismic ocean wave, was a ridge of water hurtling over the surface at 500 mph. A ship would hardly feel one racing beneath it. But when the wave reached shore and the water became shallower, the ridge could grow into a monster 50, 60, 70 feet high. People mistakenly called them tidal waves.

"You're ranting, Vail," he told himself as he sat down in the rock chair. "Take it easy. Calm down. Stick to the facts. Analyze." Outside of the explosion, nothing unusual had been reported across the bay, so it seemed reasonable to assume—if his hypothesis about the blast held—that the tank farm lay at the other end of the fault. This made the fault about ten miles long and entirely underwater except for the ends and the peninsula's tip.

No shaking, moreover, had been reported at the old people's home, nor did anything untoward appear to have happened at the gas storage facility after the blast. Perhaps just one tremor occurred there. In the church, he hadn't felt the tremor recorded at his house by the seismograph; almost certainly it had been strong enough for human senses to detect. From these and other pieces of evidence it was reasonably certain that the stone house stood precisely over the epicenter of the earthquake swarms, in the eye of the seismic storm.

What did it mean? The fault was definitely old—you didn't get new ones except on the edges of the tectonic plates, which this was not. What happened, he supposed, was that the old fault woke up at long intervals, shook itself, and then went back to sleep. There was, however, one factor of which he was forced to take account, and which could bring a decisive change—the prodigious rainfall. Suppose the rains had triggered the tremors in

183

the first place. It hadn't rained for several days, yet the tremors seemed to be increasing in number and intensity. Suppose there was more heavy rain—how large an earthquake might be set off then?

A half-dozen tiny tremors were picked up by the machine in the early evening, one large enough for Vail to feel. Simultaneously the phone rang with no one on the line, establishing the connection between the shaking and the failure of the mechanism. He reached Fred Demming after getting two wrong numbers. They commiserated about Pollidor and then Vail said, "Any word?"

"No," said Demming heavily, "and I'm worried sick. I'm starting to believe she's been kidnaped."

"Kidnaped!" Harry was startled. "But there's absolutely no evidence of that. You'd have heard from the kidnapers."

"Not yet perhaps. I did notify the police finally. There's a four-state alarm out."

"Fred, you don't sound so good. Why don't you go to Boston and wait there?"

"If she's been kidnaped," Demming muttered, "I've got to be here when they call."

Vail phoned Polly and said gently, "Any news?"

"I spent all day at the hospital again," she said in a voice weary to the breaking point, "and Bill is fine, just fine, he's going to pull through and he'll be making drinks at the computer bar before you . . . before you . . . before you . . ." She repeated herself like a broken record.

He said quickly at an interstice, "Bill's conscious?"

"Well, no, not quite. . . ."

"What does the doctor say?"

"He gives Bill every chance to get well. . . ."

Vail wanted to ask about shakings or vibrations but the ques-

184

tion would be useless. "Polly," he told her, "you ought to have somebody with you. When is Jeff coming?"

"Jeff?"

"Your cousin."

"Oh. Soon, soon."

It would be next to impossible to jolt his immediate neighbors into believing anything was wrong, he realized. Wanting to get his mind off tremors for a moment, he went down to the exercise room, where he worked out on the equipment and took a sauna bath. The heavy wood door seemed to stick a little when he opened it, and he made a mental note to sandpaper it down a hair. In his robe, he changed the paper on the drum, went upstairs, and telephoned Paul Kelly.

The seismologist said, "I tried you but there was no answer."

"Well, I got you. Listen, something is happening. There have been about a dozen tremors in the last twenty-four hours."

Kelly's voice rose. "That's hard to believe."

"You can't argue with a seismometer."

"How big?"

"Zero magnitude, mostly. But all small."

Kelly whistled. "Harry, I envy you, being right in the middle of an earthquake, even if it's a little one."

"Suppose the swarm turns into a convulsion?"

Kelly scoffed, "Not a chance. The fault must be short—a couple of hundred yards, probably." The length of the fault, both men knew, is a determining factor in the size of a quake.

"Well, I wonder about that. There was an explosion at a gas storage facility five miles away from here two weeks ago."

"I read about it. Why?"

"Suppose a tremor caused the blast? The fault extends there."

"Don't spook out on me, Harry. Nothing like that could have happened."

"No reason for the blast has been found."

185

"One will be discovered."

"I hope so, because if *I'm* right I'm sitting right on top of a potentially large earthquake. Vail's earthquake," he said with a bitter laugh.

"Vail's earthquake. That's a hot one. Listen, it's a tiny fault —the seismometer tells you that." Kelly sighed. "I hope the tremors last until I get there."

Vail said, "The earthquake's been around a long time, Paul. Those Moodus noises—well, ground noises exist here too, even without perceptible tremors. I finally heard them myself but didn't know what they were. I imagine there's a cave below the village through which the earthsounds reverberate, so the villagers could hear little tremors even though they didn't feel them. Nobody else heard them because the cave's directly under the village, because they were tiny noises, and because years might pass between the earthquake swarms that caused them. Over the years the villagers built a religion around the noises, just as the Moodus Indians did. The locals think that God—a fearsome God—lives under the ground and periodically speaks to them. They invented a scary religion to fit their fear of ground noises."

"That sounds right." Kelly hesitated. "Harry, I'm sorry I misjudged you—I thought your earthquake was imaginary. I lent you the seismometer to prove it. Now that you're back at seismology, why don't you make it permanent? There's an office for you here whenever you want it."

Vail grinned despite himself. "We'll see. When are you coming? I need some help here."

"I'll put a team together. It'll be next week before I can get seismometers back from Blue Mountain. I've only got one here —we'll need a half-dozen to do a proper job."

"Can't make it sooner?"

"Doubt it. Stop worrying, will you, Harry?" Kelly said.

"I just hope it doesn't rain."

He called Kay, then went to bed. About four, he was awakened by a loud noise which his sleepy mind finally identified as thunder. Outside the bedroom window, water came down as though the earthgod were taking a bath.

PART SIX

SHOCK

The gray sky on Monday looked like a layer of shale. The seismometer informed Vail of a dozen mild tremors during the night.

He was about to extinguish the basement light when, from the top of the cellar stairs, he saw on the wall what looked to be a shadow. Close up it became a thin line which darted two feet up in the concrete from the metal plate. The crack had broken out.

Easy, now, he told himself.

Upstairs again, he fed the cat while he decided what to do, but Judy wouldn't eat. He didn't feel like eating, either, he had to admit. The horse! He had forgotten Brioche. With oats and a bucket of water, he entered the stall. Instead of nuzzling against him as she always did, the mare shied, pushing herself against the wall and showing the whites of her eyes. When he bent to put oats in the bin she launched a hoof at him, missing narrowly.

He backed off, leaving the door open, and Brioche followed. Outdoors she seemed her normal self again, rubbing her head against him. The tremors had frightened the mare.

He made instant coffee in the kitchen, noting that the tap water still ran brown. At the butcher block table, he extrapolated the course of the crack if it continued to grow, following it in his mind as it leaped up the basement wall, appeared on the living room wall, climbed between the front windows, entered Mark's room on the wall where the circus poster was, and . . . He breathed heavily. The new crack would unite with the old crack on the outer wall, like a conspiracy to render the stone house structurally unsound, unstable, unsafe.

The kitchen clock said just past nine. He phoned the office. "Vail and Lechine," Mrs. Conner answered pleasantly.

"I'm not coming in today, and maybe not for several days," he told her.

"Dr. Vail! You're not sick?"

"No."

"Nothing wrong with Mrs. Vail or the little one, I hope."

"They're away, as a matter of fact."

Mrs. Conner's voice turned urgent. "Lechine insists you look at Walter's final drawings for propping up the abandoned factory. He left explicit instructions on Friday. He's out right now."

"Have Walter drive them over."

"He's busy on a job, too, here in the office."

"Well, it'll have to wait until I'm finished here."

"Mr. Lechine won't like that. He was quite definite that you should see them today." Vail waited. "Maybe if Walter could watch the shop I could bring them over during the noon hour."

"Fine," Vail said. "Did Robinson call?"

"No."

He dialed Summerset Villa, cursing Robinson's sleeping habits. The manager was unavailable, meaning he remained in bed.

He went to the studio—the pictures hung at every angle. Some had fallen. The easel was toppled and paint jars were strewn on the floor. He left the studio and returned to the living room with Kay's charcoals and began to sketch. He made a drawing of the wall which showed a brace fastened to it, like a Roman numeral X, with the crosspieces avoiding the windows and front door.

192

Wood, he said to himself. Where?

He visualized the pile of two-by-fours in the town square, and taking a tarp and rope from the barn, drove off. He found the wood where he remembered it, creosote-soaked pieces, about eight feet long, casually stacked in the corner of the square. The lumber had been there ever since he had lived on the peninsula, a relic of some abandoned village project. He looked about—no one was in sight.

Filthy though it was, the wood was perfect for his purpose. He carried it to the car on his shoulders, two boards at a time. After a number of trips he judged he had enough. The boards were too long to fit in the trunk, so he spread the tarp on the roof of the Rolls, tied the wood in separate bundles, and hoisted them one by one to the roof of the car, securing them there. It was a load, but the Rolls could carry it.

Vail backed up slowly and turned around. As he did, he saw a blue car almost insolently sidle around the far corner of the square, halting on the road before him. Three youths got out.

"There's Mr. Vail," Sam Wilbore said in a loud voice.

"Sure it's Mr. Vail?"

"Sure I'm sure. Who else has a shiny old Rolls Royce around here?"

"Well, that *looks* like Mr. Vail behind the wheel, but *what* would Mr. Vail be doin' with all those boards on top his fancy car?"

"Don't know. Why don't we ask him, assumin' it's Mr. Vail."

"It's Mr. Vail. Howdy," Cy Wilbore said. "Notice your load of wood. Plan to build somethin' for the community?"

"None of your goddam business."

"Oh? Well, you see, it *is* our business. Our wood."

"Our?"

Wilbore's voice lost its phony levity and became sharp. "Folks here in the village. Anyone give you permission to take it? It's stealing, if not."

"Stealing! That wood's been there for years. Nobody wants it."

"We want it," Bill Pabodie shouted, "for a bonfire on the Fourth of July."

"Come on."

"Take it easy, Mr. Vail," Cy Wilbore said. Behind red rims his eyes flickered as he reached for the door handle of the Rolls. . . . No, no, Vail cautioned himself, this isn't the late movie. Grown men don't fight, especially not with three adolescents probably armed with knives—he thought of the slashed tire. He shoved the Rolls in gear, maneuvered it around the blue car, and shot off down Point Road.

That had been an error, he realized, as he saw in the rearview mirror the blue car coming after him. He was more of a threat to them on his feet than behind the wheel of an overloaded automobile. Cy Wilbore driving, the blue car with its outsize tires and raised rear end caught up quickly. Wilbore's car began to graze the old Rolls's bumper dexterously. The car, already hard to steer because of the wood on top, shuddered and began to veer.

He had to act. Mastering the timing of Wilbore's repeated bumps, he touched his brakes lightly in unison, hoping the sturdy metal of the old English car would withstand the impacts. He heard a twang as Wilbore's bumper broke, a snap as the Rolls's bumper crushed the blue car's grille. Wilbore swung sharply, in time to avoid a collision with wood that fell from the Rolls.

The blue car again took up pursuit but halted at the edge of Vail's driveway. It came no farther.

Things could be worse, he told himself as he carried the wood to the living room. The Rolls looked undamaged, and though he had lost some lumber, enough remained for the job.

He continued to believe that everything was all right until the breeze shifted and the backyard foully breathed at him. The tremors must be roiling the undrained cesspool, agitating the contents. He turned to have a look at the yard and dropped the last load of wood.

He must have seen them earlier in the morning, assuming they were the same old mole holes—but they weren't the same. The ridges had undergone a metamorphosis and their nature had become apparent. The cone-shaped boils were of earthspouts like the ones at Summerset Villa. He remembered the configuration he had observed from the roof, the earth's insidious embrace of his arm, Punch's flattened head. His spirits sagged. Things were not all right; it was as though the quake were following him, hemming him in. To have been victorious against the boys had falsely revived his confidence. Against a trio of punk kids, he could fight. What was his strength against the earth's?

He returned to his labor, bringing in the wood, gathering tools —electric drill, portable power saw, hammer, sawhorse, nails. Kay, he thought, would be furious if she saw the room with the furniture pushed back, the rug rolled up and filthy lumber piled on the floor, leaving marks. He drilled, sawed and hammered until the wall with the crack was girdled with boards. Rubbing the sweat from his eyes, he stood back to examine the brace. Jerry-built as it was, perhaps it would support the wall if the crack continued to grow.

He heard an insistent knocking. The front door opened and Marjorie Conner stood there, consternation on her face.

"Dr. Vail! I've been out there the longest time. *What* are you doing?"

Hesitantly, she entered the room. She was done up with jewelry, makeup, false eyelashes. He stepped back, aware of what she must be thinking as she examined the brace, the room and himself. His serious tone was intended to contradict the supposition of lunacy. "A structural problem developed in the wall.

I'm shoring it up until . . ." Until what? Until the earthquake was over, but he couldn't tell her that. She probably thought him crazy already. ". . . until I can get a crew in here to rectify the situation."

"Like the problem at the old people's home?" she asked.

"A little. Did you bring the plans?"

She held up a manila envelope. "Not with *those* hands," she scolded.

Vail looked at himself in the downstairs bathroom mirror. His round face was filthy with creosote. You're a mess, all right, he decided. He suddenly realized that he was lonely.

When he returned, Mrs. Conner remarked, "My, this is a pretty place, or must be when it's in proper order." He became aware that her blouse offered more than the suggestion of ample breasts. "What a lovely staircase that is. Mrs. Vail must be very proud of the house. How lucky you are to live here."

"Lucky?" he said musingly. "Oh, sure. I like it a lot, when everything is normal."

Mrs. Conner handed him the drawings and he inspected them rapidly, standing up. He was conscious of her presence beside him—her perfume, her size (she was a bigger woman than Kay), the soft skin of her inner arm. He tapped the drawing. "This should go there." Trying not to look at her, he was unable, and found her glance darting at him. A spot of black makeup clung to the corner of her eye.

"Aside from that, okay," he said. "When is the work to start on the factory?"

"After the Fourth." She returned the drawings to the envelope and wrinkled her large, perfectly formed nose. "There's a bad smell in here."

"Oh?" Vail sniffed, smelling nothing. I'm getting so used to the stink that I only smell it when it hits me in the face, he thought bitterly. "A little problem with the sewage system, I'm afraid," he explained.

Mrs. Conner observed, "I must say you do seem to have your troubles around here."

"An old house is always a lot of trouble."

"May I see it all? I love old houses."

"There's not that much to see."

He showed her the downstairs, omitting the cellar, where the seismograph clicked and the plate tried to guard the crack. She found his study "cozy," admired the French chest and teardrop chandelier in the dining room. In the cupola, at the foot of the staircase, Mrs. Conner inquired casually, "Is your wife away for long?"

"I don't really know, as a matter of fact," he said. "She's visiting her mother in Boston. She might be gone a week or so."

"Oh. What a fine old staircase this is," she said, mounting.

"You couldn't duplicate an elliptical staircase today for thousands. They put a lot of work into it, for a farmhouse. They still had craftsmen then."

"Those were the good old days."

"My little son's room," he explained when they reached it. "And this is a guest room. Kay used to paint in here, but now she's got a studio in the barn," he said as they turned down the hall. As their eyes joined he was conscious of anxiety of a different and nicer kind than what he had been feeling recently. "Our bedroom."

"What a nice view. You can see the ocean! Is that your own beach?"

"Yes," he answered.

"Imagine, a private beach! I have to drive twenty-five miles to get to one, and it's so crowded on weekends you have to park a half-mile away. Well, that's my problem, isn't it? Look! You have a view from three sides! And not a house in sight!"

"You can see one in winter when there are no leaves." He was almost apologetic.

"My view is a factory," Mrs. Conner said. "What an enormous bed! Well, you're not exactly small, Dr. Vail. How about showing me the barn? I'm a real house freak, I tell you. I guess everybody is who lives in a small apartment."

On the way down she asked him, "Dr. Vail, have you had lunch?"

"No. I forgot."

"Neither have I. Suppose I make some for both of us?" she asked. "Mr. Lechine is out for the day, and Walter is minding the shop so I'm not in a hurry. Would Mrs. Vail mind?"

"It's a fine idea. She wouldn't mind." But she would mind, he thought guiltily. Especially she would mind *this* Mrs. Conner whose office manner was rapidly vanishing, who seemed to have forgotten that Vail was her employer. But it was good to have a woman in the house again, no, *this* woman, with her helpful way.

Walking toward the studio, Mrs. Conner said, "I don't see how you stand that odor, Dr. Vail. Good God! What are those ugly bumps all over the lawn?"

He thought briefly of telling the truth but felt certain she would neither understand nor believe him. "Some animal made them," he said with an uncomfortable shrug. The studio door stuck with a vengeance—another result of the tremors, probably—and he yanked until the frame cracked before he got it open. Mrs. Conner gave him a quizzical glance and entered.

He had forgotten the condition of the studio. Peering deep into the confusion, Mrs. Conner muttered, "I hear artists have funny ways of working. Still, if I kept my desk like this . . ."

"She must have left in a hurry."

"Maybe I should too," Mrs. Conner muttered. "Walter might need me." Back in the kitchen she regained her enthusiasm. "What shall we have for lunch?" She opened the refrigerator. "There's hardly anything to eat. Suppose I whip up a soufflé? I make a good one."

"No, that's too much trouble," he said hastily. "How about scrambled eggs?"

"You men. Now you just run along, Dr. Vail, and leave everything to me."

Vail returned to the brace and aimlessly hammered in nails. About Mrs. Conner he was hopelessly divided. Her pointed breasts and glowing eyes attracted him, and his sex life with Kay had been ruined by Seconal and his fear of shaking. Yet if he were to go to bed with someone other than his wife it should not be his secretary—wasn't that a cardinal rule? Perhaps he misinterpreted the signals: perhaps she only wanted a meal.

"Damn!" Mrs. Conner cried.

"What is it?" He scurried to the kitchen.

She pointed to the mess on the terra-cotta floor. "I don't know why, but the eggs rolled off the table. There goes lunch. No more eggs."

"We'll find something else," he said soothingly as he wiped the floor with a paper towel. "How about grilled cheese sandwiches?"

"All right?" she replied, a little dejectedly. "You go set the dining room table, Dr. Vail. I'm determined our lunch will be festive."

"Yes. Of course!"

"Can we have a little wine?"

"I think I can dig some up."

Vail was laying out placemats when she gave a strangled cry. He discovered her holding the back of her hand to her mouth: a knife appeared to have fallen from the magnetic rack. Its point was embedded in the butcher block table and the handle quivered.

"Ow!" she cried.

"Are you hurt?"

"More scared than anything. It almost flew at me."

"Just an accident. You want a bandage?" He held her hand as he examined the small cut.

199

"I'll live. It's stopped bleeding already. I must say—life in a house seems hazardous."

"Household accidents are the most common of injuries," Vail told her.

"Do you have accident insurance?" She tried to joke.

Several times as lunch progressed Mrs. Conner let her polished fingernails rest briefly on his arm, calling him by his first name. But she was glancing about as though wondering what might happen next. Finally, when the chandelier swayed and tinkled over her head, she rose hastily with their plates, ignoring his explanation about the wind, of which, he confessed to himself, there was none. "Thanks for lunch, Dr. Vail," she said with conviction. "I've got to run. Maybe you'd like to visit me in my apartment sometime. It might be safer, in several ways."

He returned to work. By late afternoon the last of the lumber was up, and the crosspieces framed on the floor and ceiling. "That's that," he said out loud to the empty house. He swept the sawdust and shavings from the floor and replaced the rug and the furniture. He put away the tools and stood uncertainly, wondering what to do. He thought about checking the seismometer again, but imposed discipline on himself. He shouldn't be skittering down the basement a dozen times a day.

In the end he decided to visit Demming. Brioche needed exercise and he bridled her in the stall. Patient Brioche required no skill to ride and he mounted bareback, his long legs almost touching the ground. As he passed the playhouse he saw that a tree had gone down just off the trail: that must have been the sound he heard when talking with Dun in the backyard a few days before.

At the Demmings' changes were evident. The lawn needed to be cut. Leaves and branches littered the poolside and floated in the water. A telephone on a long white cord beside him, Fred sat in a wicker chair, hair matted, cheeks unshaved. He was pale, and his jowls and heavy lines seemed more pronounced. The eyeglasses hung down on his nose. Newspapers, magazines, plates of half-eaten food and crumpled blankets surrounded the chair.

"Have you moved out here?" Vail asked.

Demming shifted uncomfortably. "Inside, I'm reminded of Wende."

"Pool's still leaking," Vail said, trying to avoid the main issue. Studying the bottom, he saw small cracks.

"They've been here twice to fix it," Demming said. "Something about the pool bed."

They were silent until Vail finally asked, quite uselessly, "Where can Wende be?"

"They've got her," Demming said.

"Who?"

"Kidnapers. Police found her car."

"Where?"

"At the gas station. She was supposed to pick it up but never showed. That proves she's been kidnaped."

"But, Fred . . ."

"I've got the kidnapers figured," Demming said in a monotone. "They've spent time in prison. Time means nothing to them because they've learned how to wait. That's how they can pay us back, by making us wait, too, as they did. One of these days the phone will ring and a voice will tell me they've got Wende, a thick voice, full of controlled hate. The voice will say it represents some bunch that wants to help the people . . . yes, I can hear this voice, this self-proclaimed radical hero, the voice of an ex-con, who tells me he's got *my* wife, hidden and in Christ knows what shape—raped her a dozen times, taken her with a blindfold around her face to a trailer somewhere in the woods, forced her to talk on a tape recorder and now he'll play it to me, this voice says, if I care to listen—do I care to listen? this voice asks—and she tells me, in that cool, even voice of hers, using their own lingo (what else can she do?), that she's

201

safe, she's fine, that the group has a point, yes, we ought to redistribute the wealth, give ours to the people, that we have too much, and that I should do as they say, arrange to give several million to the goddam poor and a couple of hundred thousand to them, the kidnapers, as getaway money. So! I have to bargain, because I don't personally have several million dollars to give away. Besides, there's my company and my stockholders to think about. So I can't pay. What do I do? Oh, God, I wish I knew." His eyes, small behind the glasses, began to cry.

Shocked, Vail said softly, "But you don't know for certain she's been kidnapped, Fred."

"Of course. What else could it be?"

"I don't know. Accident, maybe."

Vail went home more depressed than ever. He was fixing himself a bit of dinner when he heard the crack of a stone against the house. The kids, it seemed, waited until dusk to resume the war against him so that they would not be seen by others. He decided they wanted to taunt him into battle—though why they failed to drive up right in front of the house was not clear. Fear of the law, he supposed. He closed the shutters on the front of the house. With the brace in the living room wall the stone house was like a beleaguered citadel.

Vail ate a skimpy dinner in the kitchen. The electric clock said 7:30. He fed the cat and the bird and tried playing a record but the needle stuck. He had decided to limit his inspections of the seismometer to twice a day, and was trying to wait until later when the phone rang.

"I've been trying to get you for the longest time but the line's been busy," she announced.

"I haven't been talking. It's still out of whack, Kay."

"I called Polly. Bill's unchanged, I know. And apparently no news on Wende yet."

"Fred's talked himself into believing she's been kidnaped."

"She hasn't been."

202

"You don't know that," he said reluctantly, fearing what might follow. "Maybe she'll call."

"She won't call," Kay said with bitter finality. "Harry, I'm coming home."

"No," he said, more sharply than he intended. "Stay there."

"Oh?" She sounded suspicious. "Somebody with you? Has Marjorie Conner moved in? She'd love to, I bet." She tried to laugh.

"Kay, stop it! It's nothing like that. I want you," he lied, "but you wouldn't like it here right now."

"I knew it! They're still there, aren't they? I can't leave you alone with *them* in the house. They might hurt you."

"Kay, Kay," he said sadly, "there's no *them*. Believe me. You've got to keep away from here."

"All right. But not for long." They were silent for a few seconds then. "Don't forget to feed the animals," Kay said in a low voice.

She had upset him; he had hoped that Boston would still her fantasies. He paced the room nervously and decided he couldn't wait; he went to the basement.

The seismometer had had a busy day: the needle recorded a dozen tremors, small but steadily increasing in magnitude. The earthquake was building up. His round eyes stole to the crack. Vail blinked. The crack had been active too. Sprouting like bamboo, it reached almost to the ceiling. He quailed. Would the scaffolding above suffice?

He went to the exercise room, stripped off his shorts, and worked out with the equipment, trying to divert the rush of his mind. Crack, slide, shift, thrust, rift, slip, slump, fissure, spout, slip-stick fault . . . Stop! He turned the sauna bath on high heat and stepped inside, still attempting not to think of quakes, but the seismological words poured out inside him like linguistic lava from a verbal volcano . . . graben, hoist, seiche, fenster, klippe. Again he tired to collect himself, reassure himself that

203

there would be no serious earthquake, no destruction of his house, no fall of red stones.

He was too hot now and decided to leave the sauna. As he touched the handleless door, he felt a quick, light, deceptively delicate motion—a tremor! He pushed against the door. It stuck. He pushed harder, but the door refused to budge.

Christ! He put his muscular shoulder into the effort, without result. He retreated to the opposite wall and charged, using his whole strength, but the chamber wasn't big enough to permit momentum. He struck the door futilely and fell to his knees.

The control was outside. Heat poured into the chamber, making his lungs recoil and his skin rebel. His mouth felt like a dry hole. Beneath him, a puddle formed on the floor as sweat flowed from his naked body. *Your heart will stop.*

He rose to his feet and pressed his face against the glass diamond on the door, peering outside through stinging eyes. If he could only be there, in the room where the cool air was, so disarmingly close. He stepped back and pounded the thick glass uselessly with his fists. He had become weaker already, and his heart raged in his fiery chest.

Somehow the tremor had slightly altered the hang of the door, enough to keep him inside to die by degrees. Suppose he came at it from a different direction, corresponding to the changed position of the door? He charged low, hit the door at a shallower angle, without result. Panicking, he flung himself against the unyielding cedar door again and again.

He lay on the wood slats gasping, blinded by sweat, his head and shoulders slippery against the door, strength draining out of him. He had a vision of his body melting in the heat, like a piece of lard in a frying pan, his corpse dripping between the slats: all they would find of him was a fatty pool, streaked with blood. . . . He was growing delirious, he realized, and tried to summon his reserves.

The solution came to him almost like a reflex. Lying down, he placed his feet against the opposite wall, and, straightening his knees, gave a powerful shove with his shoulders, his whole arched body behind the convulsive effort. The door snapped open.

He fell to the floor outside and lay for a few minutes, breathing in cool air. He got on his knees, then his feet, and turned off the sauna. He put a robe over his shivering body. The mirror showed his face bright red up to the hairline, with blue pouches below the eyes. He grimaced, showing square teeth. It might be irrational but he was angry. Bastard! Son of a bitch! he raged against the quake.

The tremor had registered on the seismometer. His eyes went automatically to the crack. Like an arrow from a bow, the shaking had sent the crack up the wall until it disappeared into the ceiling. He found the tip upstairs on the living room wall, just above the skirting.

As usual, the earthquake left its talismans. The arrowheads had fallen from the mantel, the bar cart had rolled from the wall. He restored order and then, mouth grim, face set, hands shoved deep into the pockets of his robe, he mounted the stairs to his room.

During the night he analyzed the problem in his sleep and woke on Tuesday with an answer, not much of an answer perhaps, but the only possible one. If it didn't work, at least he had done his best.

Kelly's theory of earthquakes explained them in terms of high pore pressure in rocks. The heavy rains, funneling into an old fault, had increased pore pressure to the point of inducing earthquakes, minor so far, but more powerful with each passing day. As he had suggested to Kelly, it might be possible to pacify the ground by lowering the pore pressure in the fault zone.

At 7:30 A.M. Vail picked up the phone. "Charley? Vail."

"You're up early, Doctor. What can I do for you?"

Vail glanced outside. It was drizzling and the cloud ceiling looked low enough to touch. "Bring your rig to my place this morning and dig me a hole, a deep hole.

The rigman sounded bewildered. "I don't get it. Why? Besides, Lechine's got me on a rush job today, taking soil samples for a new road."

"That can wait. Remember those cones we saw on the hillside near the old people's home?"

"Can I forget them?"

"They're here too now. Water pressure's building up and I'm worried about my house."

"You're the boss."

He went to work on the living room wall, hammering more nails into the lumber to strengthen the brace. About 9 A.M. Charley arrived in his truck with a helper. "There was a blue car parked by your drive," Charley reported. "As soon as we showed it took off." Vail nodded.

Charley said, "Where do you want the hole? We'll make a mess of your lawn," he warned after Vail had showed him a spot near the giant boulder. "How far down?"

"There's water trapped down there between layers of rocks. Drill until you hit it. Hopefully, it'll spew out like an artesian well."

Charley sniffed the unpleasant air. "What's that stink?"

"Cesspool's backing up. I can't get anybody to come drain it," he added. "Everything around the house is falling apart."

Vail went inside. What he had told Charley about the house was true: one by one, the dwelling's systems were showing signs of strain and failure. The phone was erratic, and so was the electricity, which failed more and more often. The tap water ran brown and had a sulphurous smell. He drank bottled water now from a case in the pantry.

It was pointless to check the seismometer—the lengthening

206

crack in the living room was proof enough that seismic activity continued.

Pum pum pum went Charley's drill rig in the backyard.

After several tries Vail reached Summerset Villa and, with difficulty, persuaded the receptionist to ring Robinson's room.

"What do you want this time?" the manager said irritably.

"Robinson, remember I talked of scaffolding for the back of the building? You should put it up without delay."

"Not without authorization from Summerset."

With all the urgency he could summon, Vail said, "You ought to have a plan for the evacuation of the building."

"You're crazy, Vail," Robinson said, and hung up.

"You're crazy, Vail," Lechine said angrily into the phone later. "What the hell are you doing with Charley? Send him back at once. I need him."

"I do too. He's got his rig operating in the backyard, trying to rid the ground of excess pressure."

"Why?"

"Because there are tremors happening here, that's why." Vail answered. "I've got a seismometer going in the basement to record them. It's been happening for days."

"Oh, I bet. The tremors must be caused by Charley's rig, that's all. Mrs. Conner told me she'd been there. She said it was strange, or you were. Strange isn't the word for it."

"Just because there hasn't been an earthquake in this area doesn't mean there can't be a first time," Vail said, angry too now. "How can I convince you, stubborn bastard?"

"You can't. You've turned into a kook right under my nose, Vail, and you know how I feel about kooks," Lechine said excitedly.

"You can't talk to me that way, Lechine. Fuck you. Get yourself a new partner," Vail said, slamming down the receiver.

He got himself under control and went to the backyard to

check on Charley's progress. "How's it going?" he called above the steady beat of the drill.

"Pretty slow. We're hitting rock."

"Keep it up."

"Sounds nutty to me," Charley muttered. He sniffed. "If we have to come back tomorrow, I'll bring a gas mask."

As he neared the house, Dun stepped from behind the barn. "Mr. Vail?" he called.

Vail stopped. "Well, Dun?"

The old man said nervously, "Mr. Vail, beg you to stop what you're doing in the backyard."

"Why?"

Dun shuffled his feet. "Reasons."

"They better be good," Vail snapped.

"Won't you take my word for it?"

"No."

Dun's face bunched in fury. "Listen, Mr. Vail, you've got no right."

"It's my land," Vail said.

"Only the top of it."

Vail guffawed. "Who owns the rest?"

"God," Dun said stiffly.

"You mean everywhere under the ground, or just here, right here?" Vail cried.

"Here," Dun admitted. "Where the Indians were. They believed God lived right under that big rock."

"You believe that, too?"

The smile Dun's weathered face attempted failed. "Not under the rock, no. But we accept the principle. This is sacred ground."

Vail sighed. "It's because of those noises, isn't it? Your religious views, I mean. Listen to me. The noises have nothing to do with a holy spirit. They can be explained. The ground noises originate because of small tremors—tiny earthquakes which we have here whether you believe it or not. Come down to the basement and I'll show you."

The old man's gaze wavered and returned to even keel. "Don't know what you're talking about. All I know is you're not supposed to offend this ground by digging deep holes." His voice sounded stronger. "Folks in the village are upset. Don't like what you do. Want you to stop. Mean it."

Vail tried again. "Can't I get you to see that the noises have nothing to do with God?"

"Get you to see they have?" Dun paused and added, "God don't like holes dug in Him." He kicked the ground and walked off.

That afternoon the machine in the basement reported a sharp increase in seismic activity. Vail finally decided to alert the public to the imminence of a major earthquake—or to try to.

He called a newspaper in Fall River and got the city desk. Patiently, he reported that an earthquake on Old Brompton peninsula was building toward a major event, "The tremors are technically called foreshocks. When their rhythm speeds up, it can mean that a large shock is impending. At least people ought to be warned." He cited his evidence.

"In this area? You've got to be kidding. What are your credentials, please?" Vail presented them: B.A. geology, Stanford; Ph.D. seismology, Cal Tech; former professor of seismology, Cal Tech; practicing geologist in Fall River. "A reporter will phone you shortly." There was no call back—he waited an hour and phoned again. "The editor is out."

He dialed another number. "Mrs. Conner—Marjorie? Has there been a call from the local paper?"

"Why, yes. A reporter called and talked to Mr. Lechine. Something about an earthquake. Something about you."

Then the name Kip Smith occurred to him—Kip Smith, the

disk jockey entrepreneur. He switched on the radio and, hearing Smith's voice, determined to drive to WROK, a few miles outside Old Brompton.

There was no receptionist. He opened a door and found himself staring at the bearded face that talked into a microphone behind a glass plate. Smith looked up, nodded, continued to talk, and finally waved Vail in. "If it isn't the geologist! Have a seat, Harry. Is it business or social?"

"Business, if you can call it that." Vail fidgeted. He wanted to be as convincing as possible and for this reason his explanation of the recent seismic activity was belabored. Several times Smith interrupted him with announcements and commercials.

"You mean a big earthquake, man?" Smith asked finally, smiling behind his beard. "Like in San Francisco?"

"Well, no, not that powerful. Still, there could be extensive shaking, buildings could collapse, people could be hurt or killed. People ought to be warned and told to go outdoors if the earthquake happens. You could do it over the radio."

"Hey, a freaky earthquake like that would be a real trip," Smith chanted. "Man, a big quake around *here* would just have to be the beginning of the end of the world, wouldn't it? All the kids think the world's going to end anyway. I do, too. It'll just fly into a million pieces and drift off into space. Groovy! Any special date for your big earthquake?" Vail shook his head wearily. "Soon, though, right?" Vail nodded and Smith pulled gleefully on his beard. "Are you sure?"

"I'm pretty sure about the earthquake. I don't know about the world ending," Vail said patiently.

"Oh, yeah, no other way. It's been coming for a long time— nobody knew how it would happen, that's all. And now we know, thanks to you. It'll start here, spread to New York, destroy the whole country and then the world will go down in ruins and flames. I can't wait, can you? It'll be a shake-up that would be remembered a long time if there was anybody left to remember it. Great! The kids'll eat it up. I'll put it out right now, if you want to stick around."

"No, thanks," Vail said despairingly.

In the early evening, stones from the road fell upon the house again. Vail closed the wooden shutters and locked the front door. He could picture Sam Wilbore out there in the dusk, leaning back, hurling his flat white stones, trying to lure his adversary into battle on Point Road. It wasn't going to work, and he wondered when the boys would change their tactics.

The little tremors arrived continually now, according to the seismograph and his own senses. He felt them in the balls of his feet, heard them in the rattling of glasses in the kitchen cupboard, the clanging of pots in the overhead rack, the rattle of the fireplace tongs, the brief bursts from the telephone, the erratic booming of Big Ben. Occasionally, too, he heard earthsounds, deep burping, belching noises, like the one he heard when he fell from the ladder and lay with his ear to the ground.

In the basement, Vail rummaged in the cartons until he found the old Hitachi tape recorder, which he took upstairs. The batteries were dead, and he used the ones in the flashlight. He wanted to record the earthsounds. He had started the machine when he heard a knocking at the front door which persisted.

"Who is it?" he cried.

"Me. Open up. Hurry." He unlocked the door and Kay entered carrying the sleeping boy, whom she passed to him. "I tried calling you, but no answer. I decided to come home tonight and here I am. Why are the shutters closed? Why was the door locked . . ." Her startled eyes saw the scaffolding. "What in the world?"

He pointed to the crack, which had risen halfway up the wall. "I'm bracing the building."

"Have you lost your marbles?"

"You're not the first who's asked me that today. I'll take

Mark up." He carried the boy up the staircase on his shoulder. The sleeping boy wore pajamas and a robe. Vail put him in the lower bunk.

"Poor darling," Kay said in a firmly controlled voice when he returned. "You shouldn't be terrified by that silly crack. Dun could have plastered it over in minutes. It's nothing to worry about. Tomorrow you'll remove the nasty wood. . . . Oh, Harry, those boys in the blue car, they're down at the end of the driveway. I heard them yelling at me. They're drinking and carrying on."

"Let them."

"No. I'm calling the police." She went resolutely to the phone and picked it up. "Harry, the phone's dead."

"Most of the time it doesn't work now."

"Harry, we're practically marooned." Her confidence seemed to falter as her eyes darted this way and that. "We ought to get out of here."

"No," he said.

"Harry, what's *that?*"

It was a sound like a hollow gong. "That's the ground—earth noises. It's because of the earthquake."

"What? I don't believe it."

"Quiet. Just listen."

He reversed the tape and played it.

"*God, we're practically marooned. We ought to get out of here.*"

"*No.*"

"*Harry, what's that?*"

"*That's the ground—earth noises. It's because of the earthquake.*"

"*What? I don't believe it.*"

"*Quiet. Just listen.*"

He switched the tape recorder off. "The machine didn't pick up the noise."

Her control seemed to vanish. "Of course it didn't. They don't let themselves be recorded. What do you think you're dealing with?"

"Natural phenomena."

"*Them*, I tell you!"

Vainly he tried to reason with her, but she was no more responsive than Dun had been. Her face was hard with fixed belief as she refused even to look at the seismometer.

She went upstairs before he did and he heard her shrill cry, like a trumpet blast. He ran to the bedroom to see her face stare wordlessly from the full-length mirror on the back of the closet door. Their reflections were separated by the break that cut the mirror in two.

In the morning Kay dropped a milk bottle on the kitchen floor. "God, I'm nervous. That's the last bottle and the milkman didn't show up." She lit a cigarette and breathed smoke.

"We'll have to make do," he said, mopping up. "Sit down. I'll fix breakfast."

He helped Mark dress. The child's face was pale and tired. Harry chucked him playfully under the chin. "Cheer up, honey."

Mark leaped and threw his arms around his father's neck. "Okay, Daddy." Through the bedroom window he saw the drilling rig, at which Charley and his man had just begun work. "What's *that?*" Mark cried excitedly.

"That's for making a hole in the ground."

Mark slithered from his arms and ran downstairs. "Mommy! Mommy!"

She was outside when he entered the kitchen. She came in and said drearily, "Now what?"

He knew how she would regard the explanation. "I'm trying to drain the ground. A lot of water is trapped there. That's what causes the tremors."

"Tremors," she said impatiently.

"Come look." He almost had to force her down to the basement. The seismometer had recorded something like thirty tremors during the night. "You can't argue with a seismometer," he said triumphantly, "can you?"

"*They* could do that," she screamed. "All they'd have to do is jiggle the needle."

Upstairs again, Kay sat at the butcher block table with coffee. "Please eat something," he urged. Kay hadn't touched her cereal.

She slid her wedding band up and down on her finger and stood. "I'm going to the village and call the phone company. Also, I'll talk to Mrs. Wilbore about her sons. We can do something about *that*, at least."

"Don't," he begged. "Those people are trouble."

"The villagers?" she said scornfully. "I'm going. Keep an eye on Mark."

He decided not to argue. Kay got along with Mrs. Wilbore after a fashion—the clan's grudge was against him.

As soon as she left he went to the crack, and when he saw its progress his mouth contracted. The thin waving line ran to the uppermost scaffolding and disappeared. He climbed the stairs to Mark's room and lifted the circus poster: the crack had slithered into the room like a snake.

He stood at the window studying the blue car at the end of the drive. It was positioned on the Fall River side of the road, which suggested that the boys might oppose an attempt to leave the peninsula. Mentally, Vail ransacked the house for materials which would serve as a brace for the wall in Mark's room but discovered nothing suitable. If only he hadn't lost part of his wood on the road. It was possible, he supposed, that the boys wanted to frighten, not hurt him, that the incident on the road would make them more cautious, that he could slip in and out of the square without suffering injury; and yet there was clearly an element of danger, too. Even as he thought, a piece of plaster

214

fell from the ceiling and landed at his feet. The house seemed to be disintegrating around him.

He waited downstairs for Kay, whose station wagon finally bounced down the drive. "It's the damnedest thing," she muttered, waving a cigarette. "Remember when you said somebody wanted to buy our house? Well, it's Mrs. Wilbore. She was as nice as she could be, and sympathetic too. She knows there are evil things here and has always known it. They all do. That's why the boys are there—to protect us if anything happens. The boys won't come on the property because they don't want to be rude. It isn't the boys who've thrown the stones—it's the evil spirits, just like I told you. They're Indian—this used to be their burial ground—and *very* resentful against whites. Mrs. Wilbore didn't want you to buy the house in the first place because of them, and she was angry with her sister for selling it because she knew that sooner or later we'd have trouble. She'll pay a fair price."

"Why does she want to buy it?"

"She believes the spirits bring bad luck and hurt the whole community. She says she'll turn the house into a kind of a shrine to the Indians and placate the spirits."

"You believed all that?"

"Of course. It makes perfect sense."

"Well, it accounts for what Dun said but the rest is crap. They want to buy the house and get me out of here before I report the earthquake and ruin their property values. That's the whole idea, I bet."

"Harry, I want to sell the house to her. Now, today!"

His mouth turned stubborn. "We're not selling, Kay, and that's that."

He gathered rope and tarp and placed them in the Rolls. He reached the road and turned toward the village with no more

215

than a brief glance at the waiting trio in the blue car. It started to move, following him at a discreet distance.

Firecrackers popped somewhere in the village as Vail left the car and entered the square. Tomorrow, he remembered, was the Fourth of July. There was no sign of the blue car yet. He carried the first load of creosote-stained lumber and dumped it by the road. He raised his head warily and wondered where the youths were. Then the first stone hit the lumber, just missing his head. It dropped to the ground, a familiar flat white stone. He ducked behind the woodpile and glanced about. The popping of fire-crackers had ceased; the village was silent.

Another stone landed some distance away but the next pinged into the wood close to him. He had picked the wrong side of the woodpile, and Sam Wilbore threw with frightening accuracy. From the woodpile, Vail scuttled on his hands and knees to a scrapped car. He glanced up in time to see Sam Wilbore bend and heave from the old cannon.

This was no game—they wanted to kill him. The car shielded him from Cy Wilbore's missiles, but a stone banged viciously into it near where he crouched. He spotted the other two boys at different points in the square, arms back, ready to throw. He was pinned and had nothing with which to return the fire.

He ran again, ducking behind a pile of drums, but a stone caught him painfully in the calf. He looked toward the end of the square and saw a knot of villagers watching, making no move toward his assistance, like spectators at an execution. Dun was not among them. Vail moved behind some fish netting, but a stone got through, striking him in the stomach, almost knocking out his wind. He returned to the metal drums, which boomed hollowly as stones landed. He had to find a better cover and ran to the carcass of a boat. Stones flew from every direction, pounding on the old wood, splintering it. Vail was becoming desperate; he was afraid to make a run for it—if he was struck on the head he would fall, and that would be fatal—yet he could not remain where he was, crouching behind a boat while the boys, finding the range, zeroed in.

His eyes scoured the square and saw at last the battered lid of a garbage can. He ran for it in a hail of stones, scooping it off the ground, raising it as a shield into which a missile, aimed for his head, clanked harmlessly. He clung to the lid, which wrenched at his wrist as stones landed, and began to back from the square, watching for stones, catching them on his shield. He stumbled and, lowering the lid for an instant, took a stone on the muscle of his arm. Then he was back in his car as a stone smashed the rear window.

Vail drove off hurriedly, leaving the wood behind. Through the side mirror he saw the blue car gun down the road in pursuit. He tore around the square and had just reached Point Road when the steering wheel became stiff and useless in his hands. He hung on as the Rolls veered. Then it was over and the Rolls steered normally. He looked in the mirror again, in time to see the blue car twist sharply, slam into the square, and overturn.

He stopped and sat behind the wheel, breathing deeply, trying to grasp what had just happened. Wilbore's car had gone out of control at the same moment his own refused to respond. Whatever gripped one car had also gripped the other—a tremor! Saved by the quake, he thought grimly, and turned the Rolls around.

He approached cautiously, torn between a vague compassion and the angry hope that the boys had been hurt. Sam Wilbore and Bill Pabodie stood dumbly, staring from blank eyes. Cy Wilbore's head was crushed against the bloody windshield.

Vail heard running, Mrs. Wilbore's scream, his own name shouted, saw the menace in the faces of the arriving villagers, felt the hand grasp his sore arm. "Go, son," Dun said. "Quick."

The tremor he felt on Point Road had been the most intense yet. "Look what they've done!" Kay screamed at him before he

217

could tell her about the accident. A crack ran down the picture window of her studio. "Look!"

He inspected the damage solemnly. "We've had an earthquake. Didn't you feel it?"

"No," Kay shouted.

He turned to Mark, who stood there, hands slack at his sides. "Mark, did the ground shake?" The boy's lips moved but nothing came out. "Scared, huh?" He picked him up and squeezed him. "Kay, take him away from the house for a while. Walk over and see how Demming is. Okay, honey?"

"Yes," she said. "Come, Mark."

Charley had stopped drilling. Vail walked to the rig where it stood near the giant boulder. "Ground shook a little while back —we're checking the equipment. Wonder what caused it."

"It *was* an earthquake."

"Golly, never heard of a quake in these parts. Could the drilling have caused it?"

"No, but if you hit water in time it might stop a bigger one."

"Well, we're getting there. Look!" From the hole in which the drill was inserted water gushed slowly.

Vail said, "Good."

"Should hit tomorrow—no, tomorrow's the Fourth. Friday then."

"Everything's okay," Charley's helper called.

Pum pum pum went the drill. It seemed to convey a certain haste.

Vail went to the phone to call Kelly, but the line was still dead. Anyway, what could Kelly do to help at this stage? In the barn he found a few wood slats that he hammered to the wall in Mark's room, without optimism—even the heavy bracing below had failed to halt the crack's advance, and it seemed inevitable that the two cracks would unite.

Back in the studio, Vail morosely studied the broken picture

218

window, wondering if he should remove the glass before the earthquake did it for him. Wait, he concluded—perhaps the previous tremor would prove to be the worst. Staring out the window, he noticed then that the configuration of the hillside below the giant boulder appeared to have changed.

Reaching the hill, Vail saw that a small landslide had occurred at the base of the rock. A pile of mud had slipped, revealing more of the boulder. But not until Vail reached the slide did he notice the outcropping of freshly exposed rock—not the gray of granite, but the red of the rock of his own house.

At the same moment, in utter astonishment, he saw the graveyard that lay in the depression left by the mud. Five gravestones had been revealed. Four were covered with strange, almost grotesque whorls, but the fifth was plain, lighter in color, and seemed almost new. Under the gravestones appeared bits of bone, but before the new one a skull grinned brightly.

Vail clambered into the pit and emerged with the skull, which he held in his hand and studied. It had belonged, he surmised, to a small adult, probably a woman, who he was inclined to think had died in an accident, for the top of the skull looked crushed, as though by a heavy blow. Vail heard a movement and turned to find Dun standing beside him.

The gray eyes looked sorrowful. Dun mumbled, "Told them Wilbores trouble would come."

"You understand I had nothing to do with Wilbore's death? He is dead, isn't he?"

The old man nodded. "Instant. It was . . . well, you don't truck with our views, but God made the land to shake and He killed young Wilbore because he was trying to kill you. God's will and punishment was that young Wilbore should die."

"Why did they want to kill me?"

Dun blurted out, "Afraid that you, messing around with that rig of yours, would find that." He pointed to the graveyard.

Vail said, "The drilling may have loosened the hill, but the tremor was responsible for the slippage." He too was silent before he asked, "Why were they so frightened?"

On Dun's open face conflict was hard to conceal. He paused and said, "Guess you've got some answers coming. Told you there was an Indian graveyard here?" Vail nodded. "God, you see, lived under the ground and the Indians worshiped Him, and then the settlers did, or some of them. They're the ones who stayed. About a hundred years ago, guess it was, God got mad. Used to be another stone house here, before yours, but when God made the ground shake it fell into smithereens. Stones are part of a fence somewhere around, I guess. Well, a Wilbore man, farmer he was, built a new one and used up all the red stones left in the quarry. . . ."

"Quarry?" Vail asked, glancing at the outcropping of red stone.

"There." Dun pointed to the pit. "Folks here didn't want anybody to know. Figured people would blame an earthquake, just like you do. And it was a limited step God took—a warning. Ground shook here, and only here. So they decided to keep it secret, because He was *their* God, and they—we—His chosen people, and only they knew that God had shaken the ground. They burned some records . . ."

"So," Vail muttered.

". . . and nobody was supposed to sell their property to newcomers who'd find out, and especially not to sell this house where God lives underneath and sometimes makes Himself felt. The people were told that if they sold houses close by to the village they'd be killed. But a few houses were sold. Result's what you see in the graveyard." Dun took a deep breath.

Vail held up the skull. "This isn't all that old."

Dun's silence seemed interminable. Finally he said, "That was Miss Wilbore, who sold you this house. She was lonely and wanted to clear out."

"What happened to her?"

Something in Dun's face told Vail that the old man had wanted to unburden himself. He said rapidly, "Wilbores dropped a stone on her."

Vail gasped. "They did that?"

"Yes—and today Cy got his punishment. He deserved it. God forgave the Wilbores once, but not twice."

"So they put the bodies of those they executed here and covered them over?"

"That's right," Dun said. The barriers were down. "Oldest one's been here about a century. Hadn't been a killing for years before Miss Wilbore—people forgot how to carve the gravestone."

"How could they be sure nobody would find the graveyard?"

"Couldn't. Kept watch on it. Came through the woods. But never actually set foot on the sacred ground—your property. Only the Archdeacon, me now, can do that."

So Pollidor had been right—the villagers had been prowling the woods. "They didn't fully trust you," Vail suggested.

"Maybe not. Especially after Mrs. Wilbore killed her sister-in-law, or her sons did. Knew I didn't like that."

"What did they do with Miss Wilbore's money, after they'd killed her? I assume they got it."

"Yes. Well, hope was to buy the house back from you. From the common fund. We pool our money, you see. Keeps me poor, the rest are so lazy."

Vail's head was ablaze with questions. "Dun, why didn't you just clear out of here?"

Dun lowered his eyes. He said uncertainly, "Guess I believe what the others do. We're waiting for a sign from the Lord that we can sell our property and go. Besides, they would have killed me too. They'd kill me now if they knew what I'd told you, Mr. Vail. But, see, kind of look at you as a son. Don't want anything happening to you."

"Seems to me, Dun, that there's a certain confusion between religion and property values in your village. Why won't you believe me when I tell you that earthquakes, not God, are responsible for the action under the ground?"

Dun said quietly, "It's my faith."

In the house, analyzing Dun's revelations, he heard the scream. Fool, he accused himself; he should never have let Kay see the graveyard. He'd forgotten her.

Crying, she permitted herself to be led inside, Mark whimpering behind her. "It's all right, Mark," he told the boy again. "Go watch TV."

He tried to hold Kay but she shook free, saying, "Jeff's at Polly's."

"Could he give any information on Wende?"

"He hardly mentioned her. He insists she's gone to the Caribbean or somewhere and forgot to leave a note."

Every so often a little tremor shook the house. In the kitchen the dishes, glasses and pots rattled as he tried to coax a light supper down his family, without success. Mark sucked on his thumb while Kay smoked cigarettes. Judy sat in the corner and howled.

"I can't stand it. Get that cat out of here," she begged.

The cat clawed him painfully when he reached for it, then fled from the room, tail up.

Blood oozed from the back of his hand and at the sight, Kay covered her eyes. The lights flickered and he said uneasily, "The power might go out."

Mark cried, "Mommy! Daddy! Let me sleep with you, please! I'm scared!"

"We'd better let him sleep with us," Harry said, wiping his hand with a paper napkin. He heard a gust of wind and added, "Maybe it would be better if we all sleep in the living room."

"You won't agree to leave?" Kay asked. She looked at his face

222

and said, "All right, the living room. Get Mark's stuff and bring me a blanket. I'm cold."

In Mark's room, Vail eyed the advancing crack with hatred, then came downstairs with pajamas, blankets and a small mattress from one of the bunks.

The lights flickered, dimmed and went out with a certain finality. Kay moaned.

"I'll get the flashlight." It wouldn't work. "I put the batteries in the tape recorder. I'll get candles."

"Harry. Don't leave me alone," she whispered. She tucked the blanket around her.

He knew the house so well that he moved in the dark with the confidence of a blind person in familiar surroundings. He took the candles from the French chest in the dining room and went to the kitchen for Kay's matches. He returned with the lighted candles, placing them on the coffee table. The candlelight flickered on the scaffolding, which looked huge and ominous. "Who'd have thought we'd end like this—refugees in our own living room," Kay said.

Putting the batteries from the tape recorder back into the flashlight, he answered, "We ought to go to sleep early tonight. God knows what will happen tomorrow."

She lay on her back on a couch, staring up. "Sleep! You expect me to sleep. *Look.*"

The shadow of the brass birdcage began to sway slowly. At the same time, he felt the vibration through the legs of his chair. "Another tremor," he said hastily.

"Tremor! I felt nothing. And what's that?"

He heard a metallic scratching and a faint cry, nearby yet distant. "An owl," he said tentatively.

"*Ooooowell?* Since when do owls scratch?"

"Not an owl then. Something perfectly normal though, I tell you."

She glanced at him sharply. "I heard another noise. Like a footfall."

"The building creaked. It's the wind."

"Are you certain?"

"Yes."

The next tremor was the largest yet. The house groaned and Big Ben chimed once and stopped. She cried, "Did you hear that?"

"Kay," he said softly, touching the wet fingers that covered her eyes, "can't I make you believe . . ."

The hollow noise sounded again. Kay sprang into his arms like a frightened child. "Help me. Help me." Her damp cheek pressed against his.

The high-pitched sound seemed to circle the room. "I don't understand," he murmured.

Gradually her thin body relaxed and her breathing slowed. "Harry," she muttered, "it's over. They've gone. At least for tonight."

It was true that the tremors seemed to have ceased, and so had the mysterious noise. For good, he hoped. "Poor Kay, poor Kay," he murmured, stroking the fine hair of his sleeping wife.

He put a blanket over her and, flashlight in hand, explored the house, running the beam over the walls. In his study the beam passed an open place over the bookcase and rapidly returned.

The grate of the heating duct over the shelves had fallen during the shaking. It lay on the floor. He climbed up the bookcase and called into the duct, "Judy, come here."

As he listened to the cat's claws scraping tin, he wondered why he hadn't thought of it before. Terrified by the shaking, Judy had sought refuge in the hole before the lights went out, jumping from the chair to the bookcase and into the opening. Then, confused by the darkness and tremors, she had lost her way in the ducts. "Ghosts!" Vail said contemptuously as the cat's head appeared in the aperture. Judy yawned.

Vail descended to the basement, pulled up a box to sit on, and shone the light on the slowly turning drum. The smoked paper showed that there had been literally dozens of tiny earthquakes that evening, but now the needle ran straight. It continued to do so as he kept his vigil.

At last the earthquake swarm had stopped and the earth lay in stillness. Perhaps the tension in the fault had been eliminated by the steady movement of the rock; perhaps the earth was exhausted. Vail switched off the machine, placed the geophones inside the aluminum case, and closed it. He was not sure why, but the precaution seemed sensible.

PART SEVEN

QUAKE

Thursday, the Fourth of July A loud noise startled Vail from a dream. Kay stirred on the couch, and Mark breathed lightly on the floor. He had slept in his clothes and, rising, went to the kitchen. The power was still off. Daylight glowed, but if the sun was up a heavy mist obscured it. He did not know the time.

The noise seemed to have come from the sea's direction and resembled a load of gravel being dumped from a truck. He retrieved his shoes from the living room and started down the mist-arched path. Crossing Torturous Creek, he lost his footing on the stones and stepped into ankle-deep water that was almost hot.

Long before he reached the rock chair by the sea he heard the ocean and looked out at surf higher than he remembered having seen on his shore. Dead fish littered an exposed slice of beach. Through the fog billows above came the squawk of gulls in a great squadron headed inland.

Vail walked back to the house, still unable to account for the noise. The mist had lifted enough to allow him to see the stealthy shapes emerging from the wood: deer, rabbits, pheasants, skunk, badgers—animals usually invisible, moving rapidly away from the sea, oblivious to him. From the fog-fingered pond fish leaped again and again, as though desperate to join the swans whose clamorous wings announced their departure. *They know, they know*, he thought.

When he recrossed the creek, Vail understood that he had not missed his footing as he supposed. Where land should have been there was water instead, and he had stepped into it. The sound he had heard in his sleep was the clatter of pebbles as the creek abruptly shifted its course.

He remembered then his dream. Kay had sketched a kind of composite of the people around him: Pollidor's eggshell head, Polly's forehead bisected by the frown line, Dun's keen gray eyes, Demming's thin lips opening into Jeff's affected smile which revealed the two neat rows of Robinson's false teeth. Wende's clear skin cracking into Alma Benjamin's wrinkles. Only it wasn't a drawing any more but a head of stone that began to break into pieces. . . . Suddenly he feared for the residents in the cheaply constructed building on the unstable hillside. He ran.

He shook her awake. "Kay!"

"Mmmmm." She blinked. "What?"

"Take Mark and go outside. Understand?"

Eyes groggy, she sat up. "Why?"

"An earthquake's starting—a big one."

"Go away, Harry." She lay down again and pulled the blanket over her head.

He ripped it off. "I mean it. Go outside."

"All right, all right."

He should have stayed until he was certain that she got up, he thought as the Rolls pounded down the driveway. The clock on the dashboard said 6:45. He hit the brakes as the Rolls reached an ugly gash that stretched across the road. The simple break in the pavement had revealed its true nature. It was a fissure about six inches wide. The car bounced over it.

The fog vanished as he moved away from the sea. There was no traffic this early, and he drove rapidly under cloudy skies. Seeing the pay phone at the gas station, he was tempted to stop and call Kelly but decided to wait until he had completed his mission.

The crack in the road before Summerset Villa was fissurous, too, like the one at his house. He had been right, then, about the line of fault. Climbing the hill, he saw a sight that under any other circumstances would have impelled him to stop. The cones running down the slope had grown, and each spouted a plume of water. From the hole on top came a mighty gush, perhaps twenty feet in the air, like an arcane symbol.

In the lobby he found a throng of old people in bathrobes, pajamas and slippers. Their uncertain faces stared anxiously through the glass portals. Alma Benjamin rushed up to him.

"Dr. Vail! How glad I am to see you! Something's terribly wrong. Cracks have appeared all over the building, and often we feel vibrations. Look!" Over the reception desk a crack appeared in the ceiling; a piece of plaster fell, sending up a white puff as it hit the floor. A frightened murmur rose in the room. "What'll we do? I tried to wake Mr. Robinson but failed. And the phones are dead."

"Get everybody outside. Stay well clear of the building, to the side of it in case the structure slides. You'll be all right. Don't leave anybody here."

"What about Mr. Robinson?"

Vail shrugged and Mrs. Benjamin's smile was slightly sinister. He bent and kissed her. "Hurry."

"Dr. Vail," she called. She handed him a paper bag. "Your socks. I hope you like them."

He raced back toward the peninsula. He switched on WROK for news, but the station had no signal. The filling station was closed, but he stopped to call Kelly. The pay phone proved to be out of order. He thought briefly about driving to Fall River to tell the police but decided too much time would be lost. Besides, it was a fair assumption that the police would ignore him because the tremors would not be felt in Fall River unless a grand-scale earthquake developed. In that case, Lamont-Doherty would pick up the tremors at once.

Driving off, he saw Wende's cream-colored Mercedes parked in back of the station.

As Vail neared his house he encountered fog again. The fissure had widened, and the Rolls navigated it at the cost of what sounded like a broken spring and shock absorber. The car limped past the fallen mailbox and down the potted drive. He found Kay in the kitchen trying to make Mark eat. Cracks ran over the ceiling, and a seam had opened in the terra-cotta floor.

"Kay!" He felt a small tremor, quick and determined. "Go outside!"

"Oh, no," she said sounding dazed, "there's no reason. They don't come out this early."

"Kay!"

Mark pulled his thumb from his mouth and cried clearly, "Daddy's right! Let's go outside, Mommy, please! Come!" The boy seized her hand.

Her bewildered face looked back and forth at them; then Kay lowered her head on the butcher block table and sobbed.

"Where's Judy?" Harry shouted.

"She's here, Daddy, under the table," Mark said.

The animal stood stiff-legged. He grabbed it and they went outside. On the lawn, as on the hillside at Summerset Villa, squat cones ejected plumes of water. Then, with a rumble, the ground above the cesspool burst open, spewing a brownish geyser that smelled sulphurous and fecal.

"It's hell. We're in hell," Kay cried. The studio's picture window suddenly shattered and fell to the ground.

"Get up on the boulder," he yelled at her.

"Wait." She seemed to listen, and he heard it too. "Brioche

is trying to get out." She raced to the barn and returned with the terrified mare, which trembled and foamed at the mouth. "There, there," Kay said, trying to soothe her.

"I'm going to the Demmings'," he said. He thought about riding Brioche but decided the horse was too agitated. "I'll be right back. Get on the rock." He set off on the trail at a run, passing between the boulder and the black elm, whose list was obvious now. He took the creek in a leap and stumbled down the path and thrashed through the thick bushes until he came upon the fallen tree he had observed a few days before. The fog opened momentarily: he looked down, gasped, recoiled.

He saw the face of Wende Demming shrouded in the haze, her body pinioned by the fallen tree. She had been there a week, he knew with dreadful certainty. He went to the playhouse and leaned against it, unable to continue. On the night Jeff left she must have wandered out to the playhouse, the scene of her tryst, and the tree, weakened by the windstorm, had crushed her, and nobody saw her where she lay, off the trail. In death she reminded him once again of the other, the nameless one, the pale face lying beneath another tree, long ago. "She's come back. Returned after all these years. Soon she'll get up, and when spring comes we'll go to the Denali Fault as we planned. We'll bring a tent and tell the conductor to stop the train where we want to get off—that's how they do it there—and backpack our stuff to the fault. It'll be terrific camping out. Wonderful wild berries grow, they say, and the water's so pure it's as if the good Lord poured it. . . ."

A voice was speaking, a deep voice, which only after a few moments did he recognize as his own. Harry, he pleaded with himself, hang on.

Knees shaking, he proceeded down the path and reached Demming's lawn, bright green beneath the mist. "Fred! Fred!" he shouted at the silent house. Then he saw the thick eyeglasses that lay shattered on the cement deck by the wicker chair.

Through a foot-wide crack the water had emptied from the pool as though a bathtub drain had opened. On the hard bottom lay the crumpled shape of Fred Demming. The position of the limbs, the condition of the head, left no doubt that Demming was dead.

Vail found himself on the path again, brain reeling. In the tremor Fred must have dropped his glasses, groped for them in the fog, come too close to the empty pool. There was nothing that could be done for him now.

Long before he reached the Pollidors', Vail heard the mocking shriek of the burglar alarm and, seeing the house, felt certain that Polly was dead, too. The chimney had collapsed, taking with it the roof and the large glass window. He stepped into the debris. The front panel of Pollidor's computer bar had fallen off, revealing broken glass and twisted gadgetry. Polly sat on the floor, speechless, clasping her knees. The frown line on her forehead looked engraved. The alarm continued its incessant trill.

"Polly," Vail commanded, "come." She followed dumbly.

When they were out of the ruins he asked, "Where's Jeff?"

"Down on the beach with a movie camera," she was able to report.

Seeing them from the top of the boulder, Kay ran down to help.

"You poor dear!"

Together they pulled Polly to the flat top of the rock, where she sat speechless, hands clasping her knees.

"Look!" Kay cried as the boulder shuddered. Chimney stones were falling and the TV antenna went with them. A sharp metallic snap rang from the Rolls Royce, whose front end sagged as though the car had lost its spirit. The elm tree groaned.

"I'm going to the village. Keep everybody on the rock—don't go back in the house," Harry yelled at Kay as he ran toward Brioche. She had tied the horse to a pole of the clothes line. When he approached, the mare shied and reared, flailing out

234

with her front hooves. Harry seized the reins and mounted, hoping he was too big for Brioche to throw.

Horse and rider moved across open fields, around low stone fences, until the village came in sight. Vail was about to dismount by the church when he saw that the beach seemed abnormally large. A man stood on the pier with a movie camera. He rode over and shouted, "Jeff! Get away!"

Carmichael lowered the camera and turned. "If it isn't the apocalyptic geologist. What's up, Harry?" He smiled briefly.

The water had drawn back as though the sea were curling its lips. "Jeff! The water will return. There will be a big wave. Leave the pier or you'll drown."

"Expecting a tidal wave?" Jeff asked sardonically. "That's low tide."

"It isn't low tide. That's because of a quake at sea—a seaquake. The water will rush back, I tell you."

Jeff grinned. "Oh, come on. Say, this is my first earthquake. I rather like the little tremors. Think a building might fall down?" he asked with a face that hoped one would.

"Listen to me, Jeff," Vail pleaded as he turned the horse.

Inside the church, Cy Wilbore's body lay in an open coffin in front of the low altar. The congregation sang:

> While I draw this fleeting breath,
> When my eyes shall close in death,
> When I rise to worlds unknown,
> And behold thee on thy throne,
> Rock of Ages, cleft to me,
> Let me hide myself in thee. A-men.

Dun, in his russet cassock, chanted from the pulpit:

God is our refuge and strength, a very present
help in trouble.
Therefore we will not fear, though the earth be

removed, and though the mountains be carried into the midst
of the sea;
though the waters thereof roar and be troubled,
though the mountains shake with the swelling thereof.
Selah.
The heathen raged, the kingdoms were removed, he uttered
his voice, the earth melted.
The Lord of hosts is with us . . .

They were trying to propitiate the earthgod just as they must
have been in the Saturday "memorial service"—was that only a
few weeks ago? Vail could wait no longer.

"Dun!" he cried, waving his hands. "You've got to leave the
church. Take your people and go to the cliffs. A big wave is
coming and the village may be washed away."

The church creaked and trembled, as though underscoring
Vail's words.

Mrs. Wilbore screamed, "The earthgod will save us." She
pointed at Vail. "Kill him. The stone! The stone!"

"Your God will not be placated!" Vail shouted. "This is an
earthquake. It may get worse. Go to the cliffs, I tell you!"

The congregation parted, and Sam Wilbore came toward him
carrying a heavy stone from the altar, other parishioners behind
him. He raised the stone over his head, glaring at Vail.

"Wait!" Vail said in a loud voice. "Don't you see? If your
earthgod is angry with you and shakes the ground, shouldn't
Cy Wilbore's death be enough of a sacrifice for you to make?
And if He isn't propitiated, wouldn't He be an evil God, who
wants to hurt you? If He wishes you harm, how can He be your
buckler, your rock? How can He give you confidence and seren-
ity? Therefore, either your God deserves hating, not worship, for
He is the Devil, or this is an earthquake and your God has nothing to do with it. Flee!"

"Mr. Vail is right!" Dun roared. "His words are sound. The

earthgod, if that is what He truly is, will not be stilled. He will not save us. I sense the truth through the very wood of the pulpit. There is danger in Shonkawa Village. Brethren, let us take refuge on the cliffs." He removed his surplice, dropped it on the floor, and started out.

"Never!" cried Mrs. Wilbore. "We stay in church with our God. He will protect us."

Looking back, Vail saw Mrs. Wilbore, Sam, Bill Pabodie and a few others by the open coffin.

He returned by a different route, passing the pond, whose water had left its banks on the side of the ocean—a seiche was starting. When the water came back it would overflow its banks on the side of the house, and if that were accompanied by a seismic ocean wave . . . He refused to think further and pounded the horse with his heels.

Reaching the backyard, he saw that Kay and Mark had left the rock. At the same moment, the ground gave a violent lurch and Charley's drill rig toppled over. A silvery jet of water rose thirty feet in the air. The steaming water was boiling hot. On a branch of the elm, the clay bell clanked furiously.

"Where?" Vail yelled as he slid from the horse.

Polly pointed mutely to the house.

Hurriedly he entered the kitchen. The crack in the terra-cotta floor cut the kitchen in two. The butcher block table quivered on its heavy legs and disintegrated as it hit the floor with a loud crash. The refrigerator flew open and vomited its contents.

As he ran into the dining room the chandelier tinkled in the quick, hard tremors and smashed on the table, showering glass. The heavy chest rocked and crashed. All over the house objects fell, windows broke, doors slammed. He entered the living room. The door to the record cabinet seemed almost to have been lying in wait. It sprang out, hitting him painfully in the shoulder. The noise was intense: fireplace tools jiggled, tuning fork hummed, piano rumbled, Big Ben boomed incessantly. From the birdcage, green wings beating uselessly, the finch emitted a penetrating screech.

Kay cowered behind a couch, clutching the boy. The floor rippled as he tried to cross it and he almost fell. "Look out!" Kay called. He whirled in time to see the bar cart ponderously bearing down on him on its weaving wheels, bottles and glasses clinking. He jumped and turned. The heavy cart rolled across the room, then as the floor canted again, reversed itself and lumbered toward him once more. He seized the cart and hurled it at the wall, where it collapsed into a pile of bent wheels, twisted metal, and broken glass.

He recrossed the room. A large piece of plaster dropped from the ceiling, striking him on the back, and, staggering, he fell against the wall. Part of the scaffolding dropped and rapped him behind the ear.

Dazed, he knelt in terrified paralysis, unable to move, he on his island of floor, they on theirs, as the house rocked in its misery. Arrowheads flew from the mantel, pictures from the wall. A pipe burst in the ceiling and brown water poured down. The scaffolding abruptly collapsed to reveal the full extent of the crack, through which daylight showed. *Bong, bong, bong, bong,* sounded the clock.

And above it all he could hear Kay's thin, monotonous cry, "Harry-Harry-help-help-Harry-Harry-help-help-HARRY-HELP-HELP-HARRRRRIIIIIE . . ."

No! He struggled to his feet, started to fall again as a convulsive tremor struck, but made himself move across the tossing room to his wife and child. "Come on!"

Kay stood. Mark cried, "The bird!"

"He ran in to get it. I followed him," she screeched.

He carried Mark and Kay to the birdcage. "Go to the rock," he told her when they staggered outside.

Somehow he made his way back through the kitchen, ducking a jet of steaming water and a falling beam. The staircase to the

238

basement shuddered violently as he descended, snatched the seismometer from the floor, and raced back up again. Just as he reached the top the stairs collapse behind him, and he clawed his way through the door, lugging his burden, fighting his way out of the disintegrating house.

They watched the rest from the shivering boulder. The tremors came rapidly now, one after the next like birthpains, as the earth strained to release the pressure inside. Vail, counting the shocks, realized that the main paroxysm was at hand, but even so he was unprepared for its severity and brute energy. This was the dark side of the earth that he feared and admired, the pent-up fury wracking the ground, the anger in the core. The earth wasn't made for living things, he thought, but rather the shapes and forms of life—elemental, on its own—had to find their place upon it and, in the last reckoning, take it as it came, survive the vicissitudes that were visited, endure. That great ball hurtling through space was not a haven built by God, but an impersonal sphere whose workings might be discovered but never changed, whose mysteries, laid bare, only revealed more mysteries without end, whose purpose was precisely no purpose as humans understood the term, whose meaning was no meaning except existence itself. And that existence had to be clung to, even as they clung now to the rock, solid yet shaking.

From the cornfield a deep rustle sounded although there was no wind, and the ground seemed to ripple as the earthwave passed through, bouncing the surface, sending fenceposts into the air, leaving a pile of broken machinery that had been a Rolls Royce. The clay bell tolled incessantly and suddenly shattered as the elm tree tottered and swayed until, with a wooden groan, branches waving, it crashed on the barn, leaving the building in splinters. Piece by piece, the quake was destroying the stable structure of their life, and now the house itself began to rumble in protest—or was it relief that its agony was almost ended?—as great cracks appeared in the heavy walls. What remained of the chimney crashed through the roof, red stones fell down in a shower of shingles, beams broke, the cupola housing the elliptical wooden stairway collapsed, the second story became the first, red rocks rained until nothing remained but a pile of debris and a cloud of dust that hovered over it.

The mist had cleared somewhat. From above came a vast noise, like a cosmic grunt of satisfaction. He would never be certain—Kay, comforting Mark, could not confirm the sight—but in the sky he saw, or thought he saw, bright flashes that flickered and died.

The earth was still under advancing water.

On the rock they were silent in awe, and then Kay muttered, "So that was an earthquake. Jesus."

"That was an earthquake," he said.

"To think I believed all that crap about ghosts. It was unforgivable of me. I failed you and I'm sorry." Her eyes were clear and sharp.

"I almost failed you, too. I came close to panic in there," he said.

"But you didn't panic," she said gratefully. She looked at the masonry that rose from the flood. "Well, what now? Rebuild? Start over?"

"I don't think so," he said slowly. "I doubt if our insurance covers earthquakes. We've had it here. Kay, I want to go back into seismology. If I work at Lamont, we can live in New York."

"Civilization! Maybe I could do something useful there, like teach school. Mark's old enough for me to work, aren't you, honey?"

Mark said proudly, "Next year I'll be in second grade."

Kay sighed and glanced at Polly's sightless eyes. As if she had been avoiding the question, she asked softly, "What about the others?"

"Some of the villagers died, I think," he said. "Wende's dead, Fred's dead, and Jeff, probably."

"Oh, God." Kay permitted herself a tiny tear. "Just think—our whole world in pieces, just like that. You were right, but nobody listened. How different it would be if they had."

"I wonder," he said somberly. "The thing is . . ."

"What?"

"Well, what happened to our friends was exactly what you said would happen. I can't account for that. Can you?"

Kay picked up the cat and stroked it. "Look," she said, "there's a helicopter."

EPILOGUE

At Lamont-Doherty the graduate student had duty on the Fourth of July. Shortly after 8 A.M., a few minutes late, he unlocked the building and went upstairs, yawning. He reached the bank of instruments, glanced down, and did a double take. On the never-sleeping seismometers the pens were writing furiously, scratching large arcs.

The student quickly determined that the tremor had been picked up first by the seismic station at New London, Connecticut, then by other seismometers farther and farther west on the twenty-station network. Other tremors, though smaller, had preceded this one.

On weekends and holidays one telephone line at the switchboard was left open. The boy read a number on the wall, raised the phone and dialed.

"Dr. Kelly? This is Sheel."

"Sheel?" said the sleepy voice.

"Sheel, at Lamont. Sorry for waking you, but there's just been an earthquake, a sizable one, in New England," the student said excitedly.

Kelly's voice rose. "Where in New England?"

"Well, it's east of the seismic network, which would put it at sea or possibly Cape Cod or Rhode Island."

"Can you estimate its size?"

"I'd say magnitude four—or bigger. The pens have jumped off scale."

"Good God! I'll be right over. Locate it precisely, will you? Oh, notify Gold."

The graduate student phoned Gold, like Kelly a senior seismologist, and could not resist alerting several fellow students too. Then, hurriedly, he triangulated reports from three seismic stations to find the focus of the quake. The job took fifteen minutes. He had just finished when Kelly ran in the door.

"Got it?" the seismologist asked.

"Within about ten miles. It's northeast of Newport." He showed Kelly the approximate location on the map.

"Check the Wood-Anderson," Kelly ordered.

The graduate student left at a run, heading for the vault on the bluff. There, resting on concrete pillars, under perfectly controlled heat, light and humidity conditions, the special equipment was kept. The Wood-Anderson was a low-sensitivity seismometer which did not go off scale as the ones in the main building did. Its results were recorded on photographic paper which had to be kept in a dark place. Working by the red light, Sheel took the paper from the drum, placed it in a large envelope, and returned to the main building to develop the results in the darkroom.

Meanwhile, Kelly called Spring Valley Airport, ten miles away. Luckily the rental helicopter parked there was available. He summoned it.

Gold entered, with several students hurrying in behind. "What's up?"

Kelly said, "Earthquake, a biggish one, in Rhode Island. I'm going up and have a look. Want to come?"

"Wouldn't miss it. I'll dig up a seismometer."

246

The phone rang. The seismometer at MIT had picked up the tremors, and a professor wanted to know where the earthquake was. Kelly told him what he knew.

"You remember the fellow I told you about? Vail, the ex-seismologist who worried about a quake in Rhode Island? Well, he was right," Kelly said to Gold, who had returned with the seismometer in an aluminum case.

"Was the quake near where he lives?"

"Right under it, maybe. I'd better call him."

He got Vail's number from information and dialed. "Phone's out," he said to Gold.

The phone screamed and Gold picked it up. Placing his hand on the receiver, he said, "A reporter."

"Yes?" Kelly said impatiently, taking the receiver.

"Scott from the Associated Press. We have a report of a high-intensity earthquake in a small area near Fall River. Can you throw some light on it?"

"You know everything I do," Kelly said tersely. "It was a sizable earthquake."

"What about the magnitude?"

"That's not established and I won't guess," said Kelly, who did not want to be accused of having exaggerated the size of an earthquake. "It was strong, Richter scale four or larger," he admitted in spite of himself. "Call back later and we'll have more to say."

The reporter persisted. "But isn't such an earthquake unusual for that area?"

"Yes, but not impossible," Kelly said, and he hung up.

Sheel entered with his results. "The earthquake was magnitude five or even six. That's what the Wood-Anderson shows, Dr. Kelly."

A clamor rose in the room. "Five or six!" Kelly exclaimed. "Nobody even suspected a major fault there. It's one for the books."

247

A buzz sounded, becoming louder. Gold said, "The helicopter's here."

"If Vail is right—and I bet he is—the fault line is about ten miles long. Imagine it producing such a magnitude," Kelly mused as the helicopter scurried northeast at 130 mph. He leaned forward, tapped the pilot on the shoulder and shouted, "See if you can find out what happened at Fall River and Newport now that we're close."

The radio crackled and the pilot shouted back, "A few light tremors were felt and an abandoned factory collapsed in Fall River. But most people aren't even aware that there's been an earthquake."

"What about the quake zone?"

The radio crackled again and the pilot reported, "It's a lightly populated peninsula. There has been considerable damage there. The area's flooded, and they're waiting for the water to recede."

"Flooded!" Kelly said in a startled voice. He turned to Gold. "My God, is there a tsunami?"

"Could be," Gold said, staring at the map. "The quake area seems mostly under the sea."

"It adds up to an earthquake with a very shallow focus," Kelly said. "The impact was concentrated in one place, with almost no effect in the surrounding areas. That kind of event could pack a wallop."

The pilot said, "We're here."

Old Brompton Township lay below them. In the distance a radio tower had fallen. A narrow road was badly cracked, which accounted for the absence of vehicles, Kelly thought, but otherwise everything seemed normal at first, except for the military helicopters hovering over the end of the peninsula. Gold had field glasses and used them. He pointed to the mainland across the bay. "A largish building on a hill by the water has collapsed. And ahead of us there's flooding."

"A tsunami, all right," Kelly said, "but evidently just in this one place. It's like a big coastal earthquake in miniature."

"There are people up on the cliff," Gold said, moving the field glasses. "About a hundred of them."

"They're lucky," Kelly answered, staring at what remained of a village—flooded square, ruined church, smashed houses, wrecked pier. "Still, it's goodbye to property values. They'll have the peninsula to themselves. Nobody will want to live here. I wonder if anyone got hurt."

"The quake had a Mercalli intensity of ten, at least. Suppose this had been New York," Gold muttered. "There's a fault there, you know, on Fourteenth Street."

The helicopter veered, passing above a large three-story house which appeared to have survived the quake intact, a smaller house that had disintegrated into a pile of glass and brick, and finally what appeared from the rubble to have been an old stone house. A tree had fallen on an outbuilding, and half-immersed in water was a car which would never be driven again. A horse swished its tail on the side of the hill, on top of which was a large boulder. Three adults and a child had taken refuge there.

"The water's receding. They'll get to them pretty soon," Kelly said. He squinted. "Let me have those field glasses. See that big fellow who's waving? That's Harry Vail." He smiled. "He's even got the seismometer."